FOREVER CHALLENGED

BOOK FOUR FOREVER LOVED A PARANORMAL SHIFTER ROMANCE

L J HAWKE

To my editors, alpha and beta readers, critique partners, and most especially my fans, thank you. You make my world rock.

PROLOGUE

*L*ydia Hatathli tracked her quarry north. The letters, notes, and nasty messages to her social media accounts had taken quite a while to trace back. The cops weren't interested in some Native woman on a Harley complaining about a stalker. Lydia had one hell of a vested interest in finding the person. There were fake emails sent to employers saying all manner of vile things about Lydia, and she had lost a third of her clients until she was able to stop the hemorrhaging. She created a very private, very safe platform at her own time, trouble, and expense, and had gotten the hell out of all social media. Tracey Two Feathers, who everyone called Hella Girl, was one of her few remaining friends after the ugly things posted on Facebook. Hella Girl had tracked the latest attack on the "tracer" Facebook page set up to track the baddie. The last bit of nastiness had been posted from a truck stop in tiny Wharton, Missouri, sixty miles from anything but side-of-the-highway towns.

Lydia pulled into the truck stop, stowed her helmet, and stalked to the diner part, barely rating anything more than glances that slid right off of her. Riding a motorcycle in winter was bordering on suicidal, but Lydia was on the hunt. She was damn tired of doing her work in miniscule motel rooms with heaters spitting lukewarm air, but she had never gotten this close before. She sat down in a booth, ignoring the truckers eating giant breakfasts and drinking carafes of coffee as fast as they could pour them down their throats.

The server, a redhead named Polly, came by with the coffee, but Lydia put her hand over the coffee cup she hadn't turned over. Lydia ordered a Coke and the meat lover's special, complete with sausage patties, bacon, two scrambled eggs with cheese, a slice of honey ham, and two fat biscuits with butter and honey. "Sure thing, sugar." Polly was fifty if she was a day, with droopy eyelids and a cherry-red smile. Lydia smiled back.

Lydia used the restroom, came back, and was pleased to find that none of the patrons had laptops. Most of them were eating their ham, chicken-fried steaks, or steak-steaks, not poking at cell phones. Her quarry was gone, but Lydia had a plan. She had the time of the attack; now she needed a picture of her quarry. Truck stops went digital a long time ago, and they were so brightly lit they looked like the surface of the sun, day or night. Lydia took off her battered gray bomber jacket in the stifling heat of the diner and eyed both the little white cameras in each corner and over the cash register and the little black domes above each aisle of the attached convenience store.

Lydia ate her food and prepared herself for whatever came next. She paid for her food, left a generous tip, and asked to speak to the manager. She made sure all of her tattoos were covered. She took out and handed over her identification, the copies of the police reports, and the information about the exact time the person had been in two days before. No, the manager had not seen anything weird or suspicious at that time. No, Lydia could not see the surveillance tape. Lydia let the laconic Dine voice she usually used slide into cop speak, clipped and pushy. "So, you want a stalker to go free?" Lydia pitched her voice in such a way that it bounced off the wall behind the cashier's station and bounced back.

"What?" The manager's name tag said Richard, and under it tiny red and white letters, Assistant Manager. He was young, in his early twenties, with thick dark hair and a confused look on his face.

"That person has been stalking me for nearly eight months. It's all in the police reports in your hand you haven't bothered to read. I'm a woman, I live alone, and someone is threatening my life. And you won't do anything to help me." Lydia wasn't shouting, but she was projecting like hell. The servers, the truckers, even the fry cook were all staring at Richard.

The manager began to sweat. "There are privacy laws..."

"Does this look like a private place to you?" Lydia gestured around.

The trucker on the end next to the cash register, a blonde woman with a lined face, let out a guffaw and poked a bony finger at the manager. "Dick, give her what she wants. Girl sounds like she's been through serious shit; you don't need to make it worse for her."

"Yeah," said the huge guy sitting next to the petite blonde woman. He wore flannel and jeans and had a wide, serious face. "Yeah, Dick. She wants da help, someone trying to rough her up, you give her da help." He had a Jersey accent, surprising in this land of flat vowels.

Dick, threw up his hands. "Fine, whatever." He led Lydia to a back office, and lined up the recordings by date and time. Lydia found the right window, and began to zip through cameras.

Fifteen minutes later, Lydia whistled softly. "Gotcha." Her stalker wore a hoodie even when stuffing food in, poking on a cell phone the entire time, a wide, expensive model. It took six cameras, but Lydia got the stalker's height, nearly to the top of the convenience store shelves, thin build, twitchy mannerisms, a tendency to wiggle the right foot. And there, a face despite the hoodie.

Lydia tried not to gasp. Her stalker was a woman. Dark eyes, dark hair, no clear pic of the face. But a woman, nonetheless. Lydia tried to find some memory of this woman in her brain, but nothing came to mind. The woman had been driving an ancient Honda Civic, silver, a completely innocuous ride. Lydia hadn't seen that car before either.

Dick printed out some stills, and Lydia thanked him. Lydia then bought what she'd need from the convenience store--hot coffee in a carafe, energy bars for the road. Lydia filled up her saddlebags with snacks, put on her helmet and Kevlar gloves, and pulled out of the truck stop. There were only truck stops, gas stations, and the occasional motel along this stretch of little-used highway used by truckers because it was often a faster route to a lot of their destinations. These were short-haul truckers, drivers for Walmart and Costco, home supply and convenience stores, carrying loads to towns that needed food, clothing, shelter, and furniture.

Lydia checked out every motel, gas station, and truck stop looking for the Civic. She had a partial license plate from an outdoor camera, and she called it in to Hella Girl, her friend with the bum leg and a huge smile that lit up the world. Lydia and her friend had bonded in high school over their shared hatred of intramural sports, and their loves–rock music and computer keyboards. "Got your perp." Hella Girl typed so fast it sounded like one continuous noise. "Gonna run this rabbit down."

"We find the sick chick, I'll get some more clients in so I can pay you what you're worth." Lydia meant every word.

Lydia was at the fourth motel when she parked, got off, and stowed her helmet, the scent of her prey in her nose. She circled, looking for the Honda, no dice, and was on her way to speak to the crimson-haired desk clerk head-banging away to some sort of rock she could hear from across the parking lot. Then, the shot rang out. Lydia looked down, grabbed her shoulder. The woman hissed, her voice somehow loud on the wind, "Skinwalker bitch!" Then head-lights began to run over the woman's face, and the shooter turned and ran. Lydia followed her into the woods. Once into the trees, Lydia shed her clothes, changed in a swirl of light, and chased her prey. Lydia felt the burn of silver, and knew she didn't have much time, but she'd put her teeth on that arm that had held the weapon before the silver got her. She followed the sound of thrashing in the underbrush and leapt.

CHALLENGE

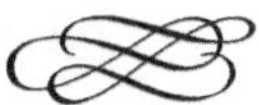

Carl glared at Lucas when Lucas pulled over his truck. They were going very slowly with the buck in the back. Lucas knew the newer model truck; it was James and Mitch Weston. Mitch usually rode a reconditioned Harley, but riding a bike in the winter was idiotic. The forecast was for snow; the reason why Lucas had been up with his father at the godawful time of four a.m. to bag a deer for Mama Ana's freezer. Lucas usually never went anywhere with his father Carl, especially not hunting, but a freezer full of sausages and steaks would be good for the holidays for his mother. His father was as cold as the wind off the mountains, his face all scrunched in on itself, his mouth a thin line. Lucas rolled down the window and asked Mitch, "What's up?"

"You bagged a good-sized buck." Mitch's eyes were crinkly, nearly shut against the cold.

"Yeah. For Mama's freezer."

Mitch gestured toward the buck. "We'll pay you twenty percent over the cost of the meat. We need it."

"Okay." Lucas held out a gloved hand to shake on it.

Carl spoke through gritted teeth. "Wait a cotton-picking minute. My license, my deer."

Lucas sighed. "You have another one on the license, Dad. We'll bag one tomorrow."

Mitch shook his head. "Not tomorrow. Weather's gonna get bad. We've gotta hurry."

Lucas nodded. "Okay." He had no idea what in holy hell was going on, but he trusted his friends. Mitch had a sharp mouth and was willing to get in a fistfight, but he had never been a bully in school. James was steady, an excellent man. They had married some newcomer. The rumor was that James was legal and Mitch was not. Lucas could care less about their sex lives, as long as it didn't involve livestock.

Carl set his jaw. "Absolutely not."

Lucas, sick of his father's cold silences and his need to tell Lucas everything he was doing wrong, had had enough. "Get out, Dad. My truck. Get out, go home. I'm selling the deer. You're being an ass." He reached across his father's torso and opened the door. "James will drive you home, and Mitch can come with me."

"Good enough." Mitch hopped out and came around to Carl's side of the truck. "Need help getting out, Carl?" His tone was even, but Lucas saw a flash of something in Mitch's eyes. Carl was dense, but the man wasn't actually stupid. Carl got out, glared back at his son, and stomped off to James' truck.

Mitch got in. "Drive as fast as you can without throwing the deer on the road."

Lucas nodded. "Where to?"

"County road. Going to the state park." James passed them taking Carl home. It wasn't far. James showed back up in the rearview mirror just before Mitch had Lucas crossed where the government land started. He must have driven like a bat out of hell to drop off Carl, then follow them.

Mitch pointed to where he wanted Lucas to park. Lucas stopped the truck and turned off the power. "Why are we on federal land?"

"Boundaries." Mitch got out, and Lucas followed suit. They wrestled the deer onto the snow. Yellow eyes stared at them. "Move the truck up. Get ahead of the line." Lucas did, and the gray and black wolves came out. James and Mitch acted as if the wolves were expected. The gaunt wolves eyed the buck, and the men backed away.

"The wolves don't eat your mama's llamas." Lucas wasn't making much of a joke. Some of the locals raised sheep and alpacas for wool and milk. Local artisans made sweaters, rugs, wall hangings, and more from the wool, and sold them for good prices. Lucas couldn't remember the last time anyone had seen a wolf, even in the dead of winter, in their little town.

Mitch nodded. "They stay across their lines."

"How do you..." asked Lucas. They got back in the truck as the wolves attacked the buck carcass. Wolves usually liked live prey, but since the buck was newly dead and it was snowing, they seemed to be happy with it.

"You don't want to know."

"Scent markers." Lucas grimaced. "I assume the piss came from wolves from a rival pack. How did you get that much wolf urine?"

"That's the part you don't want to know," said Mitch. Lucas guffawed.

Lucas looked around. "Where's your brother?" He had heard the truck pull up, but didn't see it. Lucas turned on the truck.

"Stop the truck." Lucas hit the brake, and Mitch got out and jogged back. He let out a howl, and Lucas knew something was wrong. Lucas turned off the truck, grabbed his father's shotgun, and ran out into the snow after Mitch. Mitch ran like the wind, and Lucas followed.

James and Mitch were kneeling over a mountain lion, just over the wrong way onto government land. "Shot," said James. "Get the tarp." Mitch turned to comply.

"Poor thing." Lucas racked the shotgun. "I can put it out of its misery."

Mitch stared at his friend and said very clearly, "If you shoot that mountain lion, I will take that gun away and blow your head off. Now, help or leave."

Lucas lowered his gun, stunned, while Mitch ran towards his brother's truck. Lucas literally shook himself, broke down the shotgun, and put it back in his truck. He found his first aid kit under the seat and ran towards the brothers. He nearly stopped in shock as Mitch handed something to James that looked like a thin stick. James carefully slid it into the mountain lion's body. The tawny hide had a single bullet hole just behind the shoulder. Lucas wondered how the bullet hadn't hit the heart.

"Got it," said James. "Wish I had forceps."

Lucas broke open the first aid case in his hand and handed it to Mitch. "Tweezers in there, big ones, for buckshot. Dog got shot once. He lived six more years."

Mitch fished out the tweezers and handed them to James. "Bro, here's the kit…" Mitch and James both cringed. "That was loud," said Mitch.

Lucas looked around. "What was loud?"

"Lucas, things are about to get really damn weird. If you want to bail…" Mitch found rubbing alcohol and wipes, and put them out on the lid of the first aid kit.

"Too late," said James. "Lucas, what is about to happen, never happened. Got it?"

"Got it," said Lucas, confused.

Confused changed to stunned stupid when something huge and green and glistening circled above, pulled its huge claws in, and plunged. The wolves howled and scattered, and there was a huge beating of wings. Lucas wondered if he had time to get his shotgun, and then the thing landed, spraying snow. It was enormous, with jaws that could snap Lucas in half. Its scales went from a sea green on the shoulders and belly to a deep pine on the back, head, and tail, with glimmers of gold. Lucas had to physically shut his own mouth as James and Mitch covered the mountain lion's body, protecting her from gusts of wind and snow.

"What the hell is that?" Lucas heard the shock in his own voice.

"Dragon." Mitch stood. "Help us." James, Mitch, and Lucas got the mountain lion completely on the tarp, and then they dragged her out from under the trees. The dragon sang, a great booming that shook the trees, and touched the mountain lion with a claw as big as Lucas's hand with a needle-sharp tip. Lucas's eyes tried to pop out of his head as silver gushed out of the wound, looking like mercury as it flowed over the edge of the tarp and into the snow.

The mountain lion shook, then its eyes fluttered open, shut again. "Hey, beautiful," said Mitch.

Lucas stared at the mountain lion. She was gorgeous, all tawny coat and that flash of orange-gold eyes. "She's incredible," whispered Lucas. "Thanks, Dragon." He knew about the werewolves. Some guy up north–Idaho or Montana–had tried to kill his best friend while under the influence of bath salts and Adderall while playing a video game where both were live streaming. The best friend had turned into a wolf in self-defense. It wasn't pretty. The wolf-human had been exonerated, and was found to be a perfectly normal college student. The shapeshifter college student had gone into the military, and then... "She's a 'were. Shifter. Whatever." Lucas felt his mind make another leap. "That's how you got the wolf piss."

Mitch grinned. "We mark our territory carefully."

Lucas stared up at the dragon. "That one's not from around here?" The dragon chuffed.

Mitch grinned, his eyes bright with wonder. "She's laughing at you. She's a Green, the earth ones, the magic ones." He did something complicated with his hands while James knocked the rest of the silver off the tarp with the bloody stick he still held. "Stand back."

The Dragon chuffed again and blew steam into the air as the brothers carefully wrapped up the mountain lion in the tarp like a burrito. Mitch dragged the now-shocky Lucas back to his truck, and James stepped back as well. The dragon took two steps, grabbed the tarp, flapped those gorgeous green iridescent wings twice, and launched into the air, the mountain lion securely in her claws.

"Get him home safely." James carefully poured rubbing alcohol on the tweezers, then wiped it with the forceps. He handed the first aid kit back to Mitch. James then grabbed a shovel out of the back of his truck.

"What's he doing?" Lucas struggled to keep his voice even, preventing it from sounding like a wail.

"Removing the silver. Give me your keys." Mitch opened the

driver's side door. "Scratch that, still in the truck. Get in. We've got to go have a talk with your dad."

Lucas got in the truck. It felt weird to be on the passenger side. He shut the door.

Mitch put on his seat belt and turned on the vehicle. "Your dad's being a dick for a reason."

Lucas struggled to get his brain in gear. He remembered that he'd promised to act as if what was going to happen never happened, so he tried mightily to compartmentalize. He'd been doing that for nearly four months anyway. His dad, who used to be silent and occasionally rude or abusive, was snapping at everyone, including his wife Ana, Lucas's mom. Ana had quietly told Lucas that she was moving out of the barn and into the vertical farm if Carl didn't snap out of it, and made that clear to Carl. If Mitch said something was wrong with Lucas's dad, then he was right. "Is it real bad?"

"I know this is a hell of a time to go into this, after what just didn't happen." Lucas barked out a laugh. "And you're probably shocky as hell. But, yeah, it's about as bad as it can get."

"Can you…?" asked Lucas.

"Tried that. Just…didn't work. It doesn't always work."

"Plus the drinking and smoking."

"Plus that."

"So, how long?" Lucas pummeled his brain, trying to get it to work.

"Not long. Your dad is pushing people away because he's mad, scared, doesn't think he wants or needs help, and wants to cut ties so people don't grieve so much when he goes."

"Sounds like my idiot dad." Lucas realized he had tears falling out of his eyes. He impatiently wiped them away.

Mitch drove cleanly despite the falling snow that was beginning to decrease visibility. James passed them, then went like a bat out of hell somewhere. Lucas decided not to ask. They got to the car wash and Mitch drove in. "What the hell?" asked Lucas.

"Unless you want to leave the buck blood in the bed of the truck?" Lucas nodded sharply, pissed that he'd forgotten about it. Mitch did something to his phone, then pulled up onto the track. The extremely hot water hit the car from three sides, then the soap.

"What...I need to…" Lucas was compartmentalizing like crazy. His dad. His dad was going to die very soon.

"You need to get your shit together. Ana is as strong as they come. She'll weather it just fine. I suggest you confront your dad, have it out, get the emotional storm out of the way. It's gonna suck, but this all needs to come out in the open. And tell Daddy Dearest to quit being so verbally stabby. He's pissing off everyone he comes into contact with."

"I'll kick his ass. Metaphorically speaking." The sound of the hot water washing his truck soothed him. "That's why he wanted the buck."

"We'll find you another one. Point you in the right direction, fill up the freezer. Your dad's license says you can bag another one, right?"

"Yes. I hate hunting, but I get Dad's point. Fills up the freezer. Besides, deer sausage is awesome."

Mitch grinned. "It is. Kind of pisses me off to deliver one once a month in the winter or when it snows early like now, but it literally keeps the wolves off our door."

Lucas sighed. "I've got to do the confrontation thing alone. When we get out of this thing." The second wash got all the blood off the concrete under the truck. "I'll drop you somewhere."

Mitch shook his head. "We're nowhere near our place." "Our place" was an A-frame up the mountain where Mitch refinished bikes, and his brother James was a trail guide and worked on the rescue squad. Their woman, Corinne, did websites and things like that. Lucas didn't care about them being a threesome. He cared about his own love life, which was nonexistent. "Also, I have about six people who can pick me up." Mitch meant his relatives, the Westons. Lucas didn't know how they were all related, but they lived on a huge farm.

The Weston farm was nowhere near where Lucas lived in a cabin on the edge of his mother's property. Lucas' parents, Carl and Ana, had property, and they had bushwhacked trails that connected to other ones that ended up on federal land, or heading to Lake

Conwanwin and its smaller cousin, Casree, the reservoir. Ana built a vertical hydroponics greenhouse on her land, and took the funds to build three tiny houses, employing lots of locals, and now had an author, an environmentalist who did a lot of work on federal land tracking animal migration with special software, and an avid snow-shoer and skier living in them, all paying rent and buying local goods and services. The finishing touches were going on the interior of the fourth cabin. Lucas had his own cabin near the hydroponics farm where his mother grew herbs, grains, and flax. He couldn't stand to live with his father.

Lucas nodded. "Good." It would be a pain in the ass even with a four-wheel drive, but Lucas had to get to his family. "Are you sure?"

"Dammit, you idiot. I'm trying to get you home to your family." Mitch sighed, and drove the now-gleaming truck out onto the salt-crusted road. The snow began to fall harder out of a leaden sky. "You are in no condition to drive. Ana and your dad don't need to bury you first."

Lucas felt the words like a punch in the gut. "He's…"

"Dying, yes. An asshole right now, yes. Your family needs you alive to deal with the fallout, yes. Now, shut up so I can drive in this mess." Mitch kept his eyes on the road.

Lucas shut up. He stared out into the increasingly bad conditions. "Let me text someone to get you."

"That is actually a good idea. Good, you're coming back to us. James will have his hands full, and Corinne is perfect. She'll send out a group text."

Lucas didn't know what to type, so he settled for *Mitch needs a ride from Carl Laramie's house.*

The text came back, just as terse. *Tell my idiot husband to wait inside.*

"You guys married now?" Lucas asked Mitch.

"Yes, one of us had to get her some insurance." Mitch groaned. "Laws in the US have to catch up, you know?"

Lucas snorted. "Government officials can't tie their own shoes."

Mitch blew out his breath in a choked laugh. "Not trying to be hard on you, it's just that we've always shot straight with each other."

Lucas nodded, realized his friend couldn't see him, eyes on the road in the increasingly whiteout conditions. "Yeah. Rip off the bandage time. Say, how are you at driving through blizzards?"

"Pretty good. Why?"

"'Cause we're in one." Both their phones pinged with the belated weather app warning.

Mitch grinned. "Old times," he said, referring to the time they were supposed to be back for work in the morning at the old warehouse, closed now, but they'd gotten stuck in a blizzard in a mountain pass. "Shut up some more." Mitch brought the truck out of a skid. Lucas shut up.

It took Mitch hugging the bright line on the side of the road to get to the farm. "Get a self-driving truck, you idiot," Mitch said as they slid off the road into a snowdrift from the snow from two days ago at the end of Carl's driveway.

Lucas sighed. "Waiting for this one to up and die." He cringed at the statement. Someone would, very soon. "Stay here and meet your family. I've got to see mine."

Mitch handed Lucas his keys. "Good luck, bro."

"Gonna need it." Lucas got out and began to hike, slogging through the snowdrifts. He made it to the front door because the house was lit up like a Christmas tree. He stomped onto the porch, kicked the snow out of the way to get into the screen door, and fell in the front door just as his mother opened it.

"You're a mess." Ana slammed the door with a boom. Lucas fell onto the boot bench and started pulling his boots off. They had snow in them, so they were pretty ineffective. Ana helped him take off his coat, and called out, "Hey, husband! Bring some towels now!"

"In a minute," said Carl, in the direction of the kitchen.

"Get your worthless ass in here NOW!" bellowed Ana.

Even Carl in his current pissiness didn't argue with that voice. He came rushing in, dish towels in hand. "You've been rolling in snow, boy?" Carl handed the towels to his wife.

"Dad, you say one more negative thing today, I'm punching you out myself." Lucas struggled to take off his wet jeans. "None of us deserve it." Carl looked stunned. Lucas had never spoken to him that way. "I know you're angry and scared, but get over it right now, because we've got a blizzard, and we've got three renters and two horses."

Ana turned to look at her husband. "Carl?"

"Who told?" asked Carl, his face red with rage.

"You are the biggest idiot in the entire world." Lucas got his pants off, then his socks, and pulled his shirt off over his head. His long underwear stuck to his body.

Ana looked like she'd been slapped. "It's bad, isn't it? We're gonna lose the house?"

"What? No!" said Carl.

Lucas pushed past his bickering parents. "Tell her now, Dad. I've got to change clothes and go back out in that mess."

"Not yours to tell!" bellowed Carl. "I should have been able to choose the time!"

"Four months ago would have been good." Lucas slipped on freezing water on the floor. He righted himself and stalked off to his old bedroom and the few clothes he kept there to change.

By the time he came back out, Ana was crying and glaring at Carl at the same time, and Carl looked stone angry. They looked like two hissing cats. Lucas stepped around them. "I can't get back to my cabin. There's whiteout conditions out there. I'll walk the line to the horses, get their feed and water sorted out." He put on his ski mask, then his parka. The wet boots wouldn't be good, so he stole his father's pair of heavy rain boots. Lucas stomped out the door.

Lucas walked the blizzard line to the barn. The horses stamped and huffed and were delighted to eat their dinner. He mucked out stalls and put down fresh hay. The barn was warmed by underfloor heating.

Lucas braved the blizzard back to the main house, following the line. By the time he got back inside, he felt like he had been inside a snow globe. He shook himself off like a dog and stripped and changed all over again, overjoyed that he still had old clothes in the house. The hissing cat-parents had gone quiet, a very common thing in the house.

Carl had made a series of grave errors that ended with Ana refusing to divorce him, feeling she had put over well past half the work into the farm. She wasn't wrong. Ana normally lived over the barn in the manager's quarters now. She'd come back inside to do chores.

Her vertical farm sat on the property Ana had brought into the marriage, a bridal gift from her father, Jorge. She grew grains that could be brought to Kylee's mill down on the river, seasonal flowers, some fruits and vegetables, some kitchen herbs, and flax. The flax was made into linen, and people on low-carb diets loved flax seeds for their high nutritional value. Ana had been buying Carl's property from him for the last four years–a bad harvest, new combine parts, whatever Carl's refusal to listen to anyone else pushed him to need more money.

"Are you all right?" Lucas asked his mother as he stepped across the kitchen to pour himself a huge mug of coffee. He doped it with fresh cream from the refrigerator and sugar from the little jar on the table.

"Idiot hasn't made a will." Ana's face was rigid, her back like a stick. She was making some sort of soup that smelled of mushrooms. "So, I get what I deserve in the end."

"He's downstairs?" When Lucas moved out into his own cabin his mother had built for him near the hydroponics farm, Carl had taken over Lucas's small "man cave" downstairs in the basement. Carl liked to watch Westerns. To him, that was when the world made sense.

"He is." Ana reached towards the fresh herbs that she grew in pots indoors and gathered rosemary, basil, and thyme. She sprinkled them into the soup, releasing mouth-watering odors. "Did you know?"

Lucas shook his head. "Found out today that he has...something."

"Lung cancer, got into his lymph nodes and moved to his liver." Ana's long black braid moved as she tasted the soup, then added more rosemary. "He's been getting tired, having trouble breathing. I suggested, more and more strongly, he see a doctor nearly a year ago and every month since. Man's more stubborn than a mule. I've been taking on his work for months. Thank all that is holy for Julio." Julio was the foreman, and he split his time between his apartment attached to the greenhouse and the stable. Julio was strong, hard-working, and didn't treat Ana like shit. Julio had come on about a year after Ana moved out. Carl just got more tight-lipped and cold. So, not a big difference.

Lucas set the table. He could do that. He was shivering, but the doctored coffee was helping. "Carl…"

Ana shook her head. "I'll bring down a tray. You're a giant icicle. Sit."

Lucas sat. His mother brought over the soup, a creamy sausage mushroom. "What's this about a deer?"

Lucas struggled to find words. "Carl bagged a deer. I agreed to come along to get a freezer full for you. Then Mitch bought it. The Westons–Mitch and James–they give a deer to the wolves about once a month in the winter just over the federal land boundary to keep them in their territory and to not hunt in our valley."

"Well, that's smart." Ana made up the tray and sighed. "I signed on for sickness and health, didn't I?" She shrugged, and Lucas went to open the basement door. She walked down, and he closed the door behind her.

Lucas was on his second bowl when Ana came back up, sans tray. "Asshole."

"Divorce him, Mamacita."

Ana shrugged. "Barn door, horses gone. I stayed because I've worked harder than Carl ever did, made a profit when he was losing money and nearly had the place taken away twice. Man destroyed our credit rating. I divorce him, I don't get what I've earned." She smiled sadly at him. "By the time I realized what damage I was doing to you by staying, you were already in high school and halfway moved out. My stubborn streak, I'm afraid. I suck as a mom."

"You should have divorced him when I was thirteen. Dad never got me, never will get me." Lucas cringed. "Guess that's really true now." He looked down at his soup.

Ana shook her head. "He's a stupid asshole. I like you. I love you. I don't always get you, because I'm not a game-playing gaming artist."

"Set designer," corrected Lucas. "I design the sets in which the videos are played, and a lot of the characterization. The action is up to the action people."

Ana held up her hand. "I've seen your drawings. I gave you the handheld scanner, remember?"

Lucas grinned. "I can't get back to my cabin tonight. Can't see your own hands out there. I've got deadlines."

Ana grinned. "Use my laptop. Netflix is working. I checked."

"Thanks, Mama." Lucas finished his soup, put the soup away in containers, and washed the dishes before stealing his mother's laptop and loading up the chip in his pocket. He backed up everything three ways--cloud, chip, email to himself, four ways if he was home at his cabin with a battery backup system. He worked on his new designs. For this game, the giants lived in caves, hiding from the demons. The game's storyline didn't really make sense, but that was fine with Lucas. He still made his money. Mr. Harris, his high school history and English teacher, had done up the giant's language for him, well worth the price, so he put inscriptions up about hidden scrolls and treasure. He threw garish paintings up on the cave wall, and lost himself in the world.

Lucas got the entire cave designed and the network of caves underneath. He made a map of the cave system, emailed it to the game's producer, and was astonished at the quick reply at nearly two in the morning. The game had to be out by Christmas, so there was a major push going on. He got the roughs out to the storyboarders and crashed. He slept on his mother's bed; she tended to fall asleep in front of the television on cold winter nights, reading or watching television.

∾

*L*ucas awoke to the smell of sizzling bacon. He stumbled his way into a hot shower, dressed, and went out to find waffles and bacon on the table. "Wow," he said to his mother.

"Horses are taken care of. I'll take morning chores, you take evening, deal? I know you're on deadline, and we don't have that much to do right now anyway."

Lucas grinned. "Anything for you." He kissed Ana's cheek, then sat down and grabbed the butter dish. "I take it Julio is doing fine with the plants."

Ana grinned. "Man is canning produce he can't bring to market in this storm, can you believe it? Men don't like canning. It's a bitch of a process."

Lucas grinned. "Better him than me." Ana slapped his shoulder, and Lucas pretended to be injured. Ana laughed. "Where's Mr. Grumpy?"

Ana shook her head. "Still in his man cave. He ate only one waffle and two pieces of bacon." She had a point; Carl ate like a lumberjack.

Lucas put his head down and ate. He told his mother about his work, which bored the hell out of her. She preferred comedies and a little black humor, not fantasy or science fiction. She talked about the flax, the masses of seeds they sold in big biodegradable plastic boxes and canisters, which almost put Lucas back to sleep. Finally, they finished, and then they went to wash the dishes together. Lucas washed, Ana dried.

Lucas wiped down the pan. "We gonna talk about the elephant in the kitchen?"

Ana raised her eyebrows. "Wow. Standing up to your father, now talking about death. Where's the old Lucas?"

Lucas shook his head. "I have no idea. Anyway, funeral?"

"He'll want a church service, buried in the ground. Don't expect many people to attend. His poker and hunting buddies will want a reception where they can get drunk. Not my thing, don't want people coming in and out of here, breaking stuff, staring at me, wondering if I'm really sad or not, drinking and eating, spilling stuff on the carpet."

Lucas shrugged. "I drew enough scenes of bars where people meet to drink to the dead. Pay Bill Ramos to have it at Sharky's, pay for some food and drink. Show up for an hour, then take off and let them get drunk and cry in their beer. Probably cost less, and they'll be happy."

"A wake. Your father isn't Catholic."

Lucas snorted. "Doesn't have to be. Besides, he'll be dead." He amazed himself with the stark words, but they were true.

Ana nodded. "Didn't expect it so soon."

"Did you really think banning smoking in the house would work?"

"Not really. Kind of did it to himself, didn't he?"

"Yeah. He kinda did."

SURVIVAL

*L*ydia woke up. She was laying on her side, her head piled on pillows, and she stared at a turquoise wall. Briefly, she wondered why there wasn't a Navajo rug on the wall. Then, the pain hit. She doubled over and groaned. That hurt worse, so she hissed out through her teeth like a teakettle. Someone of small stature rushed over. There was a patch on Lydia's back in between her shoulder blades, and she hissed when a hand pulled it off and put another one on. Then, a cool touch, and the pain halved. Lydia relaxed into the pillow. "Let's get some tea and soup down you while Sylvie does her magic," said a female voice. Lydia tilted her head, sucked on a straw, tasted mint. Her eyes were gummy, and hard to get open. Lydia sipped, drank, and the cup was taken away, replaced by a warm cup of corn soup. It tasted incredible. Lydia drank it down, and then the tea came back.

Strong hands walked her to the bathroom. Lydia sat on the pot while the woman washed her face. The woman drew a bath and helped her slide in, then scrubbed her down with a poof. Lydia luxuriated in being clean. "Cats," said the woman, a mass of dark hair and eyes to Lydia's blurred vision. "Always with the clean." Those firm hands dried Lydia and dressed her in a robe, and Lydia found herself back in the bed in pyjamas and warm socks, a heated blanket underneath, another over her. She slipped into sleep again.

~

*L*ydia woke again to find herself being lifted up, bathed again. A woman again, but a different one. More dark hair and eyes, much shorter hair, slimmer face, more narrowed eyes. The woman said, "My name is Stretcher. You have silver poisoning. You're on a farm, relatively near as the crow flies from the government land where you were found. You were shot. Did you decimate your shooter?"

Lydia remembered the woman cursing, taking a bite out of the woman's arm, the gun skittering across the forest floor. "Name...Lydia. Shot. With silver bullets. Bit her, but probably not fatal. She called me a skinwalker."

"Oh, shit." Stretcher narrowed her eyes..

"Stalker. Hunting her back. Bike...at hotel...blue sign...Starlight Aspen. Dumb...name. My bike, a Harley. License ...plate...2247. Retrieve...please. My clients...angry...Lydia Hatathli...First Nations Education and Web Development." Lydia closed her eyes, and fell asleep again as the water cooled the hot pain.

~

*L*ydia woke again in the bathtub. The first woman was washing her again. She looked to be a First Nations person, a curvy woman with long black hair, caramel eyes and skin, a round face, and a huge smile. Lydia opened first one eye, then the other. She wiggled her toes and fingers.

"She wakes. Lydia, I am Rachael Weston. You are on our farm."

"Remember that part." Lydia let herself relax. "Silver poisoning."

"We found your laptop in your bike saddlebag. I know some Dine, so I was able to figure out your password. We have contacted your clients, and our family member Corrinne helped your clients based on your notes. Your bike is here, waiting on your recovery, along with your clothes and things."

"Pay...you back."

Rachael snorted. "You're a shifter, so you're literally family. Very distant family. Do you know the story?"

"We were one clan, originally...then someone did something...horrible, then they tried to...kill us, and we got...broken up and scattered and...had to hide." Lydia realized that although she was in warm water, her teeth were chattering. She could barely move her limbs. "Didn't know...the silver thing...was true."

"Let's get you out. You need to get warm."

Once back in bed, Lydia was propped up on pillows so she could have blue corn chowder and mint tea. "How long have I been here?" Lydia was delighted that she had been able to speak using a complete sentence.

"Three days." Rachael pulled the comforter over Lydia's body. "You're probably going to be flat on your back for at least two weeks, probably three. Consider yourself to be a kitten."

Lydia snorted. "Ha ha."

"You can stay here as long as you like. We apologize for examining your computer, but we found the information on your stalker. Your friend Hella Girl has been frantically looking for you. We informed her that you were alive but had been shot and were recovering." Rachael put Lydia's cell phone down on the nightstand. "I suggest calling her immediately. I'll get a writing desk and your computer setup. You may not be able to work, but you'll probably be able to watch stupid movies until you're ready." She smiled, and left the room with the tray.

Lydia could barely put in her unlock code and press the key to call her friend. Hella Girl was pissed off. "So you are all right? I was ready to call the police! I thought she killed you!" Hella Girl was crying.

"No, not dead. I got shot with a bullet, and the bullet was...kind of poisonous. It's going to take me a...couple weeks to recover. Someone....else...has been helping me with my clients."

Rachael came back in and set up the little table with movable legs that could be made into a lap desk or even a standing desk that Lydia kept in her bag. Rachael took the laptop from its case and began to set everything up, and plugged the laptop into the surge-protecting power strip Lydia had in her bag.

"Who are these people? Did they kidnap you? Why isn't there a police report on this?"

"Slow down. One, they're...tribal friends. Two, have you got any hits yet on the picture of our girl?"

Lydia held the phone away from her ear as Hella Girl squealed in her ear. "No, and who cares right now? I thought you were dead and was hunting a killer! The car was stolen and ditched at a truck stop, no fingerprints, so that one is a no go. Do you remember seeing her from anywhere?"

"I don't recognize her. I don't ever remember seeing her before. But, between boarding school and college, I could have run across her and...just don't remember. Hold on." Fighting a wave of dizziness, Lydia pulled up the blurry images she had and sent them to her friend once more. "I need you to find out...who the hell she is, so we can find her. I may have done some damage. Hurt her wrist or arm, I think." Lydia closed her eyes, hearing her friend madly tapping on her keyboard. "I had a bullet wound in my shoulder. I think she's still alive."

Rachael held up a hand, and Lydia said, "Hold on."

"Do you need to use the restroom before I go?" asked Rachael.

"No, I'm fine." Lydia wasn't, not really.

Rachael smiled at her. "I'll be right back with a sealed cup with a plastic straw, some snack bars that are easy to eat and have a lot of protein, and a little bell." Rachael smiled again and was gone.

"Can't find her yet," said Hella Girl. "Where did this go down?"

Lydia said, "I'll tell you, but I don't want this traced to me." She got the story out then realized she was too exhausted to keep going. "Gotta sleep." Rachael came in with the tray and put on the night-stand. Lydia thanked her.

"You better get well soon so we can go after this bitch," said Hella Girl.

"Sleep," said Lydia. She hung up, and darkness took her.

~

It took nearly two days until Lydia was able to get back and forth to the bathroom without leaning against every object she could find. Standing up was still extremely difficult, but she could move around better. Hella Girl was still using facial recognition to find out more about the attacker. "It would have helped if you had seen her vehicle, then snapped a pic of her getting in or out of it."

"Sorry. Kind of fighting for my life at the time."

"Always with the excuse." Lydia laughed.

An hour later, Lydia had a visit from Corinne, who had finished off Lydia's contracted work. Corinne was tall and weedy, with a narrow, strong face and a fall of black hair. Corinne was very thorough and had followed the contracts to the letter. "I don't speak Dine. Had to get some help with the translations. What do you think?"

Dine, the Navajo language, was not easy to use correctly. Lydia's fingers flew over the keys with corrections. "Great job. Seriously. Just need to make it perfect for the client." The client was a cooperative that worked together to create and sell Dine crafts, such as rugs and jewelry, and digital files in Dine such as ebooks, audio, and video. Lydia was in the process of separating the digital from the physical items; they had originally been set up in the most confusing way possible by one of the co-op members who didn't understand website design. Now the site was streamlined, searchable, and nearly ready to go except for some minor tweaks.

Lydia pulled her hands off the keys, suddenly dizzy. "Sorry, I started to go down the rabbit hole. Let's look at the next one." It was far more laborious than Lydia wanted due to her own waves of exhaustion. She figured out how to prop up her bad arm so the shoulder didn't move, so she could still type. They got through the whole thing. "What do I owe you?"

Corinne laughed. "Already paid for. You are considered to be family, and you were attacked. So, you are covered." She looked closely at Lydia. "I was assaulted by a guy I dated off and on about a year ago. It hurt like hell, and took a very long time to heal. I hated every damn second of trying to recover. I suggest a recliner once you can walk better. There's one in the living room where you are."

Lydia bit down on the pain. "I would talk to you more, but I'm exhausted. Can we talk on the phone if I need any more work done? You've been doing my work as well as your own."

"Sure. Go to sleep, woman. You have ashy skin and you look like you're about to fall over."

Lydia grinned. "I am going to rest now." She closed the laptop.

Corinne took the table from her and put it on the floor, the laptop still on it. "Sleep, woman. Give me your cell." Lydia handed it over. "Here's my number. I'll put in Stretcher and Rachael's numbers. They're the ones that have been taking care of you. They're the house females here. We haven't sent in any guys because we didn't know who hurt you or why. Knocked us for a loop when we found out your stalker was female."

"Me, too." Lydia slid down under the covers.

Corinne smiled gently. "See you, girlfriend. Text me, 'cause I don't know when you're sleeping."

"Okay." Lydia let the dizziness take her down.

~

*L*ydia slept for hours, then woke up hungry. She worked her way from soup and tea to tacos and flavored waters. She was able to walk without leaning on everything, but only back and forth to the bathroom.

Sylvie visited her, a young girl with enormous chocolate-brown eyes and a shy smile. "I'm a healer. It's a huge secret. Your healing is accelerated, but it hurts a lot more. I'm sorry. I can only ask your body to heal you."

"Don't know how that works, but I get it. Or, I think I do. You have to use my energy in order to heal me."

"That makes sense. I'll do it for a short time, and since it's after lunch, you can sleep."

"Okay. Don't injure yourself healing me. And don't worry. I'm a shifter trained by a medicine man. We don't spread secrets."

"Okay. Lay back and relax." Sylvie held both of Lydia's wrists in hers, and Lydia felt the pain rise and rise.

Lydia hissed, but held it in. Finally, the pain crested and began to slide. "Can't sleep with that much residual pain," Lydia complained.

"Don't worry. It will hit you in three...two..."

$\sim$

*L*ydia smiled at Corinne. "Thanks to you, I'm back on track," she said.

Corinne grinned. "So glad I got your text. I'm here to spring you into the living room. We've got the aforementioned recliner, and all the food from the kitchen you can eat. Plus a wide-screen TV, blankets, and hot chocolate."

"Well, damn, sign me up."

Stretcher came bustling into the room. "Get up, Lydia. Time to meet the family. We're overwhelming, loud, obnoxious, and rude."

"Good," said Lydia. "Let's go."

It took both Corinne and a deceptively strong Stretcher to walk her, step by step, out of her little turquoise room with an ensuite bath to the greatroom. It was huge with a beamed sloping ceiling, a huge kitchen against the back, and a wide-screen TV. Stretcher got her into the recliner, and Corinne got her set up with the computer.

A giant man came in the side door. "Good, she's up. I'm Gunny. I'll be in and out, but whatever you need to eat and drink, just holler." He took Lydia's phone, put in his number, then handed back the phone. "Samosas up in ten."

"Good." Stretcher rubbed her head covered with very short blue-black hair shorn on one side. Her eyes crinkled. "I've got farm chores. We raise goats. Rachael raises plants." Stretcher grinned and went to wash up. Three corgi dogs rushed in from a dog door, and they all tried to kiss Lydia's fingers. Corinne picked up two and sat on the couch, and Stretcher picked up the third corgi and sat on the other recliner.

"What the hell is going on?" asked Lydia.

Corinne grinned. "This is Shawn and Wayne, and Stretcher has Rascal. This is a huge and complicated family. Rachael is married to Gunny over there. Stretcher is a sister to my two men, James and Mitch, the ones that found you."

"They keep rescuing stray people," Stretcher complained.

Corinne pretended to growl at her. "Mitch, in an enormous black wolf-dog form, rescued me, well, I rescued myself, but he prevented me from falling off the mountain. He changes into a wolf, too, and looks like his brother in wolf form. James goes wolf, and so do Rachael and Gunny. Stretcher here is like you."

Stretcher grinned. " I don't know if Lydia here is a lesbian like me."

Corinne snorted, and Lydia said, "Hetero."

"Obnoxious woman here turns into a mountain lion, just like you do," said Corinne.

"So we're probably distantly related," said Lydia.

"Hey, cuz." Stretcher bumped fists with Lydia. They both had the dark hair and eyes of the Dine, but Lydia had her father's Crow nose and his strong eyes, her mother's brow and chin, and her father's ability to change shape. Lydia looked like pulled taffy compared to a lot of the women from the rez, same cinnamon skin, but much narrower shoulders and hips.

"Your cousin does something for the government on computers involving numbers. I've no idea what the hell it is, but at this point I really don't want to know." Corinne gave tummy rubs to two dogs simultaneously.

"I make flight paths for the Martian rovers." Stretcher grinned.

Corinne snorted. "Last week, it was GPS about how mountains are changing due to climate change. I have no idea whether or not she's telling the truth, and like I said, I don't want to know at this point." Stretcher laughed, a rippling cough. Lydia coughed too. "Pumas. Always with the coughing," Corinne complained.

One of the dogs, either Shawn or Wayne, whined to be put down, went over to Lydia, and sat on her foot. Lydia put her tray down, hefted up the dog with her good arm, put the dog on her lap, grabbed the blanket from the nearby couch, put it over herself and the dog, put the tray over the dog, and reached underneath to scratch the dog's head. The exertion exhausted her, so she just sat there for a minute scratching behind the corgi's ear. The dog groaned with pleasure.

"That's Wayne. You just earned his undying love. He loves to snuggle," said Corinne.

"Tell cuz how you got them," said Stretcher.

"I hate to say it, but it was a dark and stormy night." Lydia laughed.

The samosas were excellent. Gunny set his enormous self down in his double-wide recliner and delicately ate the vegetable-stuffed pastries, served with a green sauce. The others consumed theirs far more quickly. After the food, Stretcher and Corinne went to the kitchen to do the dishes, and Gunny went to do something on the farm having to do with the third tiny house they were building in the back. The first two tiny houses were apparently full of birdwatchers who wanted to run around in the woods.

Lydia opened her laptop, checked everything, and turned in all the work she'd started on, Corinne worked on, and Lydia completed. She was surprised to find three new contracts waiting in her email box. She went over them, put on her headset, asked questions, signed everything after some back-and-forth, and settled down to build some more websites. One was for a YouTuber who was getting very popular in the First Nations community, the second a bilingual school on rez land that wanted to get all of their materials online "just like California," and the third for a consortium of wildlife rescuers who wanted to have a single website to raise awareness about wild animals and their preservation. Corinne had brought her own laptop and banged out her work as well while Stretcher went to go do her super-secret work alone.

～

everal hours later, Gunny came back in, took the dogs out, got them all back in, and toweled them off. Lydia got Wayne back and slept for a bit. She woke up to find that she felt cramped and that Corinne was gone. She put her computer aside, stretched, and was startled when Gunny came over to help her stand. "Rachael says you've got to walk around, or you won't heal properly. I wanted to get you a walker, but everybody was afraid that you wouldn't use it."

"Hell, no." Gunny laughed. "I need to…" Lydia gestured at the open bathroom door, hating her weakness.

Gunny got her back and forth to the toilet, set her up with some sort of lime-cherry tea, put Wayne on the couch, covered up her and the dog, and asked if she was finished for the day. "No, I think I've got another hour in me."

"I'll give you half an hour, and then I'm going to watch the game. Sorry if that gets your knickers in a twist, but I have money on this basketball game."

Lydia grinned. "I can watch, but I can't play. Even before I got shot."

Gunny laughed. "Neither could I. Twisted an ankle in the fifth grade, pissed off my mother to holy hell."

Lydia coughed laughter and got back to work. They had popcorn and sodas, and just to be contrary, she cheered for the other women's basketball team. Gunny was giving her dark looks by the time he was ready to start dinner, although his team won. Lydia couldn't help with the cooking, but she could work on her contracts a little more.

Gunny walked Lydia to the table and helped her sit down. It was just Gunny, Rachael, and Stretcher, the dogs under the table hoping for morsels. They had some sort of dark bread that was amazing, with a little pot of butter at each place setting, and clam chowder with sour cream, cheddar, and bacon bits on top. They had a choice of soda, water, or cherry tea. Lydia chose the tea.

Rachael talked about the goats and how the cheese-making enterprise was doing. "Our boy goats are down south eating kudzu," said Rachael, proudly.

"Less stinky," observed Stretcher.

Gunny nodded. "Best way to get rid of that blasted invasive vine. A lot cheaper than heavy equipment, too."

"So this is a goat farm?" asked Lydia.

"We've got the tiny houses, which are bringing in a pretty good income. Plus the vertical farm. Mitch, James, and Corinne live up on the mountain. James takes people on hiking and fishing trips and has some crazy people doing ice fishing and cross-country skiing in winter. Mitch refurbishes Harleys, or puts them together from kits, whichever he feels like doing at the time. He says you've got a real sweet ride, and he tuned it up for you, too. He will store it for you until the weather clears."

Lydia looked out the window. The snow was deep, but the blizzard was over when she finally was able to look outside. "Have to thank him for saving my bike."

"Did find blood in the snow," said Gunny, quietly. "Some of it isn't yours. No body or body parts. The slug was designed to fragment and send silver all over your body. It didn't hit any internal organs. Still, you are an incredibly strong woman to have survived and gotten that far. You went well over twenty miles right before a blizzard hit."

Lydia shook her head. "I have very little memory other than chomping down on the arm that held the gun, and then it all went very fuzzy."

"Silver poisoning," said Rachael. "Nasty stuff."

"Someone is hunting you," said Gunny. "We know you have an address at the house that your mom left you. But, we would like to politely request you stay here where we can protect you. Until we find out who this person is, you're in a great deal of danger, and so are all shifters. We've got to find out who's making that ammunition and shut them down."

"Be my guest." Lydia smiled ferally, and so did Stretcher.

"No, be ours," said Rachael, in a happy, singsong Disney voice. They all laughed.

After dinner, everyone cleaned up except Lydia, who went back to her recliner. Then, they watched a movie about an alien ursine race protecting a human baby from evil humans. Gunny made more popcorn mixed with miniature M&M's. The humans were soundly defeated, and the baby ended up back with his real parents. Lydia went to bed, exhausted after being awake for so long.

~

Several days later, Mitch came to speak with her about her bike. "She's a beauty. I've got her looking gorgeous and purring, and she is very safe in my garage. Don't worry about a thing."

Lydia coughed her laughter. "What do I owe you?"

"My wife's always on me about my temper, so I won't yell at you about your being family. At least Stretcher's family, she's kind of adopted." He grinned. "Had a real live dragon here. Had no idea how she managed to fly away in the middle of that blizzard, a big old Green."

"What the hell?" asked Lydia.

"They kind of like to keep to themselves. The green ones are the Earth ones, the blue ones are the ocean, and the red ones are fire. The red ones apparently hang out in volcanoes. I know, it's a shocker. And, no vampires. We are the only fangy ones around." He grinned a full canine grin at his own joke.

"Do they hoard gold and accept the ritual sacrifice of virgins?" asked Lydia, grinning back.

"No to the last two, but apparently they are rich. They have many thousands of years of history that they keep in songs. I don't know much more than that, except that we are able to hear them in our heads and call to the blue and green ones in times of great need. One of them flew you here in the blizzard."

"How can I thank that...dragon? I can't believe I said that."

"Like I said, the dragon is long gone. The best thing you can do is get yourself healthy and be a part of the greater shifter community. Are both your parents shifters?"

"No, my mother was a Dine weaver. My dad was a Crow who played in bars from Montana all the way down to Texas. He played rock and honky-tonk, whatever kind of bar it was. He had a few days with my mom, and then left, didn't come back until I was three. He didn't know he was a father, so he hadn't told my mother about the shifter thing. The medicine man on the rez checked me out, decided I was not a skinwalker but a shifter and that I was not evil, but I needed to learn all of our songs." She smiled, and began to sing. Rachael, in the kitchen, came out and sang with her. Their voices rose and fell together.

"It has been a long time since I sang the corn grinding song," said Rachael. "I am a little bit Dine as well." They spoke in Dine, then Rachael said in English, "I must go to pick more vegetables." She picked up the basket that was just inside the back door and left, all three pups following behind her.

"Wow." Mitch shook himself. "Anyway, all of us with the shifter gene are, as far as I can tell, First Nations people. Been hearing that there's some First Nations people in northern Canada who can change into polar bears, but I'm not sure."

Lydia grinned. "Are there bear shifters?"

"Yes, one of my wife's best friends is married to three," said Mitch.

"Not judging, but is it common for there to be polyamorous relationships among shifters?" Lydia tensed; she hadn't intended to ask such a delicate question so directly, or so soon. She was still on pain medication, a little patch in the middle of her back. Lydia resolved to keep a closer watch on her tongue. "Sorry, too direct."

"No, it sounds like you really haven't had much interaction with other shifters. Am I right?" Lydia nodded. "Well, my parents were monogamous, and so are Rachael and Gunny. However, there are quite a few shifter people who are polyamorous. Many animals in the wild are polyamorous. There aren't that many that are actually monogamous. And again, I don't think it really matters. It's an individual thing, or a group thing in our case. You have to do what makes you feel right in your heart and your soul."

"Damn, that's deep." James crossed the kitchen. Neither Mitch nor Lydia had heard James come in. "Our wife rubbing off on you, little brother?"

Mitch laughed. "I certainly hope so."

James went to the kitchen and opened the refrigerator. "Anyone want soda?"

"Yes, please," said Lydia. "I think there's some black cherry in there. I remember seeing it when they opened the fridge door at dinner."

"Get me a Coke," said Mitch.

"And there are my brother's real manners. A 'please' would have been helpful there." James came over to the couch with both sodas, and plopped down next to his brother. "I'm so pleased to see you looking so much better," said James. "I'm James, and this Neanderthal is my brother Mitch." All three of them popped the tops on their sodas. "Rachael and Gunny took us in after our parents died. We were part of the pack. Corinne showed up, bought a bike from my brother, got attacked, and ended up staying at our house. We fell in love, and we all ended up getting married."

"Lucky for me," said Mitch. "I was an ass. I'm damn lucky she forgave me."

"Anyway," said James, pointedly. "First of all, we'd like to officially welcome you to the shifter community. There are dogs, wolves, bears, mountain lions, and the elusive dragons, who apparently were hiding in caves all this time. We've started making connections among the First Nations and scattered tribes, trying to get ourselves together ever since that college kid was accidentally outed as being a wolf. We wolves kind of have an agreement with the government, with a few of us choosing to join the military in exchange for their not hunting, harming, or testing us. A lot of us live in these little valleys all over the place, and we stay hidden pretty well. We don't know if the government knows about the rest of the shifters, but I'm sure they'll figure it out at some point. The Canadian government knows, but they don't seem to care much about it. They consider it a First Nations affair."

Lydia nodded. "Thank you for your helpful information. My dad died when I was a kid, so I didn't learn or understand all that much about shifters. He was a loner, and I don't think he knew as much as you've just told me."

James carefully patted Lydia on the arm. "Well, then. We're here, ask us anything you want. Me, my brother Mitch here, Rachael, or Gunny, or Stretcher, if you can get her to talk. Gunny will tell you using salty language, so be forewarned."

"Oh, my virgin ears," said Lydia, dryly. Both men snorted.

"Also, I hear you've got a hacker friend trying to find the woman that attacked you. We have checked the hospitals and clinics, and no one has shown up with a mangled arm. We've also been searching in databases that we have access to, and we can't find the person either. It would be a hell of a lot easier if we knew what she was driving." James crushed his can and threw it all the way across the kitchen into the recycling.

Lydia shrugged. "I barely saw her when I was shot. I never saw the car I had seen on the tape. I didn't see what she drove up in. Hella Girl, my friend, says it was stolen and abandoned. I got shot. I feel really stupid. I should have been more knowledgeable about my surroundings."

"The wind was kicking up, and the snow was beginning to fall," said Mitch.

"Yes."

James nodded. "Also, getting shot takes a very short time, and you were poisoned by the silver. Stop beating yourself up over it. We've got people on the back roads trying to find her, but there are so many truckers going in and out of those places. We've got people getting security footage, but a lot of the smaller places don't have cameras at all. She hasn't come up on any of them."

Lydia sighed. "That sucks. And, thank you. That's a lot of time and energy to try to find this woman."

Mitch growled a little. "She attacked a shifter with a silver bullet, and called you a skinwalker. That cannot stand."

"Thank you. I know I'm saying that a lot, but I really mean it. I am half my mother's people, and I have never met my father's people. But, for some reason, I never felt I quite belong anywhere. Now I'm here, and I feel a sense of calmness and peace I've never felt before." Lydia grinned. "It could just be the silver poisoning." She coughed a laugh.

"I'm really glad you can joke about that, because I really thought you were going to die then and there," said James. "I can't imagine the repercussions if we had permitted something like that to happen. I'm stunned that a dragon was anywhere nearby and was able to help."

"I'm going to live. Then, I'm going to find out whoever the hell is stalking me, and I'm going to shoot her."

"Good to have goals," said Mitch.

James glared at his brother. "I thought the Navajo are a peaceful people."

Lydia narrowed her eyes. "Not when someone thinks it's a good idea to shoot me with a silver bullet. Or maybe it's my father's side coming out. Crow people are hard, and they don't take crap from anyone."

James nodded. "Well, first we have to find her. Could she be someone from school?"

"I went to rez schools, then went to a boarding school on a mountain where they had a lot of hiking trails. I could go out there and shift on the weekends, no problem. I went to college, made my own rugs with my mother's designs and sold them. My hacker friend is running that woman's face through all the school records, but hasn't had any hits. She's even tried aging her backwards to see if anything pops out, and nothing has come up. I have no idea where or how I would have crossed paths with this woman, but I move around. My mother died, and the house went to me, with most of her rugs. I left the house and rugs with my mother's apprentice, June, an incredible weaver. Mama said that girl is almost as good as she was."

Mitch nodded. "I understand the wanderlust."

Lydia struggled to explain her path. "I felt...haunted. Have laptop, will travel. I was slowly making my way up north to my father's people when the attacks started. The only thing that I can figure out is that I crossed paths with her somewhere and somehow she saw me change."

James nodded. "This is not going to be an easy hunt. Please, please accept Rachael and Gunny's offer for you to stay here while we look for this stalker/shooter. It would be really hard to protect you on the road, and right now you've got to take time to recover all of your strength."

"Plus, there's great food, pretty good movies, and really cute dogs," said Mitch. "We kept the girl dogs for our wife."

James mock-glared at his grinning brother. "And we promise to tell you anything we find out, and we'd like to work with your hacker friend to do everything we can to help. And, if you have any questions about the shifters, we're right here and ready to answer them."

"Cats aren't stupid, you know. We know how to take our time, recover, and spring with an attack no one can see coming. Just understand, like any cat, I deserve to be worshipped." James guffawed, Mitch snorted, and they could hear Stretcher's coughing laughter from the other room.

WORK

*L*ucas felt like he was seeing triple, not double. He was so tired he felt a little drunk or stoned, but he was neither one. He had two more clients who wanted their games completely finished and debugged by Christmas, which was crazy but the usual. The bizarre early blizzard hadn't set him back that much, because he had the sketches and knew what he wanted to do. When the blizzard stopped, Lucas finally managed to escape the claustrophobic house with his hissing-cat parents. If his mother wanted to help his father die, that was on her. He would support her. But, she told him that this was his busy time of year, and he had to buckle down and get to work. He shoveled his way to the greenhouse and met Julio halfway. He then shoveled the rest of the way to his cabin and settled in, missing his mother's cooking but not the cold infighting.

Lucas wasn't caught up, not nearly, but stopped to send a text to Mitch on the second day of the blizzard about the mountain lion. Mitch had texted back, *Female alive, poisoned, recovering.* That sounded ominous. Who the hell would poison a mountain lion? A crazed rancher? And how would they do it? Pass out poisoned steaks? That kind of shit had to be illegal. And it was absolutely certain to piss off Mitch, who had a hair-trigger temper from time to time. He thought of that ribbon of silver flowing out from under the dragon's claw. *Oh. Apparently, some of the myths about shifters are correct.*

After putting in the time at home, Lucas realized it had been days since he contacted anyone, except for a quick line to his mom from time to time. He stretched, feeling the vertebrae crack. He stripped, put his clothes in the collapsible laundry bag, took a short but blazingly hot shower, the water heated by the solar panels on the roof. He dressed again in long underwear, thick socks, jeans, and a blue sweater. He fixed himself a microwave mug omelet of eggs, shredded cheese from a bag, and crumbled bacon he'd cooked the day before. Or was it two days ago? The microwave dinged while he made himself coffee.

By the time he was done with breakfast and washed his breakfast omelet mug and his coffee carafe, Lucas felt slightly more human. He texted Mitch again. *Female still alive and healing?*

Mitch replied, *Come up for lunch at the farm. You can see for yourself.*

Well, that didn't sound ominous, that sounded friendly. Lucas texted back, *Come now?*

Two hours, was the reply back. Lucas grinned and scrambled to put his cabin to rights. When he was working designing imaginary worlds Lucas forgot about sleeping, eating, showering, or cleaning. His mother called it his pig phase. He had a small cabin, so putting things to rights wasn't that difficult. He dusted, swept, and mopped while drinking heavily from his coffee carafe. The cleaning didn't take long. With the bed made, things looked good, except for the sketch wall that covered the entire right corner of the cabin where his small computer desk sat side by side next to his drafting table. It kind of looked like a crime scene board, if the detective had been from the Lower Realms. He grinned and quick-sketched a new idea.

Lucas put on his boots, heavy coat, muffler, hat, and gloves, and stomped off to get to his battered maroon eleven-year-old truck. He and his mom had dug it out after the blizzard, and it wasn't damaged. He turned on the truck, and used a special heated scraper he had ordered online in order to get all the snow and ice off. He hopped in and realized he'd forgotten his coffee. He sighed, went back in and got it, along with a backpack with his sketch pad and colored pencils. Lucas had been over to the Weston's farm for lunch many times, and everyone seemed to either ignore or enjoy Lucas's drawing while chatting.

~

The drive to Mr. Harris' place didn't take that long. The man lived in a nice subdivision on a quiet curve of road partway to the lake, not the reservoir. Enterprising tweens and teens were out in droves shoveling snow all over the place, some with very loud snowblowers. Lucas parked the truck, got out, and very carefully made his way up the driveway to knock on the door.

Mr. Harris, a tall, bony man with a shock of brown hair on top, opened the door himself. He wore a deep blue sweatshirt and jeans. "The girls have practice," he said, in explanation. Sadie, at seven, was a phenomenal drummer. Ruby, a middle schooler, did flag team for games, which at this time of year was probably basketball. Jessica had karate, a black belt at nine, and Feria had tumbling at five, and a kids' coding club too. Lucas kicked the snow off his shoes, went in, and shut the door behind himself. "Want coffee? Don't have much time. Got to go pick up two of them pretty soon." He waited while Lucas kicked off his boots so he didn't track little puddles of wetness throughout the house.

"No, sir. Just coming for whatever language you have to give me. At this point, I don't even care what kind. I'll draw whatever you have." Lucas followed Mr. Harris to the basement door.

"Excellent," said Mr. Harris over his shoulder as he went down the stairs at a fast clip, hand on the railing. "I invented a language for a group of, shall we say, unusual beings who have been separated from everyone else for decades. I have language rules, songs, a few spells, a drinking game, and a game that involves cards, dice, and a mountain that the game pieces go up and down." The basement was done in white, gray, and maroon walls. The carpet was gray and nubby. There were five desks arranged on three walls, a dollhouse on a huge table in the middle along with a table for making doll furniture, and a barre and mirrored wall in the back, along with strange workout equipment, brightly colored balls and bands. The basement was well-lit, with can lights on a dimmer switch.

"Excellent. Maybe they'll go for having a virtual, or possibly a real-life 3D version of the game. It probably depends on how well the Christmas sales go. If the game bombs, they won't want to do the added extra level, or create a board game." Mr. Harris smiled, unfazed at finding out the board game might not sell.

Lucas looked at the writing, all curved in the middle and spiky on the tips. The game was absolutely fascinating, and Mr. Harris included a USB with the language, grammar rules, rules for the game, and a video of himself and Feria playing the game. "Feria is precocious. I'll make you a bet that this game can catch on." Lucas pulled out his cell phone. "Send me an invoice for a thousand. I know that sounds like a lot, but you have no idea how much you just saved my behind."

Mr. Harris' eyes lit up, and he quickly pulled up a file on his computer and sent it. Lucas received it in his email, linked into his payment account, and paid it in full. "Nice doing business with you, Mr. Harris."

"Anytime. No, actually, give me at least two weeks. I've got some new ideas in my brain, just gotta let it swish around in there a little more before it comes out." Mr. Harris waved his fingers around near his temples to explain the thinking process.

Lucas understood this process. "We creative types have to stick together, right?"

"You just bought us a new water heater. Just in time, too. You keep working at that pace, we might get those invisible braces for Ruby out of the way before high school. Lucas, you come on by in a week or so. I'll text you. How many games do they have you doing at the same time?"

"Three."

Mr. Harris gasped. "Don't burn yourself out, young man."

Lucas grinned. "Kind of have to. None of them will try to contact me again until March, unless it's to design a couple of new levels. You'd think with all the online gaming that the Christmas rush wouldn't be so important, but it's a down time in more than one culture worldwide."

"You remembered. Well, you were always one of my best Global History and Cultures students." The course had been a year long and counted for both advanced placement history and social studies credit. Plus, Lucas got a lot of papers out of it for Advanced Placement World News and Debate.

"Gotta go. I have lunch with friends about a mountain lion."

"A what?"

"A wildlife rescue, apparently successful. Some idiot poisoned a mountain lion across the border into the national park. She was saved." Lucas wanted to tell someone, anyone, about actually seeing a dragon, but was terrified of ending up in a little rubber room in a very special jacket. "I was there. It was...cool."

"Well, I'll keep working."

"Thanks." Mr. Harris led the way back up the stairs. Mr. Harris stopped at the laundry room and pulled the laundry out of the dryer, a *gi* for karate and a lot of long underwear. Lucas said goodbye and went to put his boots back on. He got his truck on the road just in time; a snowplow was heading around the bend in the road and may have blocked him in if he hadn't left when he did.

Lucas wanted to listen to an audiobook, but ended up listening to some screaming heavy metal to stay focused on the road. There were patches of black ice, and bridges were a real hazard. He made it to the Weston farm and parked his battered truck next to the line of all the others. He got out, stamped his way to the side door–no one much used the front door–and was surrounded by corgis before he even had a chance to knock. He petted all three of them on the head, and they danced in doggy joyful abandon, butts wriggling. The door opened, and Stretcher was there. The woman had been an angry teen and was now ex-military, so she scared the bejesus out of Lucas. "Hey."

"Get in, doofus, it's cold." Stretcher glared at him.

"Always nice to see you." Lucas stepped in and immediately took off his boots and put them under the bench in the mud room entry-way. He hung up his coat, muffler, and hat on the hooks on the wall. Stretcher wiped down the dogs' feet. The dogs followed his every move, hoping for a snuggle later on.

Lucas came to a complete halt on the smooth wooden floor in sock feet when he saw the woman sitting in the recliner, a laptop on a lap desk. She had black earphones on, and she was typing as fast as she could. Somehow, he knew that she was the mountain lion. He didn't know how he knew but decided not to figure that part out. He held up a hand.

She saw it, and one hand went to knock off her headset, and the other went to her side. "Whoa," said Lucas. "I come in peace. You're looking a lot better than the last time I saw you."

"I don't remember you," said the woman.

"That's Lucas," said Stretcher, heading towards the kitchen. "He's harmless."

"Mostly harmless," corrected Lucas. Both women coughed. It didn't take Lucas long to realize that they were laughing at him.

"She's Lydia," said Stretcher, as Lydia brought her hands back to her keyboard.

"You're the one in the woods," said Lucas, diplomatically. "I saw the dragon."

"Whoa," said Stretcher. "Draw her. I didn't get to see that." Lucas was stunned that he was having a conversation about dragons, especially one that he had actually seen, but he knew an order when he heard it. He sat down, backpack in hand, at the end of the couch. He tucked a knee under himself, pulled his sketchpad out, put the colored pencils next to his hand, and started drawing the dragon. "Wanna soda?" asked Stretcher.

"Absolutely," said Lucas. "Thanks," he added quickly. Everyone in the house was very clear about manners. He took his black cherry soda with a thank you and a smile, and caught a lap desk out of the air that Stretcher threw at his head.

Lucas had barely glimpsed the entire body of the dragon, but that moment of stunned astonishment was something he'd never forget.

He started with the head, got the dinner plate-sized eyes, realized he was going to end up stretching the drawing out across two pieces of paper. He didn't care; he had glue in the bag for these types of situations. He decided to glue the paper first, then got the contents of his brain, that one singular moment, out on the paper.

Lucas heard Stretcher stalk off to do whatever top-secret shit she did in her room, and Lydia put the headphones back on and resumed typing at a mad pace while his pencils skittered over the paper. The dogs cuddled with them on the couch. It was...amazing.

Lucas had the first sketch nearly done when Rachael came in from the cold, bushel baskets in hand. Lucas put down the sketch and colored pencils and rushed to help. "Hello, Lucas. Got four boxes shipped out today. People are hungry for the quinoa and amaranth flours. Sent a bunch of grain for Kylee to grind at the mill house by the river. What with all the diets people have going on, they love all sorts of grains other than wheat to grind. Cashew trees are tropical, and I don't think I can get them to grow hydroponically. If I did, I'd make a fortune."

"What about almond trees?" Lucas stood, walked to Rachael, and hauled one of the bushel baskets over to the kitchen.

"Good question, but no, they grow in the Mediterranean and the Middle East, then they take three years to become a cash crop. Be nice, though. A lot of these vegan-health kick types like to use almond flour in their recipes."

They put the baskets down on the kitchen counter, and Rachael took out a cutting board and knife and handed it to Lucas. She took out a plastic rolling board and a rolling pin for herself and took out three bowls. Rachael handed Lucas two fat red bell peppers, and put the fruits and vegetables she wasn't using away in the crisper in the refrigerator. Lucas washed his hands and began chopping the vegetables as Rachael put the bushel baskets out by the back door, came back, and washed her own hands. Rachael got out a bowl filled with rounds of dough that had been rising, took out a bit of flour and sprinkled it on her board and hands. She began kneading the dough, then rolling it out.

Lucas realized what Rachael was making, and diced red onion, tomatoes, and handfuls of mushrooms, then went into the refrigerator for the mild Italian sausage. He heated up a skillet and put in the tomatoes, then sprinkled them with fresh herbs, rosemary and basil. He took out another board and sliced up the sausage and threw it into another skillet, cutting it apart further with a plastic spatula. He added the mushrooms and bell peppers to the tomato sauce.

Then, Lucas took out the sausage, crumbled it, and put it in a little bowl and cooked up the onions. He scraped the onions into their own bowl, then got out the pepperoni and three types of cheese, then he sliced the pepperoni and grated the cheeses. Lucas tasted the marinara sauce and gave the wooden spoon for Rachael to taste. She approved, so Lucas put the marinara sauce in a bowl.

Rachael got the pizza shells in the oven, then took out the metal baking pan for the calzones. She made two, opened a can of sliced black olives and poured them into a bowl and made a vegetarian calzone for herself and made one with everything but the onions for Gunny. She slipped those in the oven, took out the shells, and whistled. Stretcher set the table. Gunny came in the back door, kissed his wife, washed his hands, took the pizza shells out of the oven, and filled the calzones. Stretcher and Lucas put the toppings on their pizzas while Lydia finished her typing and slowly made her way to the bathroom to wash up.

Lucas washed his hands, went to the bathroom, and offered Lydia his arm. She took it with a small smile, those big eyes of hers doing something to his heart, making it stutter a bit. Lydia ignored the pepperoni and onion but piled on everything else, making two personal pizzas for herself, heavy on the olives. Gunny got the sodas on the table, then Rachael and Lydia sang something in Navajo. Everyone sat down except Gunny, who got the pizzas and calzones out of the oven, served everyone the correct pizzas or pizza pockets, and passed around the bowl of marinara sauce for dipping. They ate the incredibly delicious food in nearly complete silence.

Corinne, Mitch, and James came in, stamping, via the back door. Gunny went over and hugged them all, making Corinne laugh and

Mitch push Gunny away with a snort. They washed up and made their own pizzas, and James said, "Sorry we're late. My *clients*." He spat out the word with venom. "They had a problem listening to any of the words that came out of my mouth. I ended up taking a dunk in an icy river, which everyone thought was funny until I texted Mitch, and he came over there roaring about hypothermia. He told them he'd sue if I contracted anything at all. That shut them up. At least two of them had apparently been reading some twaddle about the cold north, and decided ice fishing would be hilarious. What they really did was get drunk, cause problems, and attempt to leave all of their beer cans behind. I got changed, then we got them rounded up and forced them to clean up. Smoked the fish the night before and packed it, thank Spirit. Then, we got them to the airport an hour early. Mitch put the fear of God in them about leaving any negative reviews, because he took pictures of the campsite they had attempted to leave. Trash rules are clearly posted. Mitch threatened them with fines."

"Had to get this one warmed up before we could arrive." Mitch pointed at his brother. "And he smelled like fish guts." Corinne grinned, and everyone else laughed.

"Me, my truck, my blankets, everything. Mitch put my washable gear in the washer and got the truck detailed, then swung back to pick us up." James clapped his brother's shoulder.

Mitch grinned. "Family takes care of family, but he owes me one, or possibly two, because those fish guts smelled terrible."

Corinne grinned. "Had to wash everything twice. Did get my Java-Script working, though."

Lydia nodded. "That's good. That can get tricky." The timer dinged, and they fell upon their pizzas as if they had never eaten before.

"Was it the fishing guides consortium website with the dancing fish, or the glassmakers' one with all the stained glass?" Lydia asked Corinne, once they had all eaten half their pizza.

Corinne reached for the shaker of parmesan. "Dancing fish. I got that thing up and running. Traffic increased by four percent, and it had been up for only an hour."

"Damn, girl," said James. "That means we're going to the B&B for Christmas break!"

"The B&B?" asked Lydia.

Rachael grinned, piling up the dirty plates. Stretcher took them to the sink. "There is a special bed-and-breakfast retreat-type place for shifters," she said. "That's where we met our first dragon."

"I drew the one I saw," said Lucas, gesturing towards the couch.

"Bring it over here!" said Gunny. "Didn't get to see her 'cause I wasn't part of the rescue you gentlemen did."

Lydia bowed her head. "Thank you for that. I was in no position to go any farther, apparently."

Lucas grabbed the sketchpad and passed around the double-size picture. "That's exactly it!" James crowed. "That's the dragon we saw!"

"She's a beauty," said Gunny, looking over James' shoulder. James passed it over, and Gunny, Rachael, and Lydia stared at the picture.

Lydia seemed frozen. "I know what I am. I've known my whole life. My dad taught me how to hunt and fish. It shouldn't surprise me, it really shouldn't. But I hadn't heard a word about dragons until I got here. And now, three of you are saying that you saw one?"

Lucas nodded sympathetically. "I grew up around these two, went to the same schools, ate food here as fast as Gunny and Rachael could make it, but I had no idea what they were until I met you."

Rachael looked apologetic. "It's not that we didn't trust you, but we knew you would tell your mom and your father is someone we couldn't trust. If he overheard..."

Lucas bowed his head. "I get it. I don't trust the guy either."

Mitch put a hand on Lucas' shoulder. "I'm sorry about your dad. Sorry you had to find out like that."

Lucas' eyes were flat. "He smoked and drank, didn't listen to a word any doctor said to him."

Gunny grunted. "We stand ready to help. You need a toothbrush at four in the morning, call us. We'll help out financially, too. Your mother shouldn't have to end up in debt because of all of this."

Lucas snorted. "My mother is all about the insurance. That's where all of this winter money I'm making is going to, paying for insurance for myself for a year, not just a salary or rent for the cabin. I haven't asked my mother directly whether or not there's a cancer rider on the insurance policy, but it wouldn't surprise me."

"I'm so sorry," said Rachael, her eyes filling with tears. "What kind of cancer is it?"

"Lungs, and it's spread to his liver and lymph nodes." Lucas nearly shrugged, then thought better of it.

Lydia's eyes grew dark. "I'm sorry. That sounds horrible."

James nodded. "We had...someone...try to heal him with touch. Your dad didn't know what was going on because this is something we don't talk about. This...healer...said it was a no-go, that whatever it was was too far gone to help."

"Thanks for trying," said Lucas. "I hate to say it, but he did this to himself, smoking and drinking. I think whatever the hell he's angry at ate him up inside."

Rachael sighed. "The world has changed, and your father was completely unable to change with it. We talked to your mother about the way that he was treating you. I'm sorry. I think it made things worse."

Lucas reached across the table and held Rachael's hand. "No, you got them separated, which is more that I could do. Then I got out, and now I have three different companies wanting work from me. I think I'm going to fall over from exhaustion."

"Me too," said Lydia. "This...setback wears me out."

"I only have two clients, but me three," Corinne chimed in. "Got to make the money before the winter doldrums set in. Besides, I don't really want to run around in that crap out there, anyway." Corinne gestured vaguely towards the great outdoors.

Lucas grunted. "There's so much black ice on the bridges, you might as well have a sign saying *don't cross*."

Stretcher went to the kitchen, two of the dogs trailing her. She came back with a huge wooden tray, put the tray in the middle of the table, and said, "Key lime, caramel fudge, and cherry cheesecake bites." Gunny got up and came back with small plates and forks. They all dug in and laughed about the sheer amount of work they all had to do.

Lucas had a lot to think about, but he finished the sketch, scanned it with the hand scanner in his pack, and sent the scan to Mitch and James as they were all sitting around the table drinking coffee, ready to fuel up for their next endeavors. "Hey!" said Gunny. "I want one too!"

"I'll send you the file." Lucas pulled up his phone and sent it. "Don't size it to the paper; you'll need two sheets."

"Good," said Gunny. "Thanks."

The party broke up, there were hugs all around, and Lydia said, "Thank you for saving me."

"No problem," said Mitch.

"You're family," said James.

Lucas' face turned cherry-red. "I didn't save you. I almost..." He looked up, horrified, realizing for the first time what he had almost done. "I almost murdered you," he whispered.

James stepped forward to explain. "Lucas thought you were a severely wounded mountain lion a few minutes away from death with a blizzard on its way. He was trying to put you out of your misery. He had no idea who or what you really were. Mitch stopped him, and then Lucas helped us save you."

"I am so sorry," said Lucas, stammering, cringing under the weight of almost killing this incredible person standing in front of him.

Mitch went over, gave him a sideways bro hug. "Lucas, quit beating yourself up. You didn't know, I stopped you, you helped with field surgery, and everything ended up being okay."

"I...okay," said Lucas.

"That being said, if you ever try to kill me again, I'll kill you back. I am Dine, but I am also part Crow. I will defend myself." Lucas could only nod at the hardness in Lydia's eyes.

"Come on," said Mitch. "We have time for a snowball fight before we all have to go back."

"Speak for yourself, brother," said James. "I've been cold and wet once today, and I really don't plan to do it again."

"And Lucas and I both have so much work to do that we're

stunned stupid," said Corinne. "You two, boots on, coats, hats, all that stuff, then get me the hell home."

"Yes, ma'am," said Mitch, rushing to put on his boots. His brother sat down beside him and put his own boots on.

"How did you get them trained like that?" Rachael asked Corinne. "It took me years just to get them to shut the door properly."

"I withhold sex," said Corinne, sweetly. Rachael burst out a laugh, and Lydia and Stretcher both coughed their own laughs. Gunny roared with laughter, shoulders shaking, making the dogs who had run out from under the table looking to go outside stare at him, startled.

They all got out the door. Gunny followed with the dogs, and they ran around outside. Lucas followed the rambunctious dogs and the brothers and their beautiful wife, still wondering how the hell he could possibly make up for nearly killing someone. Someone who was a mountain lion, and a beautiful woman with caramel eyes and a laser stare when she wanted to make a point.

"Hey," said James, circling back, after he got the rest of his family in the car. "Lucas, seriously. If it had been a mountain lion and not a human, it would have been the right call."

Lucas froze again. He thought of all the stupid hunts his father dragged him on, how something so completely alive had gotten so dead, dropped with a single shot, and shuddered. "There aren't any were-deer or elk, are there?"

"Generally shifters choose predator species, so no," said James. He patted Lucas's face. "Hey, dude. Snap out of it. You've got so much more work to do that we probably won't see you again for a month. Go home, and get it done. Health insurance, remember?"

Lucas nodded and stumbled to his truck. He made it home, and used the new language he'd bought to make a dragon language. Using his sketch he had done at the Weston farm, he made dragons that lived in a magical cliff, coloring them every color of the rainbow.

～

*A*fter two weeks of intensive work, Lucas quit his "pig phase" and cleaned up his cabin again. Lucas went to the greenhouse to see his mom first, primarily to make sure she didn't need anything. She was doing fine. According to Ana, his dad was in the basement, still smoking like a smokestack despite it becoming harder and harder for him to breathe. He talked about something he never really considered. "So, you're growing entirely different things from Rachael?"

Ana belly-laughed. "Who do you think got me into hydroponics and vertical farming in the first place? Yes, I'm very careful not to compete with her on anything. We're here to support each other, not tear each other down. But she's been wonderful. She's been by with gourmet coffee, goat cheese, cherry cheesecake, and a good ear."

"Good."

Ana held onto her son's shoulders. "Lucas, don't spend one minute worrying about me getting through the death of your father. Your father's insurance will pay for a nurse when it gets bad, and for hospice when the time comes. The Westons have offered to help with whatever it is that I may need, but I don't need much."

"Okay," Lucas stammered out.

Ana sat down on a potting bench, and Lucas sat down next to her. "I sort of knew that this would be the ending, somewhere deep inside me. Your father won't grow, won't change, and has no interest in listening to anyone at all, especially doctors. He's willing to take the pain medication and nothing else. So he drinks, smokes, and basically gets high on pain meds in that man-cave basement of his. Don't know what the man has against sunlight. I'm going to have to fumigate the damn thing when he dies." Her eyes glistened with tears.

"This is going to sound incredibly stupid. But, why do you still love him?"

Ana choked out a laugh. "I have no idea. He certainly hasn't done anything to earn it in years. I have no reason whatsoever for loving the man. He hit me with words, not fists." She took Lucas's hand in hers. "I'm sorry I didn't see that his misunderstanding of who you were damaged you so much."

Lucas sighed. "You mean, his homophobia? I draw, I hate sports, I play poker, I don't want to drink or smoke, so I must be gay? Can he be more stereotypical in his thinking? And why should it matter? Either he loved his son, or he didn't. He obviously didn't."

"Maybe you should talk to him. You're kind of running out of time if that's something you want to do."

"What am I going to say? I'm sorry we didn't have a relationship because you're a homophobic ass?"

Ana grinned. "Yes, I think that's exactly what you should say. But not today. Are you going up to see the Westons?"

Lucas nodded. "I treated the woman that's living there kind of bad when we first met. I kinda...was Dad, made a stupid assumption." Lucas choked out a laugh. "All this time I was trying to be the opposite of him, I ended up making the same mistake."

Ana nodded. "I see. So what are you going to do to make amends?"

Lucas smiled. He pulled out his sketchbook from his backpack. "This is Lydia." He had labored hard over the blue-black hair, the firmness of her chin.

"Wow. She is First Nations, isn't she?"

"Dine, which is Navajo."

"I, too, am what they call First Nations. Mayan. We're not treated well in Mexico, so our family came here long ago to be treated even worse sometimes." Ana grunted. "Anyway, you have Mayan blood running through your veins. Respect her, respect her heritage. What are you going to do to make this right?"

Lucas showed her his drawings, one of a healthy, tawny mountain lion, one of an enormous green dragon lined with gold. "Mamacita, trust me. These pictures will mean something to her. But I'm thinking I should also stop for chocolate."

Ana laughed. "First of all, these are beautiful, very lifelike. Your skills are improving, *mijo*. Also I suggest ice cream for everyone to go along with those brownie bites Rachael and Stretcher like to make, and chocolates for your lady."

Lucas choked, stumbled getting his words out. "She's not my lady. I barely know her. I've only met her once, no, twice."

"If you plan to bring her chocolates, she's your lady. Neither one of you happens to know it yet." Ana patted his shoulder. "You should never bring a native woman dead flowers. A small plant is appropriate. Something she can grow indoors and put on her windowsill." She looked around and found a small cactus covered in thin white spines that looked like fuzz. "This, son, will grow in snow and heat, needs little watering, and will flower for a very short time once a year." She artfully put it in a carry bag and tied it with a ribbon. "Keep it safe, and don't put it next to the ice cream."

Lucas carefully slid it into the pack in front of his precious sketch pad and pencils. "I will be careful with it," he promised, and kissed his mother on the cheek. "Thank you," he said.

"Anytime," said Ana. She kissed her son's cheek then pushed him. "Now go," she said. "You're burning daylight." Lucas grimaced when he turned his back to his mother and headed back to the door, not liking to hear the same phrases father had repeated all the time out of his mother's mouth. He waved at his mother and made his way to the truck.

~

*L*ucas headed to Mr. Harris' house first. Lucy answered the door, resplendent in flaming red hair in a ponytail on top of her head, some sort of shimmering purple leotard, ballet slippers, and something plastic in her mouth. Lucas grinned; Mr. Harris must have had enough money left over from the water heater to get Lucy started on the invisible braces. "He's in the basement." Lucy slammed the door behind Lucas, then ran upstairs.

Lucas took off his boots then headed to the basement. No one was in the living or family rooms or in the kitchen, which disconcerted him. He knocked on the door to the basement to let Mr. Harris know he was coming and then jogged down the stairs.

Mr. Harris was wearing a maroon button-down with a blue Mr. Rogers sweater over it, jeans, and a very determined little girl hanging on his neck. "One more game!" said Feria. The five-year-old was big for her age and had auburn hair and slightly tilted eyes like her mother, Rhea, along with her father's slimness. Rhea had died in childbirth with Feria, which is part of why Mr. Harris doted on her and all his daughters.

"No, Feria. Ah, the man of the hour, or at least the next fifteen minutes."

Lucas grinned. "I got your text. I know it was two days ago, but I did finally show up. Do you have another language for me?"

"This one is awesome," said Mr. Harris. "You can go alien or mage, either one."

"Since the game I'm working on has both, I'll go for it. The usual price?"

"Since there's no added board game, yes. Have you heard from the gaming company?" Mr. Harris got his daughter off his neck and sent a purchase order via email to Lucas, his former student, for six hundred dollars.

"Yes, I have. They said they are knee deep in alligators right now, but they were very excited by the video about the board game. They say they can 3D print and ship it. They have some interns calling about pricing."

Feria scrunched up her nose. "Do they live in Florida?" she asked.

Mr. Harris laughed as he pulled up the script to show Lucas. "No, Little Bit. *Knee deep in alligators* means you are very busy. As we all are this time of year."

"Halloween? I'm going as Amazing Grace."

Lucas knew that the little girl was referring to Amazing Grace Hopper, the inventor of compilers, among other things, and not the song. "That sounds awesome!" Lucas had only figured out it was nearing Halloween on the drive up because of all the pumpkins, ghosts, and witches in people's windows. Calendars didn't mean a lot when you were sitting in front of the computer day after day.

Mr. Harris showed Lucas the language on his computer. "Here's the main words. They intersect, like puzzle pieces."

"That's amazing," said Lucas, meaning every word, and realized why Mr. Harris had to show him the whole thing. He would not have understood what he was looking at otherwise. Mr. Harris went over sentence structure then gave Lucas a USB. Lucas took out his phone and sent the payment.

Mr. Harris took his phone out of his pocket when it shook and grinned. "Nice doing business with you once again." They shook hands.

"Hey!" said Feria, hands on hips. "My daddy got the idea from watching me do puzzles. I'm really good at puzzles. And you don't pay me anything? I want a cut!"

Mr. Harris stared at his daughter, stunned. He'd never explicitly explained to her exactly why Lucas kept coming back to their house, what the USBs were, and that he was paid for creating languages. Lucas solemnly took out his ancient wallet, pulled out a battered $5 bill, and gave it to Feria. "For your services, milady," he said.

Feria solemnly took the money. "I'll keep him in ideas. I want my cut." She took the bill and ran up the stairs.

Mr. Harris sighed. "She's gifted. She reads at a ninth grade level, she plays chess, she can do complex mathematical equations, and I have no idea how I'm going to keep up with her. I have to pretend I'm smarter than her, and at some point, she's going to figure out that's not true."

"I can help her learn coding." Lucas had no idea why those words came out of his mouth, but somehow it felt right. "I'm better at drawing, though. Has she shown an aptitude for art or music? A lot of gifted kids do have that going on with them."

"Not so far. She is clumsy as hell, which is normal for a five-year-old, and makes thumb drawings. You know, she puts down an image of her thumb and turns it into a bunny or whatever. She likes rock music, but we all do."

"Okay. I now see that you and I are going to be doing business until we both get old and gray."

Mr. Harris laughed. "Probably. Of course, by the time she is nine, my daughter Feria will probably be doing business with you instead."

Lucas nodded. "She sure has a mercenary vibe about her."

Mr. Harris laughed. "You just gave us an excuse to hold out on her for a while. She's been trying to do extra chores to get money, and I have no idea what she's trying to save up for. I'll get one of her sisters to tell me. I'll probably go with it, as long as it doesn't blow up the house." Lucas laughed. "You laugh now, but someday you'll have one, and you'll feel my pain." Mr. Harris stretched and his back audibly popped. "Literally."

They said their goodbyes, and Lucas was extremely happy that he wasn't in Mr. Harris' shoes at the moment. He stopped at the store and bought caramel almond fudge ripple, chocolate mint, and banana cherry chunk ice creams, and a small box of chocolates. He hauled everything to the truck, made sure the ice cream and the cactus were not anywhere near each other, and made good time heading to the farm despite the black ice still on the roads.

SEPARATION

*L*ydia had been plowing through her work for two weeks. She got the one project finished and kept going back and forth on the other two. She was still exhausted but far less weak. She could move around on her own, take her own shower. She was feeling really good about that part. She was tired of Stretcher and Rachael having to help. Her pain patches were getting smaller and smaller. She could probably dispense with them in the next week or so.

The problem was the people. Everyone in the house entered and left all day long. Mitch, James, and/or Corinne would show up completely unannounced. The dogs constantly went in and out, always asking with sad eyes to be picked up and cuddled when they returned from the cold outside. People talked, answered cell phones, slammed doors, and made a massive amount of food three times a day, plus snacks. Lydia knew that the shifters ate more. She certainly did. But, she had been on the road and picking up food from diners and drive-ins, not cooking it. She had forgotten how long cooking could take. Then there were all the chores, washing and folding laundry, sweeping and mopping floors, dusting, even moving furniture to sweep underneath. Lydia was ready to scream.

Then that guy came back, the one who had almost killed her. It had taken her nearly a week for her to get over her resentment at that. James had explained just how helpful Lucas had been, in great detail. After all, Lucas had been trying to put what he thought was an animal out of its misery. So Lydia let it go. Then he was there, coming in the back door. He had his backpack on and several bags in his hands. Stretcher came out of nowhere, grabbed the bags, looked inside, and actually squealed.

"Give the chocolates back," Lucas said, in a clear, calm voice, as if speaking to a recalcitrant toddler. Stretcher huffed, then threw them back. Lucas caught the box, nearly dropped it, then caught it again. "Skies above, Stretcher. What are you, two years old?" He sighed, put the little silver and gold box of chocolates down, took off his backpack, his boots, and his outerwear, picked up the box, and came up to Lydia. "Lydia, these chocolates are for you." She took them, then put them down next to her laptop. He reached into his backpack and came out with the little barrel cactus.

Lydia took it then shoved away Rascal's little black nose. "No, Rascal, you touch this, you get spikes in your snoot."

Lucas pulled out his sketchpad and took out two double-sized rolled-up pictures. "I didn't see you except when you were wounded in your other...form. I took some liberties." Lydia looked down at herself in puma form. He'd gotten the color of her eyes a little wrong, but her eyes had most likely been closed at the time she'd been collapsed in the woods, silver coursing through her veins.

Stretcher silently slid up behind Lydia. "That's you. I bet the eyes are wrong, aren't they?"

"Yes, but in all fairness, Lucas here only saw me when I was wounded. Eyes closed."

"True," said Stretcher.

Lucas carefully unfolded another picture, this one a larger and far more detailed study of the dragon. "Whoa," said Lydia. "This is awesome!"

Lucas bowed his head. "I'm very sorry that I almost tried to kill you," he said. "It was reflex. My father kept taking me hunting, and I hated it because he thought that I was gay, and he was trying to make me into a real man. I hadn't been hunting with him in years, but that day he wanted meat for Mama's freezer, and I couldn't let Mama down."

"Are you...no, my gaydar is pretty good." Stretcher's eyes opened wider. "Oh. That's why your dad is such a dickhead."

Lucas snorted out a laugh, and Lydia coughed. "He is. Anyway, I'm sorry."

Lydia stared at both of the pictures, entranced. She was able to keep the dog's snoot away from the cactus in the nick of time. "Can you..." she asked Stretcher, handing up the cactus.

"In your room. Right," said Stretcher. She slid soundlessly away with the cactus.

"I didn't think about the dogs," said Lucas. In all fairness, neither had his mother. "Sorry about that."

Lydia waved a hand, dismissing the concern. "I could let the dog get poked, and Rascal would learn his lesson, but I really don't feel like cleaning up dog pee on my lap at the moment."

Stretcher coughed twice while coming out of Lydia's room. "I'd pay to see that."

"No, thank you," said Lydia. "Anyway, I forgave you last week. You've been mega-busy at work?"

Lucas sat down, pleased at being forgiven. "You know it. It sounded like from what you said last time I was here that you are in the same boat."

"It doesn't help that my sleeping schedule is thrown to shit, there are people in here all the time, and I keep having to take inexplicable naps." Lydia grimaced. "Plus the pain. Nowhere near like it was at first. Just enough to irritate the hell out of me. Like a thorn in your paw that you can't get out. Then there's the constant low-level exhaustion and feeling like I'm a hundred years old when I'm trying to move. I can get around on my own now, but it takes me forever to do something that used to take me two minutes."

"Sounds like working underwater." Lucas picked up a sad-eyed Wayne. He scratched the dog behind the ear, and Wayne groaned with pleasure.

"Exactly!" said Lydia. "I want to do my best work, but I've had to pay Corinne to go over what I've done to make sure I haven't done something incredibly stupid before I turned something in." She sighed. "And everything I said sounds incredibly ungrateful."

Stretcher grinned. "You're a cat. Cats like their alone time."

"She gets me!" said Lydia. Stretcher and Lydia coughed again. Lucas grinned, amused.

Rachael banged in the back door, a huge pumpkin in each hand. Stretcher and Lucas ran over to take one from her. "Skies above," said Stretcher. "Pumpkin pie, pumpkin soup, pumpkin scones...."

"Sounds great!" said Lucas, staggering under the weight of his pumpkin. He deposited it on the breakfast bar.

"I hate pumpkin," said Stretcher. "I like carving them, my knife skills are pretty good, but pumpkin guts I do not like at all."

"I hate pumpkin, blueberries, cranberries, meringue, onions, cooked green beans, squash, and turkey," said Lydia.

"You win," said Stretcher.

"Blue skies!" said Lucas. "The woman hates Thanksgiving!" Rachael laughed, and Stretcher and Lydia coughed twice.

Gunny came in the room, all bonhomie, carrying a giant box. "Maple ham," he said, depositing the giant ham on the counter with a thud. "What's so funny?"

Stretcher grinned. "Lydia hates any Thanksgiving food!" she said.

"Except salad and rolls," Lydia clarified. "And ham and duck."

"That's it. You're too strange for this house. I would put you in the last cabin out there, but it's not finished." Gunny huffed, then went out to the car for the rest of the groceries.

"My mom has one," said Lucas. Everyone looked at him. "We just finished the insides. The novelist got sick and is working from home and is coming next year instead." Lydia looked at him as though she were boring holes through him. "What?"

"Just like the tiny houses outside? Loft bed, loft storage on the other side, work area, toilet, and shower? And all those little wooden nooks and crannies that hide things like towel racks and cutting boards?" Everyone stared at Lydia. "What? Gunny showed me the plans."

"Yes," said Lucas, slowly. "The same team makes all the tiny houses and cabins around here."

Lydia whipped out her phone and a credit card. "Give me your mother's number," she ordered. Lucas recited it to her, and by the time Gunny came back with four sacks in each hand and two dogs at his feet, Lydia had a new home.

"Are you sure you should…" Rachael started to ask.

"No, let her go," said Stretcher. "It's a cat thing." Rachael shrugged, and got out a spoon and two bowls, one for the pumpkin guts, one for the seeds.

Lydia stood up and went to pack. She was not one to waste time, and she needed to get over and move into her rented cabin before someone else snapped it up. It actually took her longer to break down her computer and all the peripherals and put them away than it took for her to pack her collapsible duffel with her clothes and toiletries. She hugged Gunny and Rachael, and said, "Thank you for all you've done for me."

"Shifters stick together. And you're coming back to visit all the time, right?" Rachael took out two huge knives from their block and sat them down next to the bowls.

Lydia pretended to make doe eyes at Stretcher. "And I can give you all my undying love and gratitude…."

Stretcher stretched out a hand like a claw, and put it on Lydia's shoulder. "You do, I remove your face." They both coughed. Gunny rolled his eyes and put away the groceries while his wife cut the tops off the pumpkins.

~

*L*ydia didn't say a word to Lucas, just followed him out to his truck. He tried to help carry things for her, but she wasn't having any of it. So he settled for opening up the truck door, helping her put her things inside, and giving her a boost into the seat, his hands on her hips. He dropped his hands, afraid of offending her, closed the door, ran around the truck, got in, and put the heater on as high as he could get it.

Lucas made small talk on the way back, pointing out cabins and farms, a covered bridge, kept his mouth shut when he had to drive over a bridge or take a curve. They made it back alive, and Lucas found Ana giving the cabin the last dusting. Ana rushed to help Lydia move in. "Fastest funds I've ever gotten," said Ana. She looked Lydia up and down. "Accident?"

"Shooting." Lydia patted Ana's hand at the woman's shocked face. "Don't worry, there are people in a couple states looking for the shooter. Got myself a stalker, and it blew me away that it was a female person. Never saw her before, either."

"What does she look like?" asked Ana. Lydia showed them the picture, then texted it to them both. "I'll keep an eye out, and so will Julio." Ana showed Lydia a picture of Julio. He looked bigger in the photo than he really was in a cowboy hat, black jacket, and jeans. He had dark eyes and a small half-smile on his lips. "He helps me with the hydroponics farm."

"Like Rachael," said Lydia.

Ana laughed. "She taught me everything I know. I grow grains and nuts and have them ground into flour or sold whole for the health-conscious. I grow some flowers. I also grow flax, which is turned into linen, and the seeds are beloved by the health food crowd as well."

"Excellent!" Lydia unpacked her computer and began setting it up.

Ana grinned. "Let me take you on a two-step tour of the cabin. We have the banquet, where you're sitting at, and the table can be folded up and the other bench you've got your feet on can be pushed in to make another bed. You decide if you don't feel like climbing up into the loft. Loft on the right is the sleeping loft, loft on the left has canned food, pallets of juices and sodas, that sort of thing. There's enough food there to keep you going for two and a half weeks. Replace what you use; it is vital for blizzards."

"I will." Lydia grinned.

Ana nodded. "There's a single electric cooking burner, a

microwave under the cabinet, and an electric kettle and in a rice cooker hiding in this little cabinet over here. I suggest looking up rice cooker recipes on YouTube; it's really easy to throw stuff in there, turn the thing on, come back and have your food all done. There is a ¾ size refrigerator here, and the water filter pitcher in there is already filled up. This drawer has silverware and cooking utensils. Use any of the spices on this built-in spice rack you want. Ask my son about the grocery delivery app. That television swings out and swings back." Ana pointed up to the flat-screened television, then towards the back. "Bathroom is over there, along with a shower. Everything is run by solar panels on the roof. You have any questions or problems, you text me. If there's an emergency you call me anytime, but call nine-one-one first if it's a bad one."

"That's fantastic!" Lydia grinned. "Thank you for all your help. Lucas, please download the grocery delivery app." She unlocked her phone and handed it to him. Lucas downloaded the app and handed her phone back. "Thank you both, but I've got so much work to do, and I've also got to deal with the fact that my body wants to take a nap whenever it feels like it."

Ana said, "I know it sounds annoying considering your workload, but do what your body tells you to do. You'll heal faster in the long run." Lydia nodded curtly at her. "Come on, Lucas, all three of us have got work to do."

Lydia smiled. "Thank you, Lucas, for the ride."

Lucas nodded. "No problem. Since you can't ride a Harley in this mess, text me or my mom if you need a ride into town. We probably wouldn't leave immediately, but we can give you time to get ready."

"That would be fantastic. Bye!" Lydia said, brightly. Ana took the hint and dragged her son out of the cabin.

It didn't take long to move in and set herself up at the table. Lydia banged out her work, thinking only of how to make everything work correctly. She had learned a variety of new techniques during those boring hours on the road. Her day went very well, and she was able to get two whole web pages hammered out.

She was stunned to find fruit juices, sodas, a package of chicken breast and another of salmon, and salad fixings in the refrigerator. There were frozen pizzas, calzones, and breakfast burritos in the freezer. Lydia seared the beautiful salmon and sliced it over a salad that included carrots, greens, and tomatoes. She found a lovely balsamic dressing on the door of the small refrigerator. She grabbed some cherry water, sat, and ate her small dinner. She washed the few dishes in the sink, dried them with a towel hanging on a little wooden rack, and put everything away. She was delighted to be on her own.

Lydia managed to push through some more work before nearly falling over with exhaustion. She looked outside and saw that it had gotten dark already. She put on the television, found some microwave popcorn in the cabinet, popped and salted it, and had herself a little movie night. She swung up the table, too tired to make it up the stairs, and pushed the bench over to create the bed. Lydia found the bench was full of blankets, sheets, and pillows, made up her bed, and slid into sleep early, the darkness and quiet a cocoon all around her.

~

In the morning, she heard crunching, and looked out the window to find a hiker in a bright orange coat, black snow pants, and orange hat with snowshoes and poles making his or her way into the woods. Gender was impossible to tell, because the snow-shoer was covered from head to toe and was of average height. There were bright, chirping cardinals in the trees that swooped down to take bird food out of the feeders on tall poles. Squirrels chittered and chased each other through the trees, a mix of pine, oak, silver birch, and maple. Lydia smiled at the beauty of the natural world outside of her window. She zapped and ate a breakfast burrito she found in the freezer and drank some orange juice.

Lydia took a brief but very hot shower, reveling in the heat. She dressed in long underwear, jeans, a sweater, and warm socks, and started slamming out her work. She decided to blast some music; she preferred dance music with no words so that she didn't stop mentally and try to remember the lyrics while she was trying to work. She switched to Navajo rap while she translated a bunch of Dine to create an English version of a Dine website.

Lydia made another salad for lunch, this time with the chicken. She realized she was going to have to order some food, so she ordered pre-marinated chicken in tandoori and Italian herb flavors, more of that incredible salmon, salad, veggies, pasta, and more popcorn. A teenager with a flat face, slightly tilted eyes, and a quick smile on a 4x4 delivered the groceries. She wore a blue snowsuit with reflective patches on the back and front, and maroon snow boots. "Name's Tomma. I do deliveries all over the mountain. Whatever you need, I can get it for you. Did Ana tell you about the app?"

"Yes, and Lucas put it on my phone for me. That was fast. It's been a little over forty minutes!" Lydia handed over a five-dollar bill.

Tomma held up her hand. "You've already paid me for the delivery."

"This is for superior service." Tomma took it, waved, pulled down her ski mask, and shot off on her ride.

Lydia closed the door, shivered, and put the groceries away. She took a quick nap, then switched back to dance music. She went back to the first website and checked it for errors, then went to the third website, a First Nations artisan co-op. She took a break for dinner, and double-checked all of her work while the pasta, veggies, and chicken cooked in the rice cooker. She closed her work out, made a huge mug of mint green tea with honey, and ate her food.

Ana came by just after she put the dishes away. "How is everything going?"

"Come in," said Lydia. "Would you like some tea?"

Ana nodded, came in, stripped off her blue jacket and hung it up on the hook on the door, took off her snow boots, and sat down gracefully at the table. Lydia fixed the tea. "Busy day?" Ana asked.

"Yes, but I'm definitely getting everything cleared up. I lost a third of my contracts because of my stalker, but the police reports have made it a lot easier to get some of them back. I've got new clients now, and the money's coming in well." Lydia handed Ana a steaming mug of mint green tea doctored with honey and sat with her own mug.

"Thank you," said Ana. She tasted it. "Fantastic! Are you getting enough rest?"

Lydia nodded. "Took my nap. They're getting a little shorter, and I'm still lodgy and disoriented when I first wake up."

"There's a small apartment attached to the greenhouse, basically something like this, actually. Sometimes I catch a nap up there during the day. Made it down to see Kylee at the mill today; she grinds the grains for me. There is buckwheat flour in that cabinet over there, along with the pancake recipe on the back of the container. Goes great with some fruit. There's frozen strawberries in your freezer."

"That sounds like a good breakfast for tomorrow," said Lydia. She yawned. "Sorry, my day is catching up with me. Want to watch a sitcom?"

Ana nodded. "You know, it's been a long time since I sat down and watched something completely stupid on TV. There's the one about the space doctor…"

"That sounds good," said Ana. She called it up on the television, and they relaxed and concentrated on the medical problems humans had treating flying aliens.

~

*E*very morning the snowshoer went back out. Lydia found out the woman's name was Ryder Davis, a wildlife expert, bird-watcher, and novelist. The woman wrote murder mysteries about an animal rescuer living in Alaska. The woman inspired Lydia to get out more. Lydia turned in one of her websites, got paid, and rented some snowshoes from Ana. Unlike older-style snowshoes that looked like tennis rackets, these were metal with a hitch to put a snow boot.

Lydia got her exercise by hitching on the snowshoes and walking around the cabin every morning. At first she could barely make it to the corner and back. By the third day, she could make herself go all the way around the cabin. Her snowshoeing escapades made her shaky and exhausted, but there was still a stalker out there. Lydia needed to be in the best physical condition she could be.

Lydia kept a little telescoping baton at her side that she'd hidden in the side pocket of the recliner at Rachael's house. She didn't have much room to practice where she was, but she was determined to be able to defend herself. She felt stupid waving a baton around like a light saber in the snow, so she found a tree she could attack, holding back so she would not damage the tree. The squirrels chittered at her, confused by the insane tree-hating human.

~

The next morning after her snowshoe walk around the cabin, Lydia made it around the cabin twice. She took a hot shower, dressed, and cooked herself hot oatmeal with brown sugar and granola with dried fruit on top. She made herself more mint green tea with honey, then attacked her day. After a little online work, Lydia called Hella Girl for an update. "I've been to the databases of every school that you went to. I even aged classmates forward, and no one looks like this girl, except vaguely. When you get up to fighting speed, we're going to have to put you in the middle of nowhere and let Stalker Bitch know where you are, have you lay in wait to spring a trap."

"It's actually a good plan. I know how to make snares. But I'm still falling asleep completely inexplicably in the afternoons."

"You're recovering from a gunshot, you idiot."

Lydia closed her eyes. Even her best friend had no idea who she really was. She couldn't explain that she was recovering from a gunshot and silver poisoning. She'd still be loved, and her friend could be trusted, but Lydia knew there was a whole nation of shapeshifters out there. She could risk herself, but she couldn't risk them.

She resolved to find her father's people, to find out if any of them knew what the hell was going on when she felt better. She had to be very careful, though. The Crow were hard people, and it was possible that her father had left to become a roaming musician because their medicine man hadn't been as kind as her own had been. He hadn't said much about his past. "Yeah. Getting better, slowly."

"Gotta go. Many people are ready to slide into the pipeline." Hella Girl had made it her personal mission to get refugees from all over the world to safe places. Hella Girl looted the funds of a few cartels in order to pay for her "World Citizen Relocation Program." Lydia was terrified that at some point her friend would be found out because cartels didn't play games. But Hella Girl could run rings around nearly anyone. Hella Girl claimed the money she siphoned off was tiny in comparison with how much the cartels moved. Lydia hoped her hacktivist friend was right.

"Later." The phone went silent in her hand. Lydia put her phone away and banged through her work. Old clients came back, contrite once they had seen the police reports. Lydia was tempted to charge them a higher rate, but she let them use their old contracts, promising a rate hike in the new year. News of the rate hike got around, and she got a lot of orders coming in. She signed the contracts, added them to her calendar, and began work. Lydia's fingers flew over the keys. She ate a sandwich for lunch, took a nap, and pounded out more work.

As the foster daughter of a respected medicine man, Lydia worked with tribal elders who tried to revitalize depressed areas with shops, stores, and services using websites. There were more and more services for people visiting various national parks, including guides for hiking, hunting, and fishing, horse and burro lessons and rides, and naturalists to explain the areas and their legends. Lydia was stunned to find James on a searchable database of guides.

Lydia called to tell Corinne she had paid for the last of the help with her websites, and listened to Corinne complain that James was going out on more and more winter hikes. "I think that's partly my fault," said Lydia. "I'm linking more and more websites together, and the guide database is a part of that."

Corinne laughed. "Wow, maybe I should give you the money back for the little help I did." Lydia had managed to get her to accept a pittance for saving Lydia's contracts. "With James' extra work and Mitch selling Harleys to people down south, we think we'll be able to take two weeks off of the new year instead of one."

Lydia sighed. She had no idea where she'd be during the holidays.

However, Hella Girl had covered up Lydia's tracks very well. Lydia's website, email, and banking transactions were currently spoofed all over the world. No one knew where she was, and Lydia intended for it to stay that way while she recovered. Lydia regretted not using her friend to protect her digitally before developing a stalker, but hindsight was always crystal clear.

She looked out to the tree line, wanting to turn into a mountain lion and run out to the forest for a while. But silver poisoning made it very difficult to change back and forth. Lydia fingered the scar where the bullet had gone in above her right breast near the shoulder. Maybe staying put would be the safer option for now.

Lydia realized she hadn't been listening to what Corinne had said. "I'm sorry. My mind wandered for a second. Could you back up a sentence or two?"

"What are you doing for Halloween? It's in two days. We usually go down to the ranch, eat like pigs, and throw candy into bags whenever anyone hikes all the way to the door. We usually watch scary movies and make as many types of popcorn as we can."

"That sounds like fun. Do we have to wear costumes?"

Corinne laughed. "Gunny says their people already do when they turn furry. So, no. Just bring yourself."

"I'd like that. Will someone get me? I can't ride yet."

"Oh, I'll just have Lucas bring you. Ana and Julio like to hold the fort down on their farm. Plus, with Carl sick, they've got to stick close anyway."

"It's too bad that Carl isn't a nicer person. I've seen him around. He walks like he has a stick up his ass. He talks down to Ana, which she doesn't put up with, and he gets an ugly look on his face when he sees Julio." Lydia would have interfered, but all the arguments had been over before she could stumble farther on her snowshoes. She had seen them arguing in front of the barn, which was quite a distance from her cabin.

Corinne sighed. "News flash, but Carl and Ana haven't been living in the same house together for years. She and Julio are together emotionally but not physically, I think. Julio treats her with respect, listens to her, and it would never occur to him to hurt her in any way. Carl could have gotten Ana back if he had watched what Julio did and followed suit, but Carl doesn't think he has to change anything. He's never admitted he was wrong a day in his life."

"I know some people like that."

Corinne snorted. "Ana can handle what's going on. Sadly, from what my husbands have told me, the brunt fell on Lucas. It was impossible for the kid to please his father because the two of them have completely different personalities and interests. If Carl hadn't been a dick, he could have had an amazing relationship with Lucas. Lucas is a good guy, works hard, and is amazingly talented. People in his line of work don't get as much business as he does unless they're really exceptional. My men have played a couple of the games he's designed and say that the sets stunned them. The sets even have these secret languages that end up on the walls, doors, and computer screens. People pay extra to buy the language books, and game devotees will even start speaking the language to each other when they're online."

"That's impressive. He creates his own languages? How does he even have time to do that?"

Corinne laughed. "He doesn't. He confessed on a hike he took this last summer with Mitch and James that he's hired one of their teachers to do it. They were sworn to secrecy, but I got it out of them. Now they pay the teacher for the language book before the games come out."

Lydia laughed. "Looks like they're taking advantage of insider information."

Corinne laughed. "If there is a softer, easier way, either Lucas or Mitch will find it." Lydia heard barking. "Got to go, the girls want to walk."

Lydia said goodbye and hung up. She had work to do.

~

*H*alloween dawned clear and cold. Lydia was able to circle her little cabin twice in her snowshoes, and chose another tree to "attack." She didn't strike the tree; that would have caused snow to fall on her head and neck. She hiked back, took a hot shower, ate breakfast, and worked as fast as she could in order to get everything done before nightfall. Lydia hadn't decorated, but no one was wandering around the woods near the cabins anyway. She managed to get two entire contracts completed and sent off.

Lydia finished with some billing, then changed into a thick black sweatshirt and black jeans over her long underwear, her favorite feather turquoise necklace, and makeup. She put on all of her outerwear, difficult to do in such a tiny space. Lydia put on her snowshoes and hiked over to Lucas's cabin, just over the ridgeline. She knocked, and he said, inside the door, "I'll let you in, but I'm in my long underwear and I'm cleaning, so enter at your own risk."

"I'll take the chance." Lydia took off her snowshoes and entered. The place looked like a teen boy lived there, not a man in his twenties. Everything was dusty, there were dishes in the sink, and the floor hadn't been swept or mopped. The corner with the drafting table next to a computer with three screens was covered with drawings from the drafting table to the walls, nearly to the ceiling. "I'll help." Lydia grabbed a duster and began dusting while Lucas, in black long underwear and thick blue socks, began washing the dishes. Lydia finished dusting and went on to the sweeping, while Lucas scrubbed the kitchen.

"Sorry about this." Lucas looked like a dancer, his body skinny and lithe despite his long hours in front of the computer. "I worked all the way through a conference call, and the call ran over. This should have been done by the time you got here."

Lydia shrugged. "Happens with online business." She stopped sweeping for a minute as she got closer to his work space. Lydia realized that there was a method to his madness. The names of the projects were listed over the groupings of sketches, names like "Finite," which was apparently about a giant starship being invaded by slithering aliens, "Respite," which was a magical underground city, and "Razorworld," a prison city on an alien planet. There were characters' faces taped around each one, with names like Racel, Darviss, and Alathenon. Each place had its own map, including level maps. It was all highly detailed and absolutely fascinating.

Lydia shook herself and began finishing her sweep. The cabin wasn't that big, so it really didn't take that long, even with getting the stick vacuum under the bed and other furniture. Lucas had an electric mop, and Lydia was delighted. She followed up with a duster-mop coated with lemon furniture polish. When she was finished, the wooden floors shone. Lucas put all the dishes away, then sprayed and wiped off everything in the tiny galley kitchen. He washed his hands, then made up his bed and got the laundry started using a stackable washer/dryer set hiding in a closet in a corner of the kitchen, just like in Lydia's tiny house. Lydia finished mopping, put the mop away, and washed her hands in the kitchen sink. "Thanks." Lucas put on jeans and a dark blue sweater. "Shall we?"

"We shall." They put their outerwear and boots on, and Lucas put her rented snowshoes in the front of the truck. He grabbed a paper bag from the cabin, then locked the door. He swung by and dropped the snowshoes off at her cabin, and then drove down the hill to the road leading to the main house.

Ana flipped the lights on in the main house. "Mama must be looking in on Dad," observed Lucas.

"I'm sorry he's been such an asshole."

"Well, story of my life. Man can't see what's right in front of his face, unless it hits him like a two-by-four, then he wonders why he got beaned." Lucas looked both ways, then carefully pulled out into the main road. "Gotta watch out for goblins tonight."

The kids walked anywhere there was a sidewalk, dressed as witches, goblins, wolves, bats, a huge number of superheroes, a collection of kids in Scream masks, and one girl in the costume of a short-haired woman in a military uniform. "What's with that one?" asked Lydia, as Lucas waved and threw candy out his window directly into the kids' bags, pumpkin-shaped containers, and pillowcases.

Lucas grinned. "Amazing Grace Hopper."

"Inventor of the compiler, the woman that made modern computer programming possible? That kid couldn't have been more than six!"

"Feria is five. Her dad says she's precocious. I think the word he's looking for is *gifted*."

"Look out world, Feria's coming." Lydia grinned.

They carefully dodged children attempting to leap out in front of the truck. They chugged up the hill to the farm, distributing candy from time to time. Lucas had the good stuff, tiny miniature candy bars and mini Tootsie Roll Pops. Lucas and Lydia each had consumed a pop when they pulled into the drive. Lucas put the lollipop sticks in a small garbage bag he had in the truck, and ran around to the passenger side to help Lydia out. They went in, past two ghosts, a robot, and a flying monkey. Stretcher stood in the doorway and threw the candy overhand, and the kids laughed and leaped to catch it in their pillowcases. The kids' dad was behind them, and told them to move along after they had caught the candy.

They entered to the heavenly scents of apples, caramel, rosemary, yeast, and popcorn. "Stew's up," bellowed Gunny from the kitchen. "Come and get it." They shed their shoes and hurried to the kitchen. They formed a line, Rachael first, Lucas last. The stew was redolent of rosemary, cubed smoked chicken, corn, and potatoes, and was served with rosemary parmesan bread slathered with butter. They put their food down, Rachael and Lydia sang in Dine, and they all sat down to eat. Mitch took on door-answering duties, as he inhaled his food first.

After dinner, Lucas and James cleaned up while the popcorn-making ensued. There were toffee, peanut brittle, M&M, garlic butter, and cinnamon butter popcorns, along with caramel apples rolled in pecans. They put on *Scream* first, and they all sat down with trays with individual bowls of popcorn and apples, and cups of apple cider with cinnamon and sodas were passed around.

They watched *Alien* and *Aliens* and were debating which movie to play next when there was a whining out by the back patio. All five dogs–Corinne had brought theirs–were under the covers, snuggling, and not barking. Lydia ran to the door and opened it to find a black and white border collie mix by the back door. The dog had floppy ears and a shaggy coat, and went to Lydia's knee. It was barely able to stand in the snow. Lydia didn't think about it; she bolted out the door, picked up the dog, and carried her in.

Lucas took the dog from her, padded into the bathroom, and put the shivering canine on the bathroom rug. Rachael ran to the laundry and took out two towels for Lucas to dry off the dog, and a smaller towel and a change of socks for Lydia. Gunny got some dog food and a bowl of water, and the dog wolfed down the food and lapped up the water while Lydia dried her. Corinne, Mitch, and Stretcher put the other dogs in Lydia's former bedroom so they didn't interfere. "No collar. Don't seem to be any injuries," said Lucas. "She's malnourished, though."

"We can get her to the vet now," said James, holding up his cell phone. "She's there late because some idiot kid gave chocolate to her pooch. Pooch is fine."

"Lucas, wrap that dog up tight, and let's go," Lydia said. Lucas wrapped the dog in a dry towel, picked her up, and carried her to the door. Lydia put her boots and coat on first, then held the dog in her arms as Lucas put on his outerwear. They got into the truck and dodged the last of the trick-or-treaters as they pulled out.

The lights were on at the vet's office. Small-town vet Cicely "Sissy" Rodriguez took one look at the pooch and said, "Get her on the table." Lucas put her down, and Doc Rodriguez did the exam. "Female white and black border collie mix, long coat. She's mixed with something else because she's a three-quarter size. She's malnourished." She ran a wand over the dog. "No microchip. I'll put one in and register it to you so she doesn't get lost again."

"We gave her some water and dry dog food," said Lucas.

"Heart's fine, so's her lungs," said the vet. "Paws need some work. Hold her while I get her clipped." Lydia whispered gentle words to the dog as the vet checked the dog's nose, eyes, and teeth, then clipped her claws. "I suggest putting in some flyers and looking in the surrounding counties. Either someone moved and forgot their dog, or she is a throwaway. She's been on the road for some time."

"That's horrible," said Lydia.

"Happens more than you might think," said the vet. "I'll get her shots and heartworm medicine, which tastes like a piece of meat to her." The dog was quiet as she got her shots, and she snarfed down the heartworm medicine with no problem at all.

Lydia pulled out her wallet, and took out a credit card one-handed, her other hand on the dog's neck. "Thanks for taking such exceptional care of Luna. I'll need a harness, a retractable leash, dog food, dog bowls for food and water." Lucas and the vet smiled at the name.

"Good name. You'll want to mix in some wet food while this dog gets back up to her proper weight," said the vet. They got the dog off the table, and Lucas rushed to the outer office to get the dog's things. "What size bed?"

"That pink and blue one in the middle." Lydia paid while Lucas hauled all of the dog things out to the truck. "Thank you, Doc."

Doctor Rodriguez just shook her head. "I have no idea what is in some people's minds. That's one of the most beautiful dogs I have ever seen. She needs grooming, but let's wait until she's less traumatized, a day or three."

"Have a good night," said Lydia. She ignored her own weakness, picked up the dog, and carried her to the truck.

They were pulling into the Weston farm when Lydia realized Gunny was hiking down the driveway. "What is he holding?"

Lucas grinned. "Standard Weston care package."

Gunny walked all the way out the mailbox, threw some things into the bed of the truck, and handed in two boxes. "Got all the flavored popcorns, and two caramel apples," he said. "Dog okay?"

"Malnourished," said Lucas. The dog was bundled in Lydia's arms in a brand-new dog blanket, her head on Lydia's arms. "Her name is Luna."

Gunny grimaced. "Go home then. Call and tell Rachael how the dog did in the morning, you hear?"

Lydia nodded as the dog licked her hand. "We will."

MONSTER

*L*ydia and Lucas got the dog settled and finished off the popcorn while watching a vampire movie. Lucas drove home after Luna did her business, then curled up at Lydia's feet under the heavy comforter on the banquette-bed.

The next day, there was a pounding at the door. Lydia got up, bleary-eyed, and opened the door. Carl was there, a Marlboro hanging from his mouth. He looked skeletal, with sunken eyes. "My no-good son there?"

"First of all, put that cigarette out. I'm allergic, and so is my dog. Second, your son has helped me out twice so far. One of those times he saved my life. Third, he's not here. Fourth, if you want to be an ass, do it on your own time." She slammed the door in his face.

"Going to kick you out for having a dog!" yelled Carl through the closed door.

"Not your part of the property." Lydia pitched her voice to carry without yelling, her voice as cold as ice. She knew about the property split from Corinne, and also knew she'd paid Ana, not Carl.

Lydia grabbed her phone and called Lucas. "Your father just woke me up pounding on the door looking for you. He threatened to kick me out because of Luna."

"Wha?" Lydia repeated herself. "That idiot. Go back to bed. I'll take care of this." Lydia hung up, let the dog out to pee, dried the dog's paws, then the dog and woman went back to bed.

~

*L*ucas considered not opening the door to his father, but he knew Carl would keep pounding until he opened up or break down the door. He took the time to put jeans and a sweater on before opening the door. "What?" he said.

"Where the hell were you last night?" Carl screamed into his son's face.

"Why?" Lucas stared at his father. Carl's face was mottled, and he looked a bit green.

"Because you have to tell me!"

"Why?"

"Tell me!" shouted Carl.

"No. Is there anything else?"

Carl stared at his son like he'd grown two heads. "What do you mean, no?"

"It's a small word, really easy to understand."

"You're being disrespectful!"

"No, you are. I was sleeping peacefully until you pounded on my door, screaming at me for no reason at all. My mom is fine, or she or Julio would have called. So, I'm going back to bed, and you're going to be a lunatic asshole somewhere else."

Lucas saw the punch coming from a mile away, and he kicked the door shut against his father's fist. The fist plowed into the door, and Carl howled. Lucas waited until his father stood back, staring at his hand, to slam the door shut in his father's face and lock the deadbolt. Carl cursed, spat, kicked the stout door several times, and stalked off. Lucas stood there, letting the adrenaline leak out of him. Exhaustion won, and he crawled back into bed. Lucas found it bizarre that he was able to fall back asleep easily with a smile on his face.

~

*L*ucas woke up a few hours later and stretched. He made his bed, then coffee, then made himself a mug omelet, happy that he still had some bacon left. He cleaned up, put more sugar in his coffee, and sat down to work. He sketched the interior of the ship, room by room, making each section distinct from the last. That was why he kept being hired as a game designer. He didn't make the same rooms, tunnels, or hallways. He made everything different per level or segment, made places with people look lived-in, made abandoned places look terrifying in their cold emptiness.

His mother called just after Lucas stopped working to make himself a sandwich with chips. "Your father apparently broke his hand." Her voice was tight with rage. "Are you all right?" Lucas sat down at the breakfast table, and told his mother the whole thing, that Carl was looking for something and sounded crazy. She called Carl several names in Spanish. "Well, that did it. I used to love him, but I think it just killed the last bits. What was he thinking?"

"I have no idea what any of it was about."

"What's this your father's raving about a dog?"

Lucas told her about Luna's rescue. "Carl hurts that dog, even goes near there, I'll…" said Lucas. He had no idea what he would do, but he would do *something*.

"Not if I get to him first. I have the title to everything except for the farmhouse and grounds at this point. I was trying to leave the man his pride. But apparently he doesn't have any."

"I'm sorry he's being such an ass, Mamacita."

Ana sighed. "He's got cancer. It may have entered his brain, but this is just the sort of dumbass stuff he might do anyway. He's angry and scared, and he can't change the fact that death is staring him in the face. However, at this point he just seems irrational." She snorted into the phone. "If he thinks for one minute I'm going to help him with anything after he broke his hand taking a swing at my son, he's out of his mind."

"I am so sorry. Not for his being an ass. That's on him. But you have to put up with this idiot."

Ana sighed. "I'll buy the barn. All the horses are mine now, anyway, since Trigger Two died a few years back, and your father did not have the funds for their vet bills. I'll take charge of everything outside the house. He needs anything, he can pay for it through the sale of the barn. I am very literally not entering that house again except to get him to sign papers for the barn sale. He will definitely continue being an ass. You can press charges because he just tried to assault you. Do you want to press charges?"

"Probably not, but don't tell him that. Use it as whatever leverage you need."

Lucas listened to his mother breathe into the phone. "I should have left him ten years ago. I can only apologize for being a blind fool."

"Stop apologizing. Take care of yourself. Have Julio take over any task that you don't need to be doing. If you need me, I'm right here drawing this huge-ass spaceship."

Ana laughed. "I'll leave you to it."

Lucas reheated his grilled cheese sandwich in the microwave, and then sat back down. Carl's behavior had gone past rude to troubling. He had no idea what to do except avoid the man.

~

Ronald Foyer came by about two hours later. He was a sheriff's deputy, which had surprised his mother, his father, his teammates, and his coach. Ronald had been the boy out on Halloween toilet papering people's houses and trees, not the one catching them. Ronald was a bit wide in the shoulders, and he obviously still lifted weights. Under the lined leather sheriff's coat Ronald's arms bulged with muscles. He knocked politely.

Lucas opened the door. "Hey, Ron. Want some coffee?"

"Sure." Ron came in, shut the door, took off his boots, removed his cap, and hung both cap and coat on the hooks on the back of the door. Lucas opened a box of peanut butter cookies, put some on a little plate, and poured Ron a mug of coffee. Ron's watery blue eyes took in the cabin. "Nice place."

"Cream or sugar?"

"Sugar."

Lucas stirred in a teaspoonful of cane sugar, then brought the coffee and cookies to the breakfast table. Lucas topped off his own coffee, screwed back on the lid, and sat down at the table. "What's up?" asked Lucas.

"I saw the dent in your door. I think I know what happened, but I'd like for you to tell me." Lucas told him about Carl's yelling and hitting the door while swinging at him. He knew it might result in charges against his father, but at this point he no longer cared. "You have any idea why your dad came over screaming at you?"

"None."

"When was the last time you were at the farmhouse where your father resides?"

"Got stuck in there during the last blizzard after saving the mountain lion."

"What mountain lion?" asked Ron. Lucas gave Ron a much-abbreviated story about a mountain lion rescue, then Ron called Mitch, then James, to verify. "Well, that's interesting, but hardly relevant," said Ron, putting away his phone. "Glad they were able to get it to a rescue facility."

Lucas almost snorted. He knew exactly where the rescue facility was–the Weston's farm. "Relevant to what?"

"Your father claims that you stole something from him."

This time, Lucas did snort. "Like I said, I haven't been to the house since the blizzard. I have no interest in entering that house because my dad lives there. We found out the night of the blizzard that my dad is dying. He's known for four months, and he didn't bother to tell anybody. For four *months*. He hasn't apologized, and he stomped around the house for three days during the blizzard alternately yelling and refusing to talk to anyone." Lucas stared at Ron. "What, supposedly, did I steal? As far as I know the only things my father owns of any value are the farmhouse, the barn, and a couple of guns."

Ron raised a finger. "He says you stole three guns on Halloween night, a hunting rifle, a shotgun, and a revolver."

Lucas outright laughed. "That bastard has been forcing me to go hunting with him for years, until my mother finally made it stop. I hate guns, I don't like touching them, and I certainly didn't steal his."

"May I search for them here?"

Lucas snorted. "You can see the whole thing from here, but if you must, go right on ahead. I'll be at my desk." Lucas stood and took his coffee cup over to his drawing area. He worked on a completely new level, one that hid several caches of weapons and clues to the secret lab. He snorted at the irony.

Ron searched, even tapping the walls and floors for hidden spaces. Ron finished his coffee, washed out his own coffee cup, and went back to Lucas. "Thank you for letting me look. I would have had to get a warrant, and that's a pain in the ass. I think I know what happened to the weaponry. Would you like to press assault charges against your father?"

Lucas put down his shading pencil. "Well, locking a man up in jail who's going to die pretty soon anyway is kind of a waste of time and money."

"Yes, but it would get the assault down on record." Ron looked Lucas right in the eye. "There were bruises on you a ways back that should have had your father locked up in jail a long time ago." Lucas had, briefly, been on the football team. Lucas had hated every minute. Lucas's mom forced Carl to let him quit the team, and a lot of the hazing stopped. Lucas suspected Ron kept his teammates in line, but he'd never asked.

Lucas sighed. "My father has never admitted he's wrong, never really received any consequences. Although it's tempting, it's really kind of pointless to go after him at this point."

"I think you should do it because of your mother. He might go after your mother next. If he's in jail for a couple of days, he won't be able to do that."

"What the…" Lucas started to ask. Then, he put his head in his hands. "Mom."

"I think your mother took the guns to prevent your father from killing himself." Ron's voice was gentle. "That's not a stretch considering the fact that your father has a slow, painful, debilitating death in front of him. Now, I have a couple of choices. I could pretend that I don't suspect any of this, and let your father stew. But the man knows he's going to die, and men like that, especially ones who have never been forced to accept consequences for their behavior, may do something really stupid. Second, I could go ahead and take them from your mother and lock them up because it will be a court case. Your mother committed theft. Since she's married to the man, has the run of the household, and thought it was in your father's best interest, the charges will never stick. However, the guns will be locked up as evidence in a court case where your father can't use them. That doesn't mean he can't kill himself some other way, but at least he won't kill anyone in your family. If you press charges against your father, like I said, he'll be in jail for a night or two. It may make a hothead like him think twice." He looked sadly into Lucas' eyes. "Or not."

"Then let's do it. I take it you want me to come to the station with you to swear out the complaint?"

"Yes. I swear that your mother won't spend the night in jail, and your father will. Your mother was looking out for your father's best interests, and your father wasn't looking out for yours."

"Never has, never will. Let me get my coat."

~

It took a couple of hours to straighten everything out at the police station, and Lucas drove his mother home himself. He explained the whole thing to her in the truck on the way back.

"*Mijo*, at first I was pissed off, but then I realized that the guns were confiscated, and that your father couldn't get his hands on them. This is my fault. I didn't tell you about taking the guns this morning because I really didn't know that's what he was yelling at you about. Carl just cleaned those guns on Thursday night and had no reason to touch them." She looked out the window at the snow-capped trees. "I should have just let him keep them and blow his own damn brains out." Lucas could only pat her hand. It seems to be nothing near what she needed, but he didn't know what else to do. He dropped her off and went back to his cabin.

~

*L*ucas really wanted to concentrate and get his work done, but after the hellish day he'd had, he just couldn't do it. So, when Mitch called, Lucas welcomed the distraction. "Hey. I'm going stir-crazy here at the house. Even though I've got a heater in the barn, working on these damn Harleys is making me shiver and shake. You up for a break?"

"What the hell. You just saw me yesterday." Lucas stared at a wall. "Oh. You know."

Mitch spoke gently. "The whole town knows. Everybody knows Carl has it coming. The only people who ever hang around him are those geezer assholes that hunt and play poker with him. From what I understand, your mom was trying to help him, and he went crazy."

"That sums it up. It's really surprising that they actually got the story straight. By this time, I would have thought they would have thrown space aliens and Elvis into the story."

Mitch guffawed. "Or Elvis' space alien babies." Lucas tried to laugh but could barely get out a snort. "Come on. Shoot some pool with me, have a beer and some potato skins, lose gracefully."

"I have a better idea. Video games, but at your house, because you have a better TV. I'll swing by the bar and pick up some bar food."

"Damn, you have some great ideas. We have the stuff to make chicken nachos here, but if you can pick up those potato skins, double order, that would be great. And mozzarella sticks. Those are always good."

Lucas laughed at Mitch's enthusiasm. "Okay, I'll call it in, pick it up. See you in thirty."

Lucas called ahead, and Becks Ryland, black hair flying behind her, ran out to the car with his food. "Cold as a boar's tits out here."

Lucas took the reusable bags and signed the credit card screen. "What does that even mean?" Becks laughed and ran back inside before Lucas had the truck in reverse.

Lucas drove carefully, but the smells from the bags were making him crazy. He pulled in front of the A-frame house, lights glowing through the glass and casting shadows on the snow. Lucas grabbed the bags and let himself in, stepping over corgis. Mitch took the bags while Lucas took off his boots and outerwear. "Awesome!" Mitch crowed. Mitch divided and plated the food and took the plates to the TV tables in front of the huge television. The dogs sat under the television trays, staring with doggy love, hoping for some dropped food. Mitch went back for a new beer and gave Lucas a cola. "I know you're driving, man."

The two men fell on the food like wolves and talked about the weather, Luna the dog, and other silly things. "Where are Corinne and James?" asked Lucas.

"Date night," said Mitch. "That's why I called you. I couldn't be a manly man all by myself. You have to be a manly man around other men, so you can prove how manly you are."

Lucas guffawed. "Bullshit."

"Dude, we're scarfing appetizers in front of a giant screen with some guy in a suit giving us sports scores. I made nachos with the barbecue chicken in the fridge and Cool Ranch Doritos. We're guys."

"Good point." They watched more sports scores, washed up, got new drinks, and grabbed their game consoles and headsets.

"Wait," said Mitch. "You have an unfair advantage. I get to pick the games."

Lucas shook his head. "I know the sets, but I don't know the stories. I also know that they move everything around that I do because they like to have these weird spinning kicks to break open boxes and all that crap. Have you personally ever used a spinning kick to open a box?"

Mitch laughed. "Those things are in the game because they're fun, not because they make sense. Now, here are the games I have." He called them up. They decided on a space action game that had just come out, one that Lucas hadn't worked on. That wasn't Lucas's favorite thing because he didn't like levels of the game that all looked the same, but he went with it anyway. They joined with the blue-skinned aliens against the ones with a lot of teeth, and they were off, exploring spaceships, kicking alien ass, and getting orders from generals of many different species. They kept getting killed because the game was exceptionally difficult. Lucas's knowledge of game design combined with Mitch's sheer bloody-mindedness got them out of more than a few scrapes.

They were only six levels in and were on their way to face a nasty horde when Corinne and James came home. Mitch grunted at both of them and kept playing. Corinne kissed Lucas' cheek, and both James and Mitch growled. She laughed and ran up the stairs, James chasing her. "Keep playing," advised Mitch. "No matter what you hear."

"Eww," said Lucas. Mitch laughed, and they went after the fanged alien horde.

It didn't turn into an all-night session because Lucas was starting to see double even after drinking a can of Jolt cola that Mitch had hidden in the back of his refrigerator. Lucas stretched then put all his winter wear back on. He was hit with a wave of exhaustion, but the outside air woke him the hell back up. He got into his truck, breathed a white plume into the icy wind, put on some heavy metal, and took his time getting home. Lucas texted Mitch to let him know that he made it home alive, then he crashed after making a few notes on how to make his game designs better than the ones he had just seen. Theirs were good, but his were better.

~

*L*ucas slept in the next day, made himself a bowl of basil-tomato soup and a grilled cheese sandwich, and washed the food down with some apple juice. Rather than work on anything for his clients, he designed a space station. That cleared his head so he was able to start on his actual projects. He knew the sketch would end up being in a game later on. Lucas put down the sketch, finished off the ship, and sent it to his clients. He knew they'd want some changes, but he was feeling really good about the project.

Lucas turned to the magical underground city he'd called Respite, with its twisting walkways, numerous shops selling magical items, clothing for many races, and street performers openly using magic for their tricks. People knew where to shop by the size of the doors, and Lucas made that obvious within the game. There was supposedly a major in-game royal marriage happening within the next few weeks, and the point of the game was to either stop the marriage or make sure it was completed, depending on what part you were playing. So there were lots of little touches about the royal wedding all over the city. It was fun to make the banners with the made-up language, and he grinned as he put in some jokes about the marriage.

"Razorworld," the game set in a prison city on an alien planet, was not a fun project to make. It put him in a very strange headspace. After the few days of strangeness he had, Lucas really didn't want to work on the project. The whole thing made him think of his father as a jailbird, so he gave his mother a quick call.

"Your dad is still in jail. He gets out tomorrow morning. He's pissed as hell that you would press charges against him. I explained the whole thing to Lewis, and now Lewis is mad at Carl because I took his guns to prevent him from shooting himself. He says that man is so crazy that Carl could have shot me. Or Julio." Lucas sighed. He wondered when his mother would figure that one out. Lucas wished he had thought of it, but who wants to think of your dad that way? Even an asshole dad.

Lewis was the family lawyer, a gentle, deliberate man who dealt with Ana slowly buying the farm from Carl in exchange for cash Carl needed because of his poor decisions. Lewis was by no means a criminal attorney, but everything was going to end up being dropped anyway. No one had any interest in putting a dying man in jail, or prosecuting Ana for what was, essentially, looking out for a man who seemed to be in a savage state of mind.

Lucas decided to just say it. "Mama, I can't disagree that the man is crazy, but you put all of this in motion. I guess that you had good motives, but I strongly suggest you stay the hell away from Carl. If he bothers you, either walk away or call the police. You have nothing to say to him, and he has nothing to say to you. At least that's what I'm hearing you say."

"Yes. That's exactly what I said to him when he called this morning and started screaming at me. I told him I had nothing to say, and I hung up on him."

Lucas wished that had happened when he had been in the third grade, but now was better than nothing. "Good, good." They bored each other talking about the farm, the mill, Mitch's game night, and Lucas's three projects. Lucas hung up, stretched, and realized that he was in the frame of mind to work on the prison city after all.

~

His dad got out by the end of business that day. Lucas knew this because there was a knock on his door. Lucas, still in his long underwear, grabbed his jeans and put them on, threw on a sweater, his boots, and his coat, and opened the door. Carl stood there in his ratty black puffy coat, his right hand in a cast. "How the hell could you bring charges against me?"

Lucas stepped out of his cabin and shut the door behind him. He decided that apparently it was time to have it out. "You should have been in jail a couple of times during my childhood. You're a child abuser, Dad. You put bruises on me, beat the shit out of me with a belt, quite a few times. There's at least three times you should have gone to jail."

"What the hell?"

"Do you remember when you hit me across the face when I had braces? I was spitting blood in the sink. If I had called Child Protective Services, they would have taken me out of that house, and you would have been prosecuted." Lucas narrowed his eyes. "That's one time. Go ahead, say that never happened. I want to hear you lie."

Carl shuffled his feet. "That was a long time ago."

"Ah, so you admit it. That was one time. There's a few more of those. There's also all the times you forced me to go hunting, even when I told you I didn't want to do it, even when I cried. I know there's some sort of sick shit in your head, something cross-wired to make you believe that making me kill living things made me stronger somehow. The only thing that ever made me do was realize that you don't know me, you don't give a shit about how I think or feel, and it made me hate you."

Carl stared at his son. "We spent time together."

"How the hell is spending time with someone and forcing that person to do something horrible a good thing? What about all those sports activities you dragged me to, all the times you forced me to try out for teams? All those hours and hours and hours I spent on hard benches, being teased and belittled by the other boys. I got bullied a lot, Carl, because of you, because of what you made me do. I don't do sports, I can't do sports, I'm absolutely no good at it. My body is just not built that way. But you never got it through your thick skull that that's not my thing."

Carl continued to stare at his son. "You needed to be outdoors, not in front of a computer."

"Unless you're doing a chore or riding a horse, you're indoors too!" said Lucas, disgusted. "You don't play any sports at all! Poker is not a sport!"

Carl stared at his son, uncomprehending. Lucas sighed. "Every single minute I have ever spent with you proved to me that whatever you think love is, you're horribly wrong. You think love is forcing someone to live a life that they don't want. You think love is spending time with someone doing something they don't want to do. You think you love someone if you beat the shit out of someone with a belt. That's not love, that's control. I don't like you, I don't love you, and I'm working very hard not to actively hate you because hate damages the person doing the hating. It doesn't damage the person you hate."

Carl just stood there. His son's wrath meant nothing to him. Lucas sighed. "So yes, I pressed charges. You should have been in jail a long time ago. I didn't call the people I should have called because I was trying to protect my mother. I have no idea why she stayed. Everything she's ever told me doesn't make sense. That's your marriage, do with it whatever the heck pleases you. Just know that every fight, every nasty thing you ever said to me or to my mother, I remember them. They are in my head, and I can't get them out."

Carl worked his jaw. "You're right. My marriage is none of your business."

Lucas stared at the man who called himself his father, blew out a breath white with cold. Looked into those icy blue eyes, like the bottom of a mountain lake. "I know you don't like me. You never did. Or like what I do. I do what I want to do, I enjoy it, I'm good at it, and I make good money. Not spectacular money, but I don't feel like going to school for four years and spending twenty to thirty thousand dollars to learn stuff I don't actually use. Then I would have had to have to pay the loans back all that money with shit jobs that pay less than what I'm making now. I pay my rent on time, I pay for my health insurance, I do all the things I need to do. So go ahead and decide I'm not the person that you wanted me to be, same as when I was a kid."

Carl stamped his feet. Lucas wondered if his father was listening at all. "You are not, at all, the person I wanted you to be. I wanted a dad who loved me, who listened to me, who helped me, who wanted me to be happy more than anything else. Just in case I didn't say it in words you can understand, that isn't you. Now, get the hell away from me. I'm absolutely certain my lips are moving, and you're not understanding anything I'm saying anyway." Lucas stepped back inside, shut the door, bolted it, and leaned against it until his father left.

∽

*L*ucas spent the next week finishing up the two video games and turning them in. He got the first one back, made the changes his client wanted, then sent it back.

Finally, on Friday, Lucas sat back, his fingers cramping, and realized it was only noon. He was still exhausted, he had done everything he could, and he was waiting for more direction from a client before he could go any farther. The sunlight was streaming through his window, and Lucas realized that he probably needed to go outside.

First, though, he had to get over his pig phase. Lucas dusted, vacuumed, ran the laundry, and did the dishes. He took a quick shower, ate a ham sandwich, drank some coffee, cleaned up, put the laundry in the dryer, then decided he needed to get the hell outside. He put on his outerwear and snowshoes and started hiking towards...hell, he had no idea where he was going.

Lucas passed the vertical hydroponics greenhouse, the air burning his lungs. He had no idea why he didn't stop, but he kept going. He saw the tiny houses and started hiking toward them. To his surprise, Lydia came out with Luna. Luna seemed happy to be in the snow and apparently had gained some weight. Luna ran around in circles in a frenzy, peed in a snowbank, then followed Lydia on her slow trudge around the corner of the cabin.

Confused, Lucas hiked over to find out what was going on. Luna ran to him, and Lucas knelt and let her sniff his fingers. He patted her head and followed her around the corner. Luna barked a happy bark when she saw Lydia, who was now halfway around the back of the house. Lydia had tamped down the snow, so Lucas followed in her footsteps. "Hey," he said.

A baton came out of her hand. Lydia flicked it, then flicked it back to a small object, then shoved it back in her pocket. "Don't sneak up on me."

Belatedly, Lucas realized she had been shot and would feel the need to protect herself. "Sorry." He held his hands up. "Seriously, I was dumb. So, you like to come out here and walk around your cabin?"

"Yes," said Lydia, tersely.

"Why?"

"Because if I don't, I won't build up any stamina, and my muscles will turn to a jelly-like mush."

"You could join a gym."

"Gyms have these weird things called membership records. Someone tried to kill me, remember?"

"Okay," said Lucas, undaunted. "Exercise videos?"

Lydia snorted. "Do you do exercise videos? Besides, I'd brain myself on something in there." She pointed at the tiny house.

Lucas nodded. "Good point. You know, we have some pretty good trails."

"I'm sure you do. But, I've been both shot and poisoned. I can make it around the house about four or five times until I'm ready to collapse. I don't want someone to have to carry me. Besides, Luna is still gaining weight. She likes the snow, and she's doing well."

"How about going to the tree line and back?" Lucas pointed. "Have you been able to find where Luna came from?"

Lydia took off for the tree line, and Lucas huffed a bit to keep up. "No, she seems to have fallen out of the sky. Actually, from what the vet has been able to figure out, she was probably thrown out of a car. I have contacted the shelters, put up flyers both physically and electronically with instructions to call the vet. The vet spread the word about a lost dog too. Luna's smart and she's gorgeous, especially since she's been groomed, and I have no idea why someone would have abandoned her."

"Idiot to let that dog go."

Lydia nodded. "True."

They got to the tree line, stopped, and Lucas showed her where the two trails began. "The one on the left goes to Lake Conwanwin, and the one on the right leads to its smaller cousin, Casree, the reservoir." He pointed down to the barn. "There are several riding trails. We have two horses that do need to be taken out from time to time. Do you know how to ride?"

"Yes." They turned and started going back. Lydia stopped, turned, and swung around again. "Five more meters then we turn back around."

"Sure," said Lucas.

They walked into the woods. A squirrel fussed at them from way up in the trees, and Luna tracked it, then lunged. The dog stopped at the base of the tree, woofed twice, then ran back to Lydia. "You tell 'em, Luna," said Lydia with a laugh. Lydia turned around and started hiking back. "I am about to be very rude."

"Okay."

"You sit in front of a computer all day, like me. And, apparently, you don't do Zumba to get in shape."

Lucas barked out a laugh. "What I do is really, really stupid, and I look like a pathetic loser while I'm doing it. But it seems to work for me."

"What?"

"Tae Bo. The martial arts aerobics thing from about two decades ago."

Lydia stared at him, a little weirded out. "You mean, you pretend to do martial arts, and that's why you don't look like a big, round balloon?"

Lucas laughed. "My mom told me the only thing my dad has right is that I had to move. It didn't matter what the hell I did while I was moving, as long as I wasn't going on a killing spree."

Lydia snorted. "Prison is bad."

"My buddy Raul, his mother let him eat whatever he wanted, any time he wanted. He became diabetic and had to go on this horrible diet. Then he lost the weight and his skin hung all over. He finally got his growth spurt, and he looks like a normal person now. He went away to college; he's studying to be an engineer. Anyway, my mom said Raul's situation could happen to any kid. So, I found Tae Bo, and did it. Been relatively healthy ever since." Lucas grinned. "I blame my love of Jackie Chan."

Lydia nodded. "My mom was a weaver, but I took lots of long walks. School was really far away, so I ended up learning from home, especially after they found out I was a shifter. Our medicine man took me out hiking and riding into the desert all the time. I learned all the ancient songs, and I kept pretty healthy."

"Wish I could have been homeschooled. Wait, I take that back. All day with my dad in the house would have sucked. I did my chores, fed the horses early in the morning, curried and combed them, mucked out stalls, and took them for rides."

"What do you use the horses for?"

"Nothing, really. The land around here is played out, being worked on for too many years, farmers planting the same crops over and over without rotating crops. They used DDT on the soil way back when, a nasty poison. Dad kept trying to keep old, expensive farm equipment working, kept trying different cash crops, but my mama says the soil needs to rest. She grew crops like hay and alfalfa that people use for feed on her land, which she had before she was married. My dad finally agreed when we had some lean years and still had to feed the horses. She used her profits to buy his land, turning it over to hay or alfalfa, or just letting it lie fallow. He used his money to keep growing the crops he wanted to grow, wheat and corn, which never grew right or had much of a yield."

"He didn't listen." Lydia put her hand on Lucas' arm. Lucas left it there. It felt nice.

"No, not a single word anyone ever said to him. He lost more and more money, and Mom bought him out, bit by bit. He eventually sold the big combine for what he calls shit on the dollar. Mama pays the neighbors to cut her outside crops, says it's a million times cheaper than trying to keep those old machines working. She converted the old barn on her land to the vertical greenhouse a few years back and now makes more money in three months than my father did in a year, without all the overhead. She eventually bought everything right up to the last few acres by the road, leaving him the barn and the house, and he plows a vegetable garden every damn year. Mamacita says she bought the barn off him, too, about a week ago. He doesn't make anywhere near as much money as Mama does. He tried to grow big things like watermelons. They're long gone now, dead vines under the snow."

They got up to the back of her cabin. "Want to come in? I've got hot coffee and a cop show I'd like to see."

"I love cop shows." Lucas grinned. They took off their snowshoes, Lydia opened the door and let the dog in, and then they followed Luna into the cabin. Lydia wiped off the dog's feet with her scarf. Lucas made mint tea, got some fruit and veggies and cut them up while the dog curled up on the banquette. They noshed on fruit, veggies, and sour cream ranch dip while watching cops track an assassin all over a city. They watched a comedy about a woman who moved in with an alien and a wolf shifter, and they laughed, the dog laying over them both, brown eyes beseeching for more petting. Lucas petted the dog and found himself relaxing for the first time in days.

HORSES

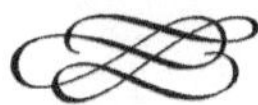

*L*ydia began to look forward to her hikes with Lucas. She did her morning hikes partly for the dog, partly for herself. She had to get stronger. Lucas would come by at random times. Like her, he had a tremendous amount of work to do, and a lot of clients that he had to please. Like Lydia, he would hit walls where he literally couldn't do anything else and needed to take a break. Then they would wander aimlessly down the trails. She hadn't made it to either lake or reservoir yet, but they were going farther and farther down the paths.

Lydia was determined to ride a horse again. She knew that it was going to hurt because she would use muscles she hadn't used in some time. If she could, she would ride a horse, and when the roads were cleared, she could ride her Harley. So, she asked Lucas if she could go horseback riding in exchange for help taking care of them. Scout and Scupper were both good horses with good steps, but were getting on in years. Scout, a bay mare with dark socks, loved dried apples. Scupper, the black gelding with a white blaze, had a thing for sugar cubes.

Lydia did everything she had done in the past. She mucked out stalls, put on bridles without a bit and a blanket and saddle, then rode the horses around the paddock, first at a walk, then a trot and canter.

She was very careful with the snow. She didn't want to injure the horses. Then she brought them back in, wiped them down, curried and combed them, checked and oiled their hooves, and fed them hay, grain, and mash. She also cleaned all the tack, a long, boring chore, and spent the time listening to Dine rock or dictating ideas and coding for websites into her cell phone. Luna lay on a horse blanket on a hay bale and thought the whole horse-riding thing was hilarious.

And, shit, did it hurt. Lydia felt like an arthritic old woman and cursed the fact she couldn't soak in a tub. She dialed up the shower to super-hot, grateful for the solar panels on the roof, and spent the rest of the day creaking around. Lydia got a ton of work done, partly because she just didn't feel like standing up. Lydia did a lot of stretching, but it wasn't until the second week that she really started to feel better. She took long naps and slept like a stone at night. Luna cuddled with Lydia under the blankets at night, keeping them both warm.

~

Ana watched Lydia curry Scout one day, bemused. "I wondered who was doing my chores. I thought it was my boy. But turns out it was you."

"New Mexico. Horses. It's a thing there." Lydia ran the currycomb down the horse's side in long, sure strokes. Scout nickered his laughter. Lydia finished, walked around front and snorted when Scout nibbled her hair, switched to the other side. "By the time I'm done with all the chores, I've got the websites laid out clearly in my mind. I just go back and make them happen. Kind of get into a flow, you know?"

Ana nodded. "My son says you were shot by a stalker that they're looking for but can't find. A woman you've never met before. You wouldn't be trying to get yourself stronger in order to be sure you could handle an attack, would you?"

Lydia checked the right front hoof, tapping Scout's leg to take a look. He obediently raised his hoof. "Why would I be doing something so intelligent?"

Ana laughed. "Well, if you're going to be taking care of my horses, I'm going to need you to text me when you can't take care of them, and I'm also going to need to knock off part of your rent."

"I'm riding your horses, too," Lydia argued. "Shouldn't I be paying you?"

Ana shook her head. "No, you're saving me a lot of time. I've got the greenhouse to run, and Hernando and Mila Gomez, they live that way," Ana pointed out the barn doors. "They took over my parents' farm when they died. My sister was already a paralegal and married to a shift boss at a power plant, so she did not want to come back to the farm. She lives in St. Louis. Hernando and Lily's son Diego and daughter Lily used the plans for my greenhouse, and built one for trees. On that farm, the only thing my father could ever grow there were fruit trees and bushes. The land is too old, rocky, and played out. So there are strawberry beds, blackberry and raspberry bushes, and peach, cherry, apple, plum, and pecan trees. And the very tiny grapes, red and black. One winter many of the trees died, so now they are growing more trees inside their own greenhouse. I must go and help them when I can, especially when they are canning, making preserves, pies, breads, many things like that. I grow strawberries because I love them so much. They make strawberry jam with them, and we split the profits."

Lydia finished with the horse, washed her hands in the sink, and then went to work on the tack. Ana sat down with her. Lydia took apart the bridles while Ana worked on the saddle. "Sounds like you are doing the work of three people."

"Sometimes."

"You still own your parent's land, don't you?"

Ana bowed her head. "My sister and I both do. But she has two toddlers, so I help out where I can. That man who runs the farm now, he worked with my father for many years. His oldest son, we could do nothing about that boy. He is already in prison. He got drunk and high, did some crazy thing with a gun. Didn't shoot anyone, but ended up in jail for twelve years. I was determined for that to not happen to anyone else in his family. The rest of them, they all work, everyone is in school, and my sister and I both get a little money that isn't reinvested into the farm. Everyone is happy, everyone makes money."

"That's incredible." Once the bridles were taken apart, Lydia worked on the metal parts first. "So your parents are gone?"

"Yes." Ana worked on making the saddle shine. "They were coming home after a little party. They had not been drinking, because everyone stopped drinking after it got dark, and the crash was at nearly nine at night. Mrs. Pewas, a high school math teacher, was the driver. She had a heart attack and ran into my parents head-on. Everybody died. It was very sad for everyone. We insisted on having a joint funeral, my sister and me. We wanted to show everyone that we did not blame the teacher. We were all Catholic, so it went well."

"That's unbelievably sad. Diabetes killed my mother, a very common disease on the reservation. My father died in a bar fight. He was a musician, and the man who was hitting people in the head with the chair was high and drunk."

Ana shook her head. "That, too, is terrible. I take comfort in the fact that I am now *Tia*, aunt, to my sister Connie's children. The extra money from the farm has allowed my sister to attend law school. She works from home, and they don't need anything." Ana smiled proudly. "And now, I am also *Tia* to my father's friend's children."

Lydia cleaned the longer leather strips first, then switched to the shorter leather. She cleaned them first with the saddle soap, then put on the oil. "You have found a good way to help your neighbors."

"And you help your neighbors by helping with the horses." Ana nodded at Lydia. Lydia grinned.

~

Two days later, Lydia was in the tack room doing the exact same thing, the parts of bridles under her hands, Luna asleep on her feet, while Ana was putting one of the saddles away. Carl came into the barn. He fed the horses some sweets by the sound of their nickers. Lydia couldn't see anything because the door was mostly closed. Carl spoke to Ana after he spoke to the horses. "My son hates me," he said, his voice heavy.

"Yes," said Ana. "I told you this would happen."

"I spent time with him, I took him to all his games…."

Ana snorted. "You are a racist, sexist pig."

"What does that have to do…"

"I admit, I was a pretty girl from the farm next door. I was seventeen, you saw me, and that was the end of that. I like that someone paid attention to me. I liked that I would have a big farm and a big house. My father told me that you were cold, but I was very stupid and I did not listen. I fell in love with you. Then every single word that came out of my mouth you ignored either because I'm Mexican or because I'm a woman. Maybe both. I admit that I was young and stupid. But I learned quickly. I told you this land was worthless, that you couldn't keep putting crops into dead land, that the soil needed to rest. My father figured that out years ago, about a year before we married, in fact. But, because I said it, you couldn't hear it. So then there were the many years of the failed crops and the expensive machines. I even got a soil sample to that man from the university to show you how bad the land was. Even hearing it from another man did nothing to you."

"That's old…" began Carl, but Ana talked over him.

"And then you were always wanting more and more horses that weren't doing anything. One, maybe two, that makes sense, but vets are very expensive. Both of these horses in that stable were from your friends. You said that you were doing them a favor. The reality is they were too old to do any work, and their vet bills are high because they're getting old. Your friends didn't want to spend any more money, and they knew you would do whatever they said."

"That doesn't have anything to do with…" Carl sputtered.

Ana kept talking over him, like a balloon letting out all its air. "I worked like a dog, managed to finally convince you to grow alfalfa to increase the nitrogen in the soil and plow it under. We grew hay and managed to make enough to stay afloat. But all along, your friends were telling you not to listen to the little woman, or some nonsense like that. I would say something, and you would come back and say something in Brandon, Skeeter, Clarence, Dabney, or Jethro's voice. And where are they now? Brandon had to sell his farm and move away because he believed the shit that he was telling you. Dabney smoked and drank himself to death, which is pretty much where you are now. Skeeter, Clarence, and Jethro, they still play cards with you, sometimes go hunting with you. And here you are, with the oxygen in your nose, and are any of them here? Do they come here to play cards with you? Pick you up and take you someplace so you get out of the house? Take you to any of your doctor's appointments? They won't, and they never will."

"What do my friends have to do with…"

"Your son? Plenty. They told you to make your son play sports, that it would make him a real man, didn't they? Told you to take him hunting and fishing with you? Told you he didn't really mean it when he said he didn't want to go? Said it was okay to take out a belt and beat the shit out of your kid whenever he'd said something you didn't like? Said if your son cried, he wasn't a real man? Or was that your dad, the one that got so depressed that he shot himself in the head? Or your mama, who never stood up to him, who died two years after he passed away of secondhand smoke, the same way you're dying now? I saw that boy try to love you, use a big heart of his to do whatever the hell you wanted, but he just couldn't."

"I raised him up right," bleated Carl.

"No, you didn't." Ana's voice was like ice, hard and cold. "There are maybe five or ten things you're good at in life and the rest you're not good at. God gave you those talents, and like it says in the Good Book, you have to spend them or lose them. You took all of your son's weaknesses and told him he had to excel at them. You told them he had to love them. But he despised hunting, hated sports, hated every damn thing you tried to force him to do. I told you this over and over and over, but because I'm a woman, because I'm Mexican, you decided that I was wrong, that you didn't have to listen to a word coming out of my mouth."

Carl tried to talk again, but Ana raised her voice and plowed on. "I saw his strengths, I saw what he could do. I saw that his drawings and his affinity for computers and games could make him a lot of money. And it has. He's doing fine. He doesn't have to live in that cabin, he doesn't have to pay rent here. He can live anywhere the hell he wants to. But he loves me and wants to stay to be sure I'm okay. I think he's afraid to leave me alone with you. He loves me because I didn't force him to be something that he is not. He loves me because I let him be who he is. He loves me because I wanted what was best for him, what would make him happy. And you didn't, not one day in your life."

Carl stood there, huffing. "I was raised that way, and it worked for me. I turned out just fine."

Ana laughed, an ugly, cutting sound. "You're fine. Right. So, now you're going to die. You're going to have to pay people to come in and take care of you, because I'm not wiping your ass. You're still not listening to the words coming out of my mouth. Your son is not going to come over and hang out with you and watch your stupid movies with you. He is not going to be with you when you die. And those friends you decided you wanted to listen to aren't going to come over and wipe your wrinkled ass either. So, you're going to have to pay a complete stranger to take care of you, and you're going to die alone."

"You turned my son against me."

"Bullshit. You did that all by yourself. Did you just listen to anything I just said to you? I told you all these years to keep your hands off my son. The day you hit him across the face when he had braces on, what did I do?"

"He was talking back to me."

"No, he was trying to find out what you wanted him to do. He was trying to turn himself into the perfect little robot that did whatever the hell you wanted so you would quit hurting him. Answer the question, Carl. What did I do?"

"You moved into the barn."

"And what did I say to you?"

Carl shuffled his feet. "You said you would wait until I was asleep and slit my throat if I ever hit my son again."

"The only reason why I haven't done that is because you're already dying and because my son is old enough to defend himself. Look at your cast, Carl. You broke your hand because you took a swing at your own son. Everybody in town knows what you did. Nobody much is talking to you right now, are they? Get stares and glares?"

"It's your fault. You stole my guns!"

"All you had to do was come to me and ask me in a reasonable tone of voice where they were. You never asked me a single question. You just went over and decided to take a swing at your son. You see, I know what a hot-headed bastard you are, and I was afraid that the cancer would get into your brain and you would decide that you needed to shoot someone. It wouldn't necessarily be you, either. It might be me, your son, the horses. Now, the police have your guns, and you can't shoot anyone. Are you really angry because someone took your guns, or because you can't take the easy way out?"

Lydia heard Carl make some sort of inarticulate noise, and then there was a sound of a body hitting the barn floor. Lydia told Luna to stay put, got up, and looked out of the door. Carl lay on the ground on his left side. He was cradling his right hand, the one in the cast. Lydia walked up to Ana, who was in a crouch with one foot behind her, ready to move again. Lydia looked down at Carl, looked back at Ana and said, "Do you want to press charges?"

Carl huffed and puffed and sat himself up using his good hand. "Yes, I do!" he said, spittle flying out of his mouth. He used his oxygen bottle and his good hand to stand up completely.

"I wasn't talking to you. I was talking to her. You took a swing at her with the hand in the cast. You're very lucky you didn't connect with anything. First of all, she'd have one hell of a lawsuit against you because she would have a broken jaw. Two, you would have probably broken the bones in your hand again."

Lydia knew she had guessed right when Carl used his oxygen tank to stand up, turned on his heel, and stalked out, dragging his oxygen behind him like a dog on a leash. "Are you all right?"

Ana nodded, came out of her crouch, and stood up. "Three more months, maybe two now. Pressing charges sounds like filling out a lot of paperwork, which doesn't seem like a lot of fun. Besides, I'm still married to him, and if he had to pay a fine, I'd have to pay myself." Ana huffed out a laugh.

"I'm going to finish cleaning the tack. Don't ever be alone with that man again. Call me, call your son, call the guy that lives in the apartment attached to the greenhouse. Julio, right? That's probably the last time Carl has the strength to actually do any damage, but you need a witness to everything he says and does."

"I already called some people. He's refusing the chemo or radiation, but the doctor only offered it because she had to. No oncologist in the world is going to touch anything that far advanced with surgery. Carl knew he was sick, he knew he had trouble breathing, but he didn't see a doctor until it was far too late. He does see the doctor so he can get pain meds, and there's a company that delivers the oxygen." Lydia nodded.

Ana smiled ferally. "Carl can't drive in the condition he is in, so I've hired Roberto. Roberto is twice Carl's size, and he moves into people's houses and helps them die. Whatever the insurance doesn't pay for, and I bought a cancer rider years ago for both of us, will come out of the money I just paid Carl for the barn. He'll have his food delivered; if he wants steak, whiskey, who cares? He can have whatever he wants, and with the money I paid him for the barn and the horses, he should have plenty."

Ana put her hand over her eyes, and Lydia touched her shoulder. "Remember the man you thought you married, and forget about this one. The only thing he should be saying to you or your son is 'I'm sorry.' Don't be surprised if he tries to fire Roberto. Make sure that you're the one that hired and pays him, and so your husband can't fire him. Get Roberto a backup or two. No nurse can work 24/7. Also make sure that Roberto and his backups know they can quit anytime Carl becomes physically or verbally abusive. The man's probably going to be a menace until the day he dies."

"Good advice." Ana raised an eyebrow. "You are wise for one so young."

Lydia grinned. "My last name is Hatathli. Among my people that is a name for a medicine man. I had one who taught me right from wrong, a quiet man, kind and gentle to my mother and to me. He became my father after my own father died. He never married or moved in with my mother, but they were together for many years."

"You're very lucky to have had him."

"I know." Lydia looked at the spot on the floor where Carl had fallen after he attempted to hit his wife with his hand in a cast. The man was dangerous and should not be around others. Ana had been right to take his guns. Shooting a gun was the kind of stupid action a helpless, dying, angry man would take. Lydia gave Anna a quick hug, then went back into the tack room with her dog to finish cleaning the tack.

~

When Lydia got back to her cabin, she worked on several websites, rotating through, doing page after page. Despite the disruption, what she wanted to do was clear in her head and she knew how to do it. She reheated tamales she had made the night before and ate them with some fresh salsa she had gotten at the farmer's market when she had gone into town with Lucas during the last week.

Her medicine man father rarely answered the phone. He often forgot to take his phone with him because he spent a lot of his time in places where he couldn't receive a signal. He had a huge territory to cover, some of the most remote houses on the rez. He did sweats, sang over people, taught Navajo and wilderness survival to the children, and helped wherever he could. If your house was falling down, he showed up with wood, nails, and a hammer. If you were starving, he would bring you the tamales or the chicken that he had been given for his services. Renault Hatạthli had a heart the size of their sacred mountains.

Lydia left a message for Renault in Navajo about the strange occurrences she was going through. Living near such a dangerous man put her on edge, and she was already being hunted. But she didn't want to leave Ana and Lucas. Although they had each other, she was the daughter of a medicine man. She would be needed.

Lydia did more work until her eyes crossed, then she decided she needed to leave the house. She put on her snowshoes and took the dog for a walk, then she called Mitch to get her bike back. Mitch said, "There's no damn place for you to park the thing there, it's been snowing on and off, and there's ice everywhere. If I let you die, Stretcher would kill me. Then Rachael would. I'd be dead twice."

Lydia huffed out a laugh. "Well then, how am I supposed to get around? We're in the middle of nowhere, so Uber isn't exactly something I can use here."

"Where do you want to go?"

"Since I'm not driving, a beer would be good. And bar food."

"Okay, this is what I'll do. I'm going to call Lucas first, and see if he can get his head out of the crap he said now. Chances are, he can't. He told me once that he works for eleven different companies, and most of them are trying to get a game out by Christmas. It's little late in the game with Thanksgiving coming up at all, but they're dumb at figuring out how much time things really take to do. Lucas is one of the best at what he does, if not the best. I bugged him to change his rates, and he's nearly doubled them over the past year-and-a-half, plus bonuses, and he didn't lose a single client. Anyway, I'll make the call, and if he doesn't want to hang out, I'll come and get you myself. We'll go to a bar, we'll shoot some pool. I'll make sure you get home alive."

"Doesn't your work kind of dry up during the winter?"

"It does not. I buy bikes from insurance companies and turn them into refurbished or custom jobs. I build bikes all winter and sell them from spring to fall, and sometimes I have custom jobs that people commission in the winter. I do sell a few bikes in the winter, mostly from people down south. I put them on trailers and the moving company hauls them to the clients. Anyway, I'm going to hang up now." Then he did.

Lydia laughed, changed her sweater, petted an appreciative Luna, and did a little bit of cleaning. Pretty soon, there was a honk. Lydia put on her boots and outerwear and got into the back of Mitch's king tab truck. Mitch and Stretcher were in the front, and Corinne and James were in the back.

The conversation on the way over was about Thanksgiving, the giant honey ham they'd already ordered, an argument about buttermilk versus cheesy herb biscuits, how many pies and what kind that they had to make, and a lot more. The arguments were fast and furious, and somehow Lydia was pressed into voting. Lydia found herself agreeing to help make pecan pie and cheesy herbed biscuits because Lydia had her own killer recipes for those. She refused to have anything to do with the turkey, but was strongly against deep frying the giant bird. Lydia had a duck in cherry sauce recipe that she knew and volunteered for that.

The argument stopped when they got to Sparky's, and they got out and launched themselves towards the food and the beer. They ordered cheesy marinara breadsticks, potato skins, mozzarella sticks, and nachos loaded with pulled pork, bacon, cheese, lettuce, tomato, and sour cream, with guacamole on the side. Lydia found herself with some red local craft beer that she never tried before which had the faint taste of cherries underlying the hops. Her second beer was a dark ale.

After they had eaten, Mitch and James circulated around the room, shaking hands and slapping people on the back because they knew a lot of the people there. Corinne, Stretcher, and Lydia ended up shooting pool, laughing their heads off, talking about everything from television to YouTube videos to nothing at all.

For once, Lydia felt a part of. Stretcher and Lydia were the same, and Corinne knew the secret about both of them. Lydia realized how long it had been since she'd gone cougar and realized that was tearing a hole in her life. She blurted it out, right there in the bar, while Corinne was shooting the seven ball into the corner pocket. "Stretcher, I've got to change, or I'm going to go crazy. It should be enough time since the silver." Silver poisoning interfered with shifting.

Corinne looked up and said, "You're in a sweater and jeans, just like the rest of us." Lydia and Stretcher both coughed. "Oh," said Corinne, when she realized they were laughing at her.

Stretcher nodded. "Come back to the house with me. Bring the dog, let her play with the corgis. Leave your computer behind for a day or two. You have to be what you are, or you won't be able to tolerate the rest of the world."

Lydia smiled. "Sounds like a plan. I completed two contracts this week. I think I can handle a bit of a break."

"Can I paint your toenails?" asked Corinne.

"She likes giving mani-pedis," Stretcher told a stunned Lydia. "We deserve it."

"We do?" Stretcher coughed, and Corinne laughed.

Corinne, the designated driver, drove them all back to Lydia's cabin to pick up some of her things, Luna, and the dog's things. Luna was excited to be going on a trip. She was even more excited to realize that she had corgis to play with at the Weston farm. "Go on," said Corinne. She got herself a beer out of the refrigerator. "I'm staying in the farmhouse, watching television and playing with the dogs."

"Thank you kindly." Lydia left the dogs playing together, stripped naked in the mudroom, went out on the back patio, and changed with Stretcher. Lydia felt whole, complete, and her pain level suddenly plunged to near nothingness. Stretcher coughed, turned, and Lydia followed her into the night, a darkness that was alive to her senses. As a human, she felt like she couldn't smell anything compared with what she was able to scent as a mountain lion. They followed the trails of rabbits, foxes, and deer. Wolves too, of course.

Stretcher apparently liked to play games with the wolves, climbing in the trees and falling on top of them. Lydia hid behind rocks and leapt out in front of the pack, and exchanged nips to tails and ears. She kept her claws sheathed, though, except for when she clawed a tree. It took her a while, but she got her claws razor-sharp. The winter wind was no longer cold and biting but a caress to her senses that brought the scents from all over the forest. All manner of animals hid from her, and Lydia reveled in the sense of power and mastery.

Sadly, the silver moonlight began to fade. They all went back to the mudroom, dressed, and went to bed. James and Mitch piled some blankets on the women, who lay back on the recliners. The men took the guest room, and everyone went to sleep.

~

In the morning, Corinne fed them brunch, some sort of layered egg and cheese thing with a lot of veggies inside. They ate pieces of it like lasagna, with crisp bacon on the side and glasses of orange juice. The dogs all hid under the table, eager to snarf down any bacon that may fall to the floor.

Gunny and Rachael had only a few things to do in the morning. They binge-watched Netflix while Corinne went crazy with the mani-pedis. They went through cases of soda, then ate every snack in the house. At night, they changed again, and ran free through the woods. Stretcher and Lydia took turns stalking each other, then stalked the wolves. The snow smelled so clean and fresh, moonlight dancing on its surface. Animal tracks beckoned. Bit by bit, Lydia learned the trees and trails. It was becoming her land, and that refreshed her...and scared her. She didn't want to stay, did she? She pushed the thought aside and ran in the night.

HUNT

Carl went out with his friend Jethro and Jethro's rifles, and they bagged a deer each, probably the last time Carl would ever go hunting. He came back to the ranch, wheezing and crowing about all his hard work. Ana came over, told him that drinking beer in a blind at 4:30 in the morning and shooting a deer who couldn't see him coming wasn't hard work.

Lydia had been cleaning tack and came over to help. Disgusted, Ana called Lucas and asked him to come over to finish cleaning the tack, while Ana and Lydia butchered the deer so the meat would not go to waste. Lydia hung up the hide, stretching it out. She knew deerskin had many uses. Ana and Lydia made deer sausage together and dog food. Hours later, they had everything in the freezer.

Ana then called all of Carl's supposed friends and said that if any of them took Carl hunting again, she would personally hunt *them* for being complete idiots. They cleaned up all the blood and offal, and Lydia rejoiced that she would never have to do anything like that again unless she wanted to. She was certain she had no desire to be a hunter, except when she had four feet. Then, it was about the chase, not the kill. The rabbits all lived to run another day.

Lydia got her dog from the barn, went back home to her cabin, and showered. She put all of her clothes in the washer and started the load. Luna hated the scent of blood. Lydia then spent a peaceful morning pounding out work, the dog at her feet. She took a break, baked some ravioli, drowned it in some tomato sauce and olive tapenade, popped the top on a Dr. Pepper, and watched a cop show while eating her lunch. Lydia washed up, and then went back to work.

Lydia was just finishing up a contract when Lucas came over, looking for a hike. Lydia put on her boots, grabbed the dog, put on her snowshoes, and they all headed for the trail. They saw rabbits, deer, and once, a silver fox peeping out on their nearly-silent hike. They made it to the small lake, iced over and ringed by birch, oak, maple, and pine trees. Houses and cabins lined the other side, but none were too close together. There were a few docks with canoes and kayaks tied up on them, and a few boathouses. There was a wide trail that went around the lake. The snow had been tamped down, snowshoers and the winter birdwatchers having already been by. Luna had tremendous amounts of fun sniffing at the lakeshore.

Lucas stared out at the frozen water for a long time, his hands in his pockets, his breath making plumes in front of his face. "What is it? You have a powerful thing going on in that brain of yours." Lydia rested her fingers on his arm.

"I hate him. I've been to see Father Monaghan three times in the past month. He told me to pray for forgiveness. Father Diaz was a bit more helpful. He told me that I have every right to hate my father, that his behavior is just wrong. The man is not kind or loving and has so many snakes in his head that if anyone tried to take them out, it would take a very long time. Father Diaz explained that living with that many snakes in your head has got to make anyone even crazier than they already were, so essentially I'm hating someone who's already living in the hell that he's made in his own head."

Lydia didn't know what to say, so she just listened. She was lethally pissed at her stalker, but her situation hadn't been going on long enough to have decades worth of hate built up. "There is nothing I can do to my father, Father Diaz said, that would be worse than what my father has already done to himself in his own head. He said to ask God to take a little tiny bit of the hate away, and to do that every day until there's nothing but a kind of residual oil slick left." Lucas stared out at the water some more, his face twisted with hurt and more than a little bit of raw rage.

Lydia nodded, took back her hand. "I would like to meet Father Diaz. He seems to be a very intelligent man."

"Do you think he's right?"

"I got nearly the same advice in Navajo from the medicine man that eventually became my other father when my first one was killed in a bar fight. The man who did it was high on drugs and alcohol at the time, and he went to prison for killing a man and injuring three others. I think my father's killer is still in prison. I haven't tried to find out. At any rate, I hated him so much for taking my father away from me. But I was given pretty much the same advice, and I began to throw pebbles into the ravine near my mother's house. Each pebble was a tiny piece of my hate. I threw them until I didn't need to throw them anymore. I think it took about a year." She looked where the dog had been digging in the snow and found a pebble. She handed it to Lucas, who wordlessly hurled it at the lake, where it skittered and bounced across the frozen whiteness. "You'll have to throw a lot more rocks. Be careful not to fill up the lake."

Lucas snorted. "I'm sorry that you came here to get away from someone who was stalking you, and then you ended up with all our family melodrama. Have they been able to do anything to track the woman?"

"No, and there are quite a few people looking. Gunny and Mitch have people, and I have a person. My stalker's not in any database that they can find, they haven't been able to figure out what vehicle she is driving, and at this point she knows damn well that someone is looking for her. I'm hoping she doesn't know whether I'm dead or alive. That may be why we haven't heard anything from her. The only two people I communicate with are my best friend, who's been helping track this person down and Renault, my second father, the medicine man. I've been calling him on a special phone my friend sent to me that should be impossible to trace. And my computer has special software on it that spoofs where I am. Corinne was working on my contracts for a while, so maybe the stalker-attempted murderer thinks that my business was taken over by someone else."

Renault had been calm, the words rolling around his mouth before he said them. "You have found a new family. Some of its members need you. You are strong. Others will take their strength from you. There is little for you here, and you are not safe here or on the road. Stay." Lydia let those words reverberate in her head. As always, Renault thought of Lydia's best path and her ability to help others. She hoped she would live up to his amazing example.

They began slowly walking around the lake, Luna was in heaven, finding all sorts of things to sniff. "So how are you going to catch your stalker person?"

"We are going to wait until I'm stronger, much stronger. Then we shall see."

"Riding the horses, doing the chores, that's to get you stronger," Lucas theorized.

"And hiking in snowshoes. My problem right now is that I'm feeling much, much better because I was able to change last night and the night before last. It's really easy to get cocky when recovering from something serious. You feel so much better than you did in the beginning, so then you think you can fly or something."

Lucas laughed, making Luna bark, circle his heels, then run out further into the snow. "Kind of like getting a Superman cape after a long illness, then thinking you can jump off the roof."

"Did you jump off the roof?" Lydia grinned.

"No, because my mom is the smartest woman alive. One year, I got tonsillitis three days before Halloween. She knew that once I felt better, I would be running around like a whirling dervish. She gave me a Superman cape, and told me that little boys can't fly, but if I behaved myself she would take me to the lake to let me run around all I wanted. It worked. It was a day like today, all frozen whiteness, so she tied that cape around my neck over my coat and let me run my little heart out."

Lydia smiled. "What a wonderful memory of your mother. Mine

are a lot quieter. I'm an adequate weaver, but certainly not talented like her. It was never my path; we both realized it. But I was good at hooking rugs. You know, using loops of yarn to make a rug."

"You are a hooker!" Lucas shouted. "I knew it!"

Lydia punched his arm, laughing. "You are such an idiot!"

Lucas rubbed his arm. By some sort of unspoken agreement, they turned around and began to walk back. Luna ran out ahead, pink tongue lolling out of her mouth. "What does it feel like to, what did you call it, change?"

Lydia shrugged. "I've never really been able to put it into words. It's just magic. It's just what I am. I was five years old when the first change happened. My father knew it was coming, and he had taken some time off to be with me. He showed me how to walk, run, pounce, and hunt. As a human, I don't like to remember having taken a life as a mountain lion, so I don't generally hunt unless I'm starving. I will fish, however. My claws are damned useful where there is a stream with a lot of trout."

"So, the cute furry things are safe." Lucas grimaced.

"Yes, and so are the large, fast things. Deer are actually overpopulated in a lot of areas because there aren't as many predators as there used to be. It's actually cruel to have too many of them because they starve to death in winter. But, like you, I have no urge whatsoever to hunt. Stalk, yes. Kill, no."

"Good. Speaking of food, I'm not actually at a stopping point, but there's only so many hours I can push myself in a day before my eyes start to cross."

"That's the problem with being creative. You can only push the brain and the eyes for so long before they give out on you. I'm working faster these days because Corinne showed me this dictation program where I can dictate my words. It took a while to learn how to speak in code, but I can get a whole lot of lines down faster than I could with typing. Cleaning them up is a pain in the ass, but I get a whole lot more done than I used to."

"Well then, we still have about an hour before I would normally head out to get something to eat." Lucas laughed as Luna treed a squirrel. The squirrel chittered at Luna, bushy tail twitching.

"You had me at food. I hate to tell you this, but I'm pretty much always hungry, I kind of graze all day long. You have no idea how many snack bars, nuts, and containers of hummus with pita bread I go through."

"Well then, what do you think? Fish? Chicken?"

"As long as it's not a cow. I primarily eat chicken or fish and occasionally relapse into bacon or sausage patties. The sage ones are delicious."

"Then it's the diner. Corinne's friend Dana might still be working. Dana is going to school, but she still waits tables." They both increased their pace, realizing that they were hungry. The dog ran on ahead towards the trail, then stopped to bark at a squirrel. They both laughed. "They've got amazing chicken burgers with this olive tapenade. They've also got home fries and chocolate mint shakes. I know it sounds stupid to have a shake in the middle of winter…"

Lydia slid a little, then righted herself. "The only thing stupid about that sentence is that a person wouldn't choose to have chocolate mint anything." Lucas laughed.

They made it back to the end of the trail, Lydia let the dog back inside her tiny cabin, and they hiked to Lucas's truck. They took off their snowshoes; Lydia put hers against her front door, and Lucas put his in the truck cab. They got in the truck then headed off to an early dinner. Dana wasn't there; she was home studying. Piper was there, a high school student, all angles, pale makeup and black hair streaked with blue. The chicken burger was excellent, and so were the fries and shakes. They finished with warm apple pie with cinnamon ice cream and laughed their heads off. They each had stories about crazy clients, impossible jobs pulled off in the nick of time, and clients that had no idea what they wanted.

They talked about the creative life, Lucas envious of Lydia's life on the road. "It's not what you think it is. You have to get cheap hotel rooms because as you know, after the first of the year neither one of us are going to be working for the next two months. There are only so many beige rooms with cheap art that smell like musty cigarettes no matter how many times you ask for a non-smoking room you can stand. All those little ticky-tacky boxes are just the same. When I could afford it, I stayed at a bed-and-breakfast. There are some gorgeous ones all over the place, hidden in hollers, on the tops of mountains, by lakesides. I stayed at little ones that didn't cost so much. Now that was fun."

"I stay put because of my mom. My dad wanted me to join the military and said it would toughen me up. His distant second choice was for me to go to college, become a vet tech or get my degree in agriculture. I did briefly consider the military just to get the hell away from him, but then I realized that I would be finding him over and over again."

"Not everyone is like him. Most of the military people I talked to are perfectly normal. They like to be squared away, do what needs to be done in the order in which it needs to be done. They are very cool to work or be with. But, the military is a very distinctive thing, something you shouldn't do unless you really want to. Kind of like a calling, like being a priest or something."

"I get that. I'm Catholic, but I have no urge whatsoever to be a priest." He smiled. "So, I pissed the hell out of my father by moving out into the cabin that Mom built on her land the day I graduated. I started doing gaming work when I was fourteen, worked my way into a job when I was sixteen. I'd been a taxpayer for two years by the time I moved out. My mama made sure that I had insurance, not just food on the table. She made sure I had stuff to do over the two months I have for downtime, as well as actually taking some time to do absolutely nothing. Now, that really pissed my father off."

Lydia laughed. "Isn't there some sort of 'On the seventh day he rested' thing?"

Lucas guffawed. "Yes, and my father actually does a lot less than it looks like. He pretends he does more, but my mother's been running things since day one. To hear her talk about it, it took her a year just to figure out what to do, how to do it, and in what order, but she grew up next door. I sincerely doubt she was sitting on her hands." He sucked down the rest of his shake.

"My mom did the traveling thing to sell her work. Maybe that's where I got the bug. Anyway, she had to sell her work, so we traveled all around the Southwest, went to every fair and flea market, found stores willing to sell her rugs and wall hangings. The minute she found out she could sell her weaving online, that's what she did." Lydia grinned. "And from a ten-year-old cell phone, too. Bought the cabin, settled down."

Lucas grinned back. "So, little Lydia went on buying trips with Mama?"

"The yarn was locally-sourced. Wool from local sheep, alpacas. I carded and spun and dyed until I felt my hands would fall off. When my mom's work started selling, we were able to have local girls do most of that stuff, but we both still carded late at night. It's very calming."

"What the hell is carding?" asked Lucas. He held up a finger. "Wait, stupid question. Rubbing the wool between two cards with metal spines attached to get all the wool going in the same direction so that you can spin it into yarn." He grinned. "Medieval Arts. My school let me take some classes online because they didn't have the art stuff I needed. I had a lot more time to do that once my mom drew a line in the sand and removed me from all sports." Lucas smiled a thin smile.

Lydia nodded. "Never my thing, either. I can hike, but if you tell me to run, I'll just give you this look." She aimed a flat stare at him. He barked out a laugh. "I can climb like a goat. I can stalk, leap." She grinned. "I can get into trouble with the best of them."

"So, no track team for you."

Lydia grinned. "Once my mom's work started to sell, she knew I needed a much better education. She sent me to some out-of-the-way school for girls, with a very specific contract saying that they would never prevent me from speaking Navajo, contacting my family, or force me to attend any religious services. Also, they put in there that I needed to take frequent hikes out into the desert. My mother explained it as some sort of ADD thing, that the excess energy I burned on my hikes somehow caused me to concentrate better in school. They bought it hook, line, and sinker because I actually do get extremely nervous if I'm not able to hike and go cougar."

"You needed to change." Lucas was getting more comfortable with the word and about saying it in public. Both Mitch and James somehow seemed more free around Lucas now, more relaxed. He hadn't realized it, but keeping that particular secret had driven an invisible wall between them. Now, they openly talked to Lucas about going out into the wilderness and running as wolves. It sounded so cool that Lucas was jealous of their genetic difference that gave them freedom.

"Yes. They immediately said that I was really right-brained, a real artistic type. There was no giant loom there, but I could hook rugs. I designed and hooked these huge things, tapestries that they hung on the walls. I then moved to actual tapestries."

Lucas scanned everything he learned in his medieval arts class in his mind. "Wouldn't you need a loom for that?"

"And that's where it gets interesting. Because I was there, the school's board wanted to win some prize. Somehow they got their hands on an old loom. I had to call one of our people to help me put the thing together correctly and to clean everything and make it work properly. Yas was old, one of the best Dine weavers. His work sells for even more than my mother's. He helped me thread that thing, and I showed him the YouTube videos of how to make a tapestry. He helped me make the design, people harvesting the sacred corn, the sun high overhead, Coyote hiding in among the stalks. It won several prizes, and the Navajo Nation bought the tapestry from the school, which paid for my tuition for nearly a year. I made less sacred tapestries of the beautiful things all around me like fruits and flowers, mountains and landscapes." She grinned. "I know this sounds strange to you, but I'm not a weaver. I think I was weaving it out of my life."

"I get that. You grew up with it, but it wasn't your path, and you were getting it out of your system." Lucas grinned and threw down his half of the bill as the server took away the plates.

Lydia put her half of the bill down, plus a hefty tip, and said, "Are we going somewhere?"

Lucas grinned. "Have you ever played pool?"

Lydia snorted. "Of course." They headed out, night already falling.

It took a while to get a table at the country bar. They were both full after dinner, so they had some dark ale and watched people line dance. Once they finished their beers, they danced too, stamping, clapping, and laughing their heads off.

Lucas spied an open pool table, and dragged her off in the middle of a song. Lucas called stripes, then Lydia proceeded to kick his ass. They played two games, then went back to dancing when a couple of different people longingly eyed the pool table. They switched to Coke mid-game, so driving home wasn't a problem.

Lucas dropped Lydia off. "Thank you for a much better ending to that difficult beginning of a day," Lydia said, her hand on the door handle.

Lucas grinned. "I feel exactly the same way. If you're the cure for that, then you and I are going to be going out a lot."

"We artistic people need to get out more."

"Have a good night, Cougar."

She grinned at him. "I'm only two years older than you." He laughed. She slid out of the truck, shut the door, hiked over to the door of her tiny house, and opened it. Luna came out, wriggling. Luna had her second time at the groomers, and her fur was coming in beautifully without matting. Lucas made sure the dog was nowhere near the truck before he backed out and headed to his own cabin.

Lydia sang to herself as she readied for bed, then opened the door to let the dog back in. She laughed as Luna shook snow onto the floor. Lydia mopped it up and dried off the dog with a towel she threw in the wash. Lydia heated up a mug of tea, then the dog and human climbed into bed. Lydia put on a cop show, Luna's head on her lap. It had been a good day in the end.

Lucas seemed nice. He was artistic like her. He was able to smile and joke. Considering what he was going through, that was impressive. He was also honest to her, as clear as a mountain lake. She liked the lines of his cheekbones, his rangy build, and his laugh. That laugh came from deep inside the belly. He didn't try to hide or cover up anything. He was young, younger than she was, mentally and emotionally. He'd been stunted by his father, and had been too close to his mother's orbit. Lydia suspected Lucas desperately needed to see the world. He also had friends, hobbies, and a lot of work to do. He was as busy as Lydia was, which made Lydia happy.

Lydia had gone to a coed school, had lost her virginity to a White Mountain Apache who was only at school for six months. Sweet, shy John was now both a painter and whitewater rafting guide, and was already married with two kids. She followed him on Facebook. There were a few fumbling tries with women, which were just as satisfying with the attempts at sex with men. She liked her partners tall and lanky, preferably with some muscles, a sweet smile, kind eyes, and a belly laugh. True hardness had never attracted her.

Love, well, that had happened a few times. Crushes, mostly. Lydia's cool self-containment and artistic bent put off a lot of people. Most people who were busy like her were self-involved, needy, controlling, or didn't share her artistic, right-brained thinking. She tried dating the left-brained people, and it just didn't work for her. Sleeping with one once or twice, fine. Anything more than that left her cold.

A nerdy boy living in the middle of nowhere may have had some sexual experiences, but he would have had to be careful. Everyone knew everybody else in these small towns. Lydia had been able to go to boarding school, and therefore, had been able to have some fun without everybody judging her. There was also the possibility that he was a very good Catholic. Lydia didn't want to be someone's only experience. She'd have to dig a little deeper without embarrassing the hell out of Lucas. She sighed, put Lucas out of her mind, and watched her cop show.

*I*n the morning, Lydia's back hurt on the left side; she had pulled something the day before. She let the dog out, did some very careful yoga, let Luna back in and toweled her off, took a hot shower, dressed, ate an omelet, washed it down with some orange juice, and threw herself into her work. Lydia was shocked to find two more contracts in her inbox. It was one thing to talk to clients, to figure out exactly what they wanted, and give them a quote. It was something else entirely to have customers ready to pay money. Conversations she had with possible clients months ago were bearing fruit. She added those to her calendar and started knocking out her work.

Lydia wanted to take a walk in the frigid air, but her back hurt like hell. She did some more stretches, let the dog out again, made herself a pulled pork sandwich with barbecue sauce and veggies. She added some corn chips and drank down a Dr. Pepper. She let her dog in, and carefully put her feet back up in order to begin work again.

Ana came over in the afternoon with some sage sausage. "For all the work you did yesterday," she said with a smile. Lydia let Ana in, let the dog out, shut the door, then carefully made her way back over to the banquette and sat down. "Pulled a muscle working on the deer?" Ana's voice was sympathetic.

"I learned a lot of skills. Hunting, fishing, tracking, climbing, wilderness survival. I need to take my time with that deer, but the anxiety level in the house...I wanted to get it done more quickly."

"Understandable, and I'm sorry you were hurt." Ana put the sausage away in the little refrigerator, let the dog back in, grabbed herself a can of soda, and sat down. "I'm sorry my family drama has affected you. I'm especially regretful because you were stalked in the past, and now you have idiot Carl to deal with. I won't charge you a penalty if you want to get out of the contract and leave."

Lydia shook her head, then regretted it as she moved her back slightly, and it twinged like a plucked violin string. She sighed. "A little family drama isn't going to make me leave. To be blunt, I need time to get into proper physical condition, and my condition today makes it very clear to me that I'm not ready yet. I just have no idea when I will be ready."

"Stay here as long as you like. This is a new cabin, not even on the website yet. Have you had a chance to meet the other people staying in the cabins?"

Lydia nodded. "The birdwatcher goes out very early in the morning, and she nodded her head at me once. I haven't seen the writer. I don't even know if he comes out at all."

"He doesn't because he has missed two deadlines. Eddie has to have a novel in by the end of the month or he's toast. He's also promised to help someone else with their project, so he's co-writing something else as well. Essentially, he doesn't have time to eat, much less socialize. He hired Rennie, our local fitness guru, to make him relatively healthy meals and snacks, package them, and deliver them twice a week. Eddie is apparently a creature of habit, and likes to eat the same thing at the same time on any particular day of the week."

Lydia nodded her head. "That actually sounds like an interesting idea. I'd like some variation in my diet, but sometimes when you dig deep into something, your brain just forgets to eat. And standing up long enough to cook or make something seems to be an impossible task."

Ana laughed. "I've been there a time or two myself. Come to think of it, that's a service my son would probably enjoy. He'll probably end up spending less money and eat more healthy food at the same time."

"A mother plots to make her son more healthy." Lydia spoke in a stentorian voice. "That's never happened before."

Ana threw her head back and laughed. "You're absolutely right. Maybe I should have Rennie mock up some meals and send the two of you some e-flyers?"

"That would work. This may sound strange to you, but I'm trying to keep a low profile. My stalker may think I'm dead. Corinne took over my work for a while, so the stalker may think that Corinne is running my business. I bought everything on a really private credit card or used electronic transfers through purchase orders."

"I've never had anyone on the run stay here before. I don't know the proper etiquette." Ana's eyes were sympathetic.

Lydia chuffed laughter. "After me, you can contact the US Marshals, and they can send people to hide here from the witness protection program."

Ana laughed. "That is just what I need, some wise guy. Someone like that would stand out here, like some mobster's wife in leopard print and heels trying to walk in the snow." Lydia snorted at the image. Ana reached out and laid her hand over Lydia's. "I am genuinely sorry that my family business has intruded on your stay."

Lydia smiled. "There is nothing to forgive."

Ana looked deep into Lydia's eyes. "I also know that you are becoming friends with my son's friends, and by extension, with my son. You have probably been to more places than my son, seen more things. If you do choose to enter into some sort of relationship with him, help him grow. I will not be so stupid as to ask you not to break his heart. He has such a large one, and it will be sad to see it broken, but he must fall in and out of love to make it stronger. He had only a few friends in high school, but he did date. He has had several girl-friends, mostly girls from our church."

Lydia picked her jaw up from off the ground. Ana laughed. "Do not look so surprised, Lydia. Geeks date, even in small towns. I know that my son is no longer a virgin, and it does not bother me. I was a fool to marry so young. I was seventeen. I moved only a short distance away from my family. I was a child who thought she was a woman. I want to be sure that my son knows himself."

"That's...inspiring. My mother wanted the same for me. She sent me to boarding school because there were so few opportunities where we were, how we lived. I met people from all over the world."

Ana nodded. "When my father and mother were still with us, we did not have much money, but my son went away with them on little vacations. He has seen the world around us, the Grand Canyon, and went gambling in Las Vegas for his twenty-first birthday. My son speaks fluent Spanish. He has people he works with online from all over the world. During his downtime, as he calls it, in January and

February, he translates video games into Spanish. He does not get paid much for this, but the people who play those games are very grateful. He has been to Mexico many times. We used to go back and forth for a very special time, the Day of the Dead. I could not bear to do it this year because Carl is dying, and I do not want to celebrate his life. My parents would be horrified."

Lydia moved a pillow behind her back and winced. "Please, Ana, do not be hard on yourself. You're in a very difficult situation. There are no manuals for this type of thing."

Ana sighed. "I wish there were. I'm a good Catholic. I'm in love with my foreman, Julio. But I sleep at the barn, and Julio sleeps with the plants. Carl became very jealous because he is not stupid. I have spent the night with Julio several times for him to hold me in the dark while I cry. We have done nothing that we should be ashamed of." Ana's eyes flashed. "Carl has made assumptions, and trying to correct them is pointless. He doesn't listen to the words coming out of my mouth. So, I gave up."

Lydia decided to confront the issue head-on. "Even being Catholic, there are certainly grounds for you to divorce Carl."

Ana laughed bitterly. "I should have done so many years ago. Father Monaghan says that I must stay married, no matter what Carl does, but he is an old and bitter priest. Father Diaz was the one that insisted that I separate out the property and my own money, to prepare for the day that Carl sins so much that I would have no choice but to divorce him. Father Diaz only came a few years ago, so, sadly, he was not there when Carl was at his worst. I am certain he would have sanctioned the divorce at that point. Julio and I have both been to Father Diaz, and he has carefully instructed us how to behave appropriately. Father Diaz says that Carl is a very sick man in his head. I have had as little contact with him as I possibly can over the years. I thought Carl would die hunting, driving home drunk, something like that. Father Diaz has told me to forgive myself for praying for such a thing, that sick people make other people around them sick."

"Why did Lucas stay? I'm certain you told him to see the world."

Ana sighed. "My son is a private person. He is very intelligent and sensitive. Would it have been much better if he had gone away to college? Yes, it would have, but he took so many advanced placement courses in high school that he had an associate's degree by the time he graduated. He took art and gaming design and said it would be point-less to spend more money and end up many thousands of dollars in debt. Art school is not cheap. This was actually a very intelligent decision."

"I agree."

"Lucas does love me, he loves the farm, and he has good friends. I suggested he move out and get an apartment in the town. Lucas did for a while while I was building the cabin on my property. I expected Carl to die much sooner than he has and that my son would want to move into it someday." She barked out a laugh. "Someday was sooner than I thought. My son had one roommate who stole from him, another who brought home both girls and boys at all hours of the day and night. He said that he was very tired of paying money so that he couldn't sleep or get his work done."

"Been there, done that."

Ana laughed. "So, Lucas is in a position to pay me more money when he's making it, and not have to pay me when he's not, unlike with a traditional lease. I am putting that money in an account for property improvements. If he does marry and chooses to have chil-dren and does not wish to leave the property, it would be very easy to add rooms to that cabin."

Lydia laughed when Ana waggled her eyebrows. "I have no idea what's going on between myself and your son, yet." She smiled, letting a little of her inner cat show on her face. "And if you say one word to me about dropping babies because you want to be a grandmother, I will remove your face."

Ana gave Lydia a tight smile. "And if you ever deliberately hurt my son, I will remove your spleen with a spoon."

"I would expect no less." Lydia gave Ana a tight nod.

"Good, then we understand each other." Ana stood, stretched, crushed the soda can, and put it in the recycling. She petted Luna, who groaned with pleasure, and rolled over on her belly for a scratch.

"Traitor." Lydia made a face as Ana rubbed the dog's tummy.

Ana laughed. "Never underestimate the power of the tummy rub." She stood, stretched out her fingers. "Sadly, I must pick strawberries. Again."

"Did you put the boxes at head height with the runners hanging down so you just have to reach up and pick them?"

Ana looked off into the distance, thinking about the layout of the greenhouse. "I hate it when other women are right."

Lydia laughed. "I do too. I would prefer to be perfect in every way."

Ana let out another one of her belly laughs. "I like you."

"Good, because I like you too."

THANKSGIVING

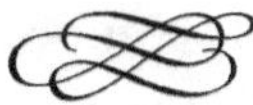

*L*ydia had to get to the Westons for Thanksgiving a day early because another blizzard was coming. Mitch had his own shopping to do, so Luna ended up at the groomer's for pampering while they filled up two shopping carts to the brim. Lydia had agreed to make pecan pie, cheesy herb biscuits, and a duck in cherry sauce. Luckily, she was able to get all of the correct ingredients. Mitch went wild getting ice cream, sodas, and snacks, as well as asparagus, mushrooms, breadcrumbs, sausage, sage, cranberries, and other food for side dishes. "Turkey's out of the freezer and ready to be cooked. Apples. Apple pie, mmm." Mitch grinned wolfishly.

Lydia grinned as she got the fixings for an apple-walnut salad for herself and anyone else who so desired it. She also got what was needed for peanut butter, double chocolate, and toffee nut cookies. "Is anyone allergic to nuts?"

"Too late, my time has come…" sang Mitch, in a horrible Freddie Mercury impersonation. Lydia swung at him and he danced away. "Nope, I can't think of anyone with any allergies."

They made it to the front, their carts groaning. Mitch snorted at her when she tried to take her own things out of the cart. "One thing you need to know about Gunny and Rachael, they look like simple folk, but they do have some money. The other thing you need to know is that we have a blizzard coming, and we're going to need all of this food. I'm paying with the family credit card."

They got all of the food into their reusable bags and headed out to the truck. Lydia put the cart back while Mitch made sure everything was not going to roll around in the back of the king cab. "I love this truck," said Mitch. The snow began to fall. "Better get in before we end up getting in trouble." Lydia climbed in. Mitch put on some head-banging rock music, turned up the heater to high, and drove slowly down the street to pick up a clean, brushed Luna. Luna cuddled in Lydia's lap under a blanket as Mitch slowly drove straight to the farm.

James and Gunny rushed out to help them unload. The snow had already coated everything. "Cold as a witch's..." Gunny looked at Lydia.

Lydia laughed. "Cold as a warlock's steel blue balls." Gunny raised his eyebrows, then belly-laughed. They slipped and slid but managed to get inside the house with all of the goodies. They all got out of their outerwear, and Luna rushed to go play with all five corgis. James and Corinne had brought their two.

"Sweet stars, Mitch." Rachael stared at the piles of food on her counter. "You do know that it takes more than three days to starve to death, don't you?"

"Cookie ingredients!" Corinne held up bags of chocolate, peanut butter, and toffee chips. "Can we get started on those?"

Rachael shrugged. "Why not? We can also get the pie crust made, and probably cut up a whole lot of stuff."

"Oh, no," said Gunny. "I sense a lot of knife-wielding and cutting boards in our futures."

"Great ESP," said Rachael. Gunny snorted. They all washed up at the various sinks around the house, James put on some eighties rock music, then they all sat around the giant dinner table with cutting boards, knives, bowls, and piles of apples and vegetables as Foreigner wanted to know where to find love.

Gunny and Mitch were experts at peeling vegetables, and Lydia cut the carrots and cucumbers and diced potatoes. Lydia put one aside. "Leave one of the potatoes whole."

Corinne pointed a measuring cup at Lydia. "Omigod, she hates mashed potatoes. The woman really does hate Thanksgiving."

"We can cook them up cut up like that, bake them with herbs, serve them with butter and chives and sour cream," opined Rachael.

Gunny glared at Mitch when Mitch opened his mouth to whine. Mitch closed his mouth with an audible click.

"That sounds great," said James, also glaring at his brother. "We have a lot of bacon in the freezer. We can sprinkle bacon on top."

Mitch grinned. "You had me at bacon." Stretcher went to get the bacon out of the freezer and put it into the already-stuffed refrigerator. They would need it for breakfast for the next few days anyway.

Lucas came in, to a whirl of doggy barks and love. "Mama kicked me out. She fed me homemade turkey sandwiches with cranberry dressing, then said she wanted a quiet holiday with Julio. Asked me if I knew where my girl was." Lydia grinned at that one.

Rachael went to the mudroom, gave Lucas a hug, and took the bags of vegetables from him. "The more the merrier."

"Let me get my sleeping bag while I can still get to the truck." He kissed Rachael's cheek and headed back out to his vehicle.

Once they had potatoes, carrots, cucumbers, and apples ready to go, Lydia made the walnut apple salad, the sage sausage and sun-dried tomato dressing for the duck, and rubbed the duck with olive oil and oregano. She decided to stuff the duck in the morning.

Lydia started on the peanut butter cookies while Gunny marinated chicken breasts in Greek yogurt, cardamom, turmeric, and other Mediterranean spices. Gunny put the reusable plastic bags of chicken in the refrigerator, and took out some chicken legs and marinated them in a tandoori spice mix.

Corinne showed Mitch how to make a double mouth-watering pie crust so there was a top for the pie. Mitch and James were happy to make the chocolate cookie pie crust; they had fun banging on the packets of chocolate cookies with a rolling pin. Corinne baked several pie crusts in between bouts of cookie-baking. Lydia went ahead and made the rest of the cookies and cooled them on racks.

The multi-flavored chicken went into the oven, and James made the *roti* bread. The apple walnut salad went well with the Indian meal. They had green chutney, an Indian mint and cilantro sauce, with the chicken, and a small green salad with cucumbers.

They stood and sang, then sat down to eat the delicious meal. The conversation ran light, mostly about the blizzard, which forced a whole lot of people to go to visit their relatives a day early. About raising dogs, while all six of theirs under the table waiting for chicken to rain down on their heads. About other blizzards that happened with other Thanksgivings, which often resulted in epic snowball fights with forts and giant snow people. James had gotten in trouble when Mitch had made some anatomically correct snow animals, and Mitch had been caught in the act later that morning. Mitch had to correct all of his snow animals, and had developed a nasty cold after having been outside for too long.

Corinne told the story about selling Girl Scout cookies in a late snowstorm. "I was a Girl Scout for about a year, but I nearly won the entire county that year by being pathetic. We were in an upper-middle-class neighborhood unused to little girls shivering on the front porch begging for people to spend money." She made pathetic goo-goo eyes, and everyone laughed.

Stretcher and Mitch cleaned up. Lydia wasn't allowed to help clean up at all because she had done so much baking. They decided to do an action–space–holiday movie rotation. Rachael made a to-die-for cinnamon-laced hot chocolate, and Gunny made both peanut butter cup and peppermint ice cream sandwiches with what was left of the chocolate cookies.

The movie rotation went well. Everyone covered themselves up with blankets, draped themselves over the furniture, then the dogs draped themselves over the people. Belly rubs abounded for the dogs. Mitch, Stretcher, Lucas, and James, bored by the holiday movies, broke out a puzzle and did it on the kitchen table. Gunny supervised and insisted that they do the edge pieces first.

The sleeping bags were rolled out in front of the couch after the first round of movies. There weren't enough bedrooms. "Just kick me out of the recliner when you want to sleep, Corinne," said Lydia.

Corinne yawned. "Not sleepy." Lydia laughed.

They got through the next action movie, where Liam Neeson talked about his "particular skills," then people started to trundle off to bed. Gunny and Rachael went off first, then Stretcher. Lydia watched the next holiday movie, breaking the cycle, with Corinne while the boys worked on their puzzle. They both enjoyed *Last Holiday*, then Lydia went to bed in the guest room with Luna at her heels.

They woke up to the amazing sound of sizzling bacon. Gunny was already in the kitchen, and made a pot of coffee and a second of hot chocolate. Lydia couldn't let the dogs out; the snow was blocking the door. There were pee pads in the mud room; the dogs used those. They moved the puzzle onto a card table, Gunny made omelets, the turkey had already gone into the oven, and everyone made stuffing or pies. Lydia wouldn't have to put her duck in for quite some time.

Mitch, Gunny, and Stretcher took turns with Rachael, Lydia, and Corrine to dig out a hole in the snow out the back door. The dogs were delighted that they had somewhere to go. Everyone got warmed up, Rachael poured out peppermint hot chocolate, and the kitchen smells drove everyone crazy.

After brunch, Rachael gave Lydia a hook rug kit, a beautiful long rug of winding flowers with a royal blue border that included two wooden latch hooks and all the yarn. "How did you know?" Lydia asked, tears in her eyes.

"Lucas crowed to Mitch about how he knew that you were a hooker, and Mitch couldn't stop laughing when he got the explanation. I thought you'd want something better than a 1980s middle school girl pattern."

"This is lovely and amazing. Thank you." Lydia hugged Rachael, and Corinne teared up. Lydia started the border of her rug as they started the cycle up again, this time with a fourth round of Marvel movies. Everyone loved superheroes. Lydia enjoyed hooking her rug and took turns with the puzzle, a fantasy epic with elves, dwarves, humans, and a beautiful elven woman on a steed, holding a glowing sword aloft. The jokes were constant, along with the apple cider loaded with cinnamon Rachael had on the stove. Mitch passed Lucas a piece. "This one is the edge of her robe."

"Thanks." Lucas added it to the puzzle. Rascal sat on his food. "Oof, dog." He scratched Rascal's head and ended up on the floor giving the dog a tummy rub. "You are so spoiled!"

James snorted. "You're the one spoiling him." He snicked in a piece. "Finished this corner."

Mitch popped the top on another cola. "So, what's it like dating a hooker?" Mitch asked Lucas.

James groaned. "Old joke, bro. Move on."

Lucas sat up and popped his back. "You'll have to ask her."

"Hey, Lydia. Are you and Lucas dating?" Mitch put down his cola after drinking half. James punched one of his shoulders and Lucas pushed the other one. Mitch threw up his hands. "Hey! Easy on my gorgeous body!" Corinne doubled over, gasping with laughter.

Lydia smiled enigmatically. "If hiking around in the snow is dating, then yes." Lucas grinned, his face lighting up, and Mitch punched his shoulder. Lydia stood. "Lucas, want to help me with the stuffing?"

Lucas stood up as if he had been goosed. "Whatever you need."

"He's got it bad." Mitch sighed and shook his head. Lucas and James both glared at him. "Just in the corner for my man, you know?"

"Are you stepping out on us?" James asked his brother. Corinne choked, Rachael let out a peal of laughter, and Mitch gave his brother the finger. "Classy, bro."

Lucas washed his hands and began working on the sage stuffing while Lydia prepared the duck. He got out a small bowl, the bread-crumbs, and the sausage. Soon, the sausage was sizzling, and Lucas heated the butter in the microwave. The smell of sage sausage permeated the room. Mitch sniffed. "I'm hungry."

James groaned. "You're always hungry."

"Mitch, stuffed mushrooms in the freezer. They've got that sage sausage in them. Heat them up." Rachael pointed in the general direction of the freezer.

James shook his head. "Only enough for you, bro."

"Your loss." Mitch hustled to the freezer.

Lydia had Mitch stuff the duck, then it went into the bottom oven. The top one had the turkey. Then the side dishes and pies went in. Everyone sang, then sat down for a table-groaning, mouth-watering spread. Gunny carved both birds with an electric knife, and Mitch and Corinne passed down the plates. Mitch audibly groaned. "This is nearly as good as the Harley Sportster Iron 883. That bike rides low, great for new riders."

Corinne shook her head. "That's an all-black bike. I prefer red."

"Air-cooled engine, dropped handlebars. A nice bike. A rebuild?" Gunny asked, while putting the meat on the plates.

"Yes, nasty accident. Rider's spending the holidays in the hospital. I want to have it done by the time he gets out." Mitch added potatoes to each plate.

"Nice." Lydia added bacon-wrapped asparagus to the plates. "I hope he gets well soon."

"She, and she's doing great." Mitch passed another plate.

"I'm thinking about refurbishing a Mustang." Rachael smiled and added Italian bread to the plates.

Gunny grinned. "The electric blue one."

"You peeked?" Rachael punched his arm. He rubbed it; Rachael had one hell of a punch.

Stretcher coughed. "Don't ask any more." Eyebrows raised all over the table. Lydia got the point. Gunny had bought the car and stored it to give it to his wife over Christmas.

"Nice, Gunny." James grinned.

"Great touch." Mitch passed another plate.

Corinne cleared her throat. "What are we watching after lunch?" The suggestions poured in.

They passed the dishes and talked about movies, books, music, cars, trucks, and Harleys. They laughed their heads off, put away the leftovers, ran the dishwasher, washed up, and staggered back to the couch and puzzle.

The males decided to play Splendor, a deceptively simple board game having to do with gems, merchants, lords, ladies, and fun. Lydia stretched her shoulders and hands and sat down. Lucas quietly explained the rules of the game, and Lydia sat next to him to learn the strategy. The key seemed to be attracting a patron and/or purchasing the most expensive cards. Within two hands of playing on her own, Lydia won three times in a row. "Ringer," Mitch complained.

Lydia grinned. "Females have brains, and they think ahead."

Lucas laughed. "Exactly." They smiled at each other.

Mitch groaned. "Stop looking at each other like that! Who wants pie?" Everyone raised their hands. "Can I get some help here?" James groaned, got up, and helped his brother with the slivers of pie—apple, pecan, and blackberry.

Dinner was sandwiches made from leftovers and chips, then they got serious about the board games. Risk was on one end, Monopoly on the other, and people sometimes traded seats. Some joker put Parcheesi in the middle. Lydia suspected Mitch, but she wasn't sure because she had to get up to use the restroom.

Someone put the music on "random," starting with Gunny's iPhone, and Gunny apparently liked everything from rock to country and some soul. Corinne and Lydia got up to dance whenever they heard either Shania Twain or Aretha Franklin, making everyone laugh. There was some spontaneous line dancing when "Achy Breaky Heart" came on, along with a ton of laughter. Lydia knew the entire dance, and taught Corinne and Lucas the moves. Soon they had the song on replay and were kicking up their heels. Rachael joined in, and so did Gunny. The dogs tried to help while James joined in, and Mitch laughed so hard he cried.

Then, everyone simultaneously abandoned the games for movies. Gunny and Mitch were in charge of the various flavors of popcorn, along with peanut butter pie Rachael had hidden from everyone. They ate and argued over what movies to see. The holiday movies were taken out of the rotation in favor of Patrick Swayze movies, superhero, and classic murder mysteries like *Clue* and *Knives Out*. Lydia made headway on her hook rug, the dogs had more belly rubs, and, in the middle of a superhero fight scene where everyone was giving their own commentary, Lydia realized that she had been made part of a family without even being aware of it.

~

The next morning the snow finally stopped, but everyone had the intelligence to stay put for a while. The snowplows would just throw more snow and ice up, making digging out something that had to wait. "Hot chocolate with cinnamon is in the blue pot, the Mexican version in the red one. Coffee in the black one." Rachael pointed them out. They lined up and got their hot drinks while Rachael and Corinne filled up the plates with a breakfast of sage sausage, bacon, eggs, and cheesy biscuits with butter and honey. Lydia rubbed her stomach as she sat down. "I love the food, but now I'm spoiled. And so is Luna." Luna sat under Lydia's chair where she could cadge bits of sausage.

Corinne laughed. "One of the many good things about being a part of this family." Rachael's eyes teared. Gunny put a hand on her shoulder.

Lydia sat there, making a decision. Staying meant family, shifter family. And Lucas, so kind and hard-working. He had helped make most of the food, and he had been on the line to wash dishes every single time. He was always ready to rub a dog's belly or hand out dog treats. He helped set up and put away the games. He touched people's shoulders or arms and gave gentle smiles. He was an extremely nice guy. Lydia hoped she didn't have a type. It was better to see people's hearts. And everything she saw pointed to someone she could fall for, hard.

They drank hot chocolate and engaged in a gigantic video game war on the wide-screened television and an old-fashioned role-playing game with a starship at the kitchen table. Most people went back and forth, and there was a lot of yelling, cheering, and smack talking. They received a text that the snow plows had gone through on their route, and they went out in pairs to begin digging themselves out. Corinne and Lydia took the second shift, being intelligent women. Lydia took the back while Corinne used the snowblower in front. The dogs thought it was really fun to run out and "help" the diggers.

They finally dug their way to the street, and they used the snowblower in shifts in the back until they got to the goats. The goats still had food, but the indoor stalls needed to be mucked out. The goats had been nice and warm with their wooly coats combined with the heated flooring in the barn. The goats thought it was hilarious to run back and forth to the house, bleating.

Gunny and James dug out the trucks, and Mitch, Stretcher, Corinne, and Lucas went with them to see if any neighbors needed help. Lydia, exhausted by all the digging, stripped out of her wet clothes, took a hot shower, put on dry clothes, and took a nap. Luna decided she needed to help Lydia with that, too, and snuck in under the covers.

〜

It was dark again when Lydia woke up, bleary-eyed. Two of the dogs were gone, and so were James, Corinne, and Mitch. Lydia was surprised when their absence felt like a blow. She stumbled to the back door, let Luna and the corgis out, then went into the kitchen. Stretcher was in the kitchen, and she pointed to the teakettle. Lydia nodded, poured herself a cup, and realized she and Stretcher could probably have an entire conversation without saying a single thing. Lydia let the green mint tea steep while she let the dogs back in, toweled them dry, and threw the wet towel in the hamper. She stumbled back, doctored the tea with honey, poured herself a mug, and put the remaining cookies on a plate. She and Stretcher sat in silence, eating cookies.

Rachael ambled into the kitchen, yawning. She poured herself some of the tea and got out a quarter of a chocolate peanut butter pie she'd kept hidden. Rachael brought over a knife, three plates, and three forks. Lydia and Stretcher ate completely silently.

Rachael said, "Cats." Both Lydia and Stretcher coughed. "Lydia, you don't have to go home. It's going to be a bear to dig your way up to that cabin, and you've done way too much digging today." The front door opened, and Rachael said, "What the hell?" Lydia knew who it was when she heard his boots stomping on the floor, and she smiled.

Lucas came into the room, reusable shopping bags in his hand. "Lydia, I went to see my family, dug my way to my cabin, then came to get you. If you want to hang out here, I brought food. I figured the manly men would have eaten you out of pretty much everything."

Rachael laughed, and Stretcher and Lydia coughed. "Thank you," said Rachael. "We dug ourselves out, then collapsed. I don't even think we ate lunch. And I don't think any of us have the energy to cook. Shockingly, we're even out of turkey, stuffing, and cranberry sauce, and we ate that entire honey ham as sandwiches."

Lucas pulled the items out of the bags. "You'd be crazy if you wanted to cook right now. I've got pulled pork and cheddar, both already shredded, tortilla chips, salsa, this red bell pepper and this yellow one…"

"Shut up and make the nachos," said Stretcher.

"Be nice, or I won't give you dessert. I have a chocolate mint French silk pie with a chocolate cookie crust, with crumbled peanut butter cups and a ribbon of chocolate on top."

Stretcher let her jaw drop. "Damn. I take back anything bad I've ever said about you." Lucas snorted out a laugh.

Lydia managed to stumble around the kitchen enough to get more plates, and Lucas made the nachos, piled high. Lucas cheated and used the microwave, so it didn't take long at all. They ate ravenously, washed it down with sodas, and then rolled their overly-full selves over to the television. Lucas talked about visiting with his mother's friends next door, his mother, and Julio. "Too loud there. Glad I spent Thanksgiving here."

Lucas kindly cleaned up, which involved putting the plates in the dishwasher as they'd almost literally licked their plates clean. He plated the chocolate mint pie, brought it to the women, and was surprised by their movie choice about an alien, her human lover, and a battleship. Lydia showed Lucas how far she had gotten on her hooked rug, but was too exhausted to do any work on it. Lucas rubbed Lydia's feet, making her groan with pleasure. Lucas went to the bathroom and came back out with lotion.

They started the next movie, about a trio of women, an evil New York tycoon, and a heist. Lucas rubbed lotion into Lydia's cracked feet, put her soft, warm socks back on, then asked her to turn around. Lydia put her head on a pillow in his lap and he started on her hands. She relaxed, snoozing from time to time.

When Lydia woke up, it was the middle of the night and the snow was falling again. Lucas leaned back on the couch's built-in recliner, and Lydia's head was on a pillow right next to his hip. Luna was on Lydia's feet. They were all covered with heavy blankets. Lydia moved Luna, stumbled to the bathroom, went back to the couch, and lay back down where she was. She grinned as she felt Lucas' hand stroking her hair, and Luna crawled back onto her feet. Lydia purred with happiness, and fell back asleep.

The next day, Gunny cooked everyone a farmer's breakfast of bacon, eggs, and biscuits, and grinned when Lucas joined them at the table. "I must have been tired. Slept all the way through."

Lucas laughed. "Lydia almost did that, too." The new snowfall wasn't deep, and Lucas and Gunny made quick work of the snow while Rachael and Stretcher let the goats and dogs play together. Lucas and Lydia said their goodbyes, got all Lydia and Luna's things, packed up the truck, and headed back.

"You can stay in my cabin," said Lucas. "But, I get it if being around that many people would make you want to be alone for a little while."

Lydia smiled. "Actually, I'm way caught up on my work. You?"

Lucas grinned. "Nowhere near done. In fact, I'm in a horrible time crunch. But I got a bunch of food delivered. Rennie sent me an e-mail, I bought the stuff, and Rennie says she wants you to try it to see whether or not you like it."

Lydia grinned. "I'll need my computer and more dog stuff. How do you feel about dog hair?"

Lucas smiled sadly. "I just couldn't handle getting another dog after Bo, my ancient black Lab, died. It would be very nice to have a dog again."

"Then, we have a plan." Lucas dropped off Lydia and Luna at his cabin, then snowshoed his way to Lydia's tiny cabin, got in the loft window, and packed Lydia's things, plus more dog food. He made it back to his cabin, soaked through and exhausted after all the activity in the snow. He took a hot shower and went back to work.

Surprisingly, Lucas was able to block out having a dog and a woman in his place when he needed to work. He spread himself out over his drafting table and computer, put in some earphones, and worked, often with Luna at his feet. Lydia slept a lot, completely exhausted after all the exertions of the last few days with shoveling snow. Lydia did take the dog out to snowshoe a little bit, but the drifts were very deep and therefore dangerous. She kept herself very close to the cabin.

Lydia watched stupid movies, played video games, watched cop shows, ate chips and dip, and sampled the three-section meal boxes stuffed into Lucas's full-sized refrigerator. She found chicken marinated in some sort of dill Greek yogurt that came with sliced cucumbers and carrots and pasta with some sort of amazing sun-dried tomato sauce. There was a tandoori chicken with *roti*, and little samosas stuffed with potatoes and lentils, with a basil-mint chutney and tzatziki sauce. There were boxes with roasted potatoes, rosemary chicken, and grilled asparagus.

Lydia ignored the turkey with cranberry sauce and chestnut stuffing. She held off eating the pulled pork fajitas with lots of red bell peppers, salsa, and sour cream. She zapped the chicken and pasta in the microwave and dipped the veggies in the yogurt and sun-dried tomato sauces. Lydia called and put in her order with Rennie for the next week, figuring it would take time for Lydia to dig herself out and for Rennie to make everything.

Lydia and Lucas slept together, but it wasn't very sexual. They kissed, stroked each other's hands and faces, but both of them were just too exhausted to do more. Lydia had been pushing herself to recover, and her body was getting really tired of being pushed. She'd also been working nonstop, even before she started being harassed. The stalking had taken its toll, then the gunshot and the silver poisoning, then finding out that she was part of a much larger shifter community had drained her mentally and emotionally, not just physically. Yes, she had known about the shifter wolves, but she had no idea there was a larger society as a backdrop to the rest of them. Lydia didn't even have any idea there were other cat shifters. Her father's people may or may not be friendly.

Lucas built worlds. More accurately, he made those worlds come alive under his hands. He created various cities, towns, and villages or levels if there was a space station or habitat, devised transportation systems, determined if the people used magic, technology, or both, and what each species was or was not able to do. He set up a framework for the story to happen. That was a huge job, and he did it very well.

The game creators would give him some basics, and then he was off and running. He sketched out each level, village, or whatever it was by hand, scanned each sketch with a handheld scanner, then put the entire system together. He included all sorts of things that could lead the plot twists, like hidden panels and switches leading to hidden doors, trapdoors, ladders, tubes, and the like. There was a certain order to the tasks, and changing the order of them created new storylines, tasks, and dangers. The idea was to allow plenty of opportunity for the game designers to develop far-reaching storylines that could be told in a multiple of different ways, with the maximum amount of gameplay available.

Over a lunch of pulled pork sandwiches, carrots, hummus, and Cool Ranch Doritos, Lucas explained it to her. "I've played plenty of games that sucked. I have no control over the storylines. I can't make people create an interesting story. What I can do is set up the conditions to where that could happen as easily as possible. I do that for every game I make, even the rush jobs. I can always add levels, buildings, and missions later. A good designer sets everything up to where that is as easily done as possible."

"How do you keep track of it all?" Lydia ran her Doritos through some red bell pepper hummus.

"I keep track of which game has caught on and which hasn't based on which clients come back to me asking to create twenty or thirty more levels and scenarios. That's what keeps me busy during the rest of the year. Some of it is designing new games not aimed at the Christmas market or new levels for Lunar New Year for Asian markets. I keep busy creating new scenarios for games I've done before. Once a gaming company has a best seller, it's very important to add levels to the current best seller and to create new games based on the same universe, usually using whatever characters didn't die in the first one." Lucas ate the end off the carrot stick he was waving around.

"Why are you working so hard? You only have so many hours in the day."

"You're absolutely right. This is going to sound stupid because I'm still young, but eventually I'll have to quit taking on new clients. That's going to be a bit sad because I love new challenges. However, at some point I am going to run out of hours in the day. In fact, that situation is rapidly approaching. Mr. Harris can only come up with a certain number of new languages a year. It is a long and complicated process. I just told Mr. Harris to create a variety of different scripts. They had to be read by human eyes, something visual, and use the sounds the human tongue and throat could make. Mr. Harris could get bizarre, like having a language be the rippling patterns on the skin of an alien."

"Whoa." Lydia grabbed two carrot sticks, one for each hand.

"Exactly. Mr. Harris has been working on that one for nearly a year. He's getting very good at being a linguist. He reads papers on obscure and even inactive languages and steals their structures whole-sale. Then he makes a script, some way for humans to read that language." Lucas paid the man as much money as he could because Mr. Harris had daughters and, therefore, an unending supply of bills.

Lucas didn't have to go far for inspiration. There was a beautiful woman sleeping, eating, stretching out, watching movies, and playing video games on his bed. From time to time she would do actual work, but she did it sitting up. He knew rescuing her computer before the blizzard hit would be important; he had borrowed the key from his mom, and had been very careful with her equipment.

Lucas felt his work was important and not just as a way to pass the time for geeks. Humans were able to work with what they understood, and if he could push human understanding, help people comprehend the universe better, then Lucas would have made a real contribution. When the aliens did show up, which Lucas figured would probably not happen in his lifetime, he really hoped they'd be ready as a species to understand beings who probably wouldn't be remotely humanoid, unlike the games that he was designing.

In his downtime, which Lucas hadn't had since late summer, he read science and technology magazines online and tried to figure out how things worked. A lot of the stuff he read blew his mind, and Lucas tried to put as much of it as he could into the games. He drew aliens that lived in lava vents under the ocean, as his new job was making a habitat in the alien ocean. He populated it with intelligent octopi aliens and other sorts of creatures, and had a lot of fun as he did so. He made the world as bright and colorful as he possibly could, mimicking the human ocean.

Lucas put in another order to Rennie, who came over in an ATV and stuffed his refrigerator as full as it could get. Rennie's cloud of wiry black hair was crushed under her helmet. In fact, the only thing he could see of her was her melted chocolate eyes, her flat nose, and her salted caramel skin. She took off her gloves, did some Tetris thing with the inside of his refrigerator to get everything in, and shut the door. Luna sat at her feet and watched the food going in lovingly. "Hi, I'm Rennie," she said to Lydia. Lydia unfolded herself from the bed and shook Rennie's hand. "I'll get your order next week to your cabin. Probably take you that long to dig yourself back into there."

Lydia laughed. "True. In fact, I really should suit up and do a little bit of digging. If I go out for an hour or two, I can come in and defrost in between."

"I also brought Lucas's Korean wedding tea. Lucas here likes it, not because he's going to a Korean wedding, but because it has caffeine in it and it keeps him the hell awake."

Lydia laughed. "I thought that's what this stuff is for." Lydia pointed to the cases of Mountain Dew and Red Bull that Rennie had pulled inside from her ATV.

Rennie grinned. "Anything that works, right? Nice doing business with you, Lucas. See you next week, Lydia." She closed the front of her helmet, went out of the cabin into the snow, got on her ATV, and was gone.

"What's her story?" Lydia asked Lucas. Lydia let the dog out so Luna could run around in the snow for a few minutes, and shut the door against the frigid air.

"Rennie? Well, culinary school is expensive. Rennie is sixteen, and she isn't stupid. She knows she's going to have to save up a lot in order to go. Her mom is a nutritionist, so she's known what to do to create a well-balanced meal since she was eight. She also teaches fitness at the community center, so she's making money."

Despite the fact she was shivering, Lydia made a bowl of butter brickle ice cream. She stole a Mountain Dew, let the dog back in, wiped the dog down, then sat down on the bed again. She was nearly done with the website and quite eager to get it up and working for the client. She went through her final checklist, sent the link in to her client, then started watching a movie about a group of teenagers who could fly.

Meanwhile, Lucas got a lot more of the ocean world done, then switched to an alien university. That one was much tougher because he wanted to be sure at least some of the aliens didn't breathe oxygen. The third one was a pretty straightforward elven princess rescue, something that had been done to death but still kept getting made and, apparently, purchased. Since it was with a company he worked for before, he used the elven language that he had used previously.

Lucas threw in a lot of in-jokes about things from the previous game onto banners and wall hangings and such.

Two Mountain Dews, a Red Bull, and an Italian sausage pasta bake later, he was ready to completely give up. His eyes were crossing, his stomach felt strange, and he was ready to lie down on his face. He let Luna out, used the restroom, let her back in, toweled her off, and was surprised to see that Lydia was awake.

Lydia sat up, yawned, and stretched her hands over her head. "How many games have you designed since October?"

"I am going to assume you're talking about the Christmas season that actually started in September. If I include what I'm working on now, that will be twelve."

"What the hell? That's a tremendous amount of work."

"To be fair, I'm actually cheating." Lucas stretched, walked to the kitchen, scooped out two bowls of peanut butter chunk ice cream, and brought it over to the bed, along with a cola for each of them.

Lucas sat down on the bed. "Whenever I'm not working, I'm sketching. I work on sketches until they're nearly complete games. By the time I get an order for a new game, I usually have something that will fit. Or, at least partially fit. It's very rare that someone comes up with something I've never even considered before. In fact, a good percentage of what I do is a continuation of an earlier game, with a storyline based in the same universe. There's usually a whole bunch of stuff that I've come up with that I never used, so I just stick it into that part. Some wall hangings, hidden alcoves, and secret rooms later, I'm done."

"I'll make you a bet what you do is not remotely as easy as you just made it sound." Lydia finished her ice cream, stood, stretched. Lucas liked the way her nearly flat stomach peeked out from under her long underwear. Both of them were wearing their long underwear indoors, along with thick socks. Both of them usually had a blanket draped around their shoulders too.

Lucas smiled at the compliment. "It is and it isn't. I'm designing the sets, the look and feel of the game. The characters, all the things they do within the game, the storyline, none of that is mine. I'm the set designer. I get everything ready to where they just put the characters in and move them around and everything works. I tell them where all the hidden stuff is, secret levels, all that part. I send a message first with some sort of map, they approve it, throw in a couple of pictures of a level or something. Then I continue, and I've never had a client look at what I've come up with and not pay me. I'm actually on a retainer with most of my clients. This is just when I do the bulk of my work."

Lucas stretched and heard his back pop. He got up, washed the bowls and silverware and put them in the drying rack, and brought back over two black cherry sodas. They bumped cans, opened them, and sipped. "Want to watch something really stupid?" Lucas asked Lydia.

She grinned. "I thought you'd never ask." They picked a cop movie, propped themselves up with pillows, and started watching with Luna on their feet. Lydia put her head on Lucas' shoulder. Lucas very deliberately relaxed himself. If he jumped like a scared rabbit every time Lydia touched him, she'd stop. And Lucas most definitely did not want her to stop.

DIGGING OUT

They took turns digging their way between Lucas and
Lydia's cabins, and Lydia moved back in. Lydia finished off
her last contracts, snowshoed with the dog, and kept coming back for
hot showers. Lucas missed her, but knew that he really didn't have
time for her that week. Besides, she had her own work she had to
get to.

Lucas put his head down and did as much work as he possibly
could do. He would get something worked up and turned in, only to
get a request for a new level, hidden tunnels because there was a
conspiracy theory afoot, or some other such thing to alter on a game
that he'd already done, as well as working on the other games he was
trying to finish. He was in a race to get everything done by mid-
December, the absolute last second that it could be done.

He consumed a lot of caffeine, ate his way through the food in the
refrigerator, and missed Lydia sitting on his bed, watching silly TV,
the dog at his feet. He hadn't felt lonely before. Alone, but not lonely.
That was how a game designer lived, or so he thought.

Lucas occasionally snowshoed around his house, or worked a little
on the trail between his cabin and the main house. Ana and Julio had
been digging as well. Ana showed up at Lucas' cabin with an entire

chicken dinner of herbed potatoes, biscuits and honey, brown sugar carrots, and a carafe of Mexican hot chocolate. "How are you doing?" Ana asked her son. "Sorry, stupid question." She fingered his overly long hair. He'd kept up with shaving and literally set his timer to remind himself to take hot showers. But he hadn't made it into town for a haircut.

Lucas grinned. "Money, Mamacita. At this rate, with all the bonuses I'm making by getting things in on time, I'll have the insurance for the whole year paid by the end of next week, including accident and cancer insurance riders. I should also be able to pay you about three months' rent in advance. I'll be stunned if I'm not able to pay you six months in advance by the time all the bonuses are calculated. I'm so glad that I've been drawing nearly every minute that I'm not actually working, at least not intensively. I've been able to really get stuff worked out to where I could just open one of my sketchbooks and grab a new idea right there."

Ana grinned. "Money is good, son. Remember what I said about savings." She patted his hand, then put the side dishes and biscuits in the microwave, zapped them, and put the steaming dishes out on the little table.

"Mamacita, you would have more money for advance rent from me if I weren't putting some of it in savings." Lucas got out the plates and silverware.

"Good," said Ana. Lucas got out spoons for the side dishes, added knives and forks. They sat down and had a delicious meal. Ana talked about the hydroponics farm, and Lucas talked a little bit about the different worlds he had created. Ana talked about the next door neighbors, their efforts to dig themselves out after the blizzard, and the antics of the various kids in that family.

Finally, Ana confronted the subject she had been talking around. "Your dad went down pretty quickly. I left a Thanksgiving meal for him, and his nurse got paid for round-the-clock care for the blizzard. There are three nurses now because Carl is having a lot of trouble breathing. I think that we should visit him, be sure we're never alone with him, but I don't think Carl can hurt anyone anymore. Maybe with words, but we've heard it all before, haven't we?"

"Give me another week, ten days at the most. I'm nearly done. I can see the light at the end of the tunnel."

"Sounds good," said Ana. Ana heated up a pocket apple pie in the microwave, Lucas added some cinnamon ice cream, and they split the dessert. "I heard that you and Lydia were living together, but I see that is not true."

"It isn't. We did live together for about three days while we were digging a trail to get her back to her cabin."

"So, nothing happened?" asked Ana.

Lucas glared at his mother. "If it had, what makes you think I'd tell you?"

Ana laughed, one of her full-belly laughs. "That one is trouble, but I think she is good trouble for you." Lucas glared at his mother some more, then they cleaned up the mess and washed the dishes. They had eaten everything that she brought.

Julio came with his ATV to drive Ana and her freshly washed containers back. "You know, we can eat dinner together," Lucas said to Julio.

"Not my place yet," said Julio. Lucas nodded. It wouldn't be long now.

～

*L*ucas catnapped rather than slept throughout the next ten days. He had a ton of work to get in, and he was determined to earn as many bonuses as he possibly could. He ate because he set alarms to remind himself. When he ran low, Rennie came with more food and drinks. Rennie understood that Lucas was in his zone and didn't bother chatting with him.

Lucas looked like a mountain man when he was finally done. He had everything in on time and no new orders pending. Lucas slept for two days straight. Then he took an extremely hot shower, shaved, and went for a haircut in the village. Juliet at the haircut place razzed him about his nonexistent sexual relationship with Lydia, not that he wouldn't jump at the chance, but Lydia was the kind of woman who was definitely in charge. And the kind of fierce female who could literally claw his face if she were upset.

Lucas went home, his heart stuttering in his chest. It felt like he was approaching a firing squad, but he had made a promise to his mother. After doing a reconnoiter to be sure that there was a nurse there, Lucas went to go talk with his father.

Lucas was absolutely stunned. Carl's face was skeletal. He had a tube in his nose to help him breathe hooked up to an oxygen tank. Carl was in his recliner, dressed in warm flannel pajamas and covered with a blanket. Lucas had never seen his father without a variation of jeans and a long-sleeve shirt, except for the few times his father had worn a suit coat to go to church or a funeral. There was an IV in his arm, and while he was there Wyland, a large black man with close-cropped black hair, kind eyes, and a sad smile came by and told Carl that he would be coming by with this injection a bit later. Carl nodded.

"Lucas, it's good to see you. Come sit down," he said. Lucas continued standing, working to unclench his jaw. "Please."

Lucas had never heard that word come out of his father's mouth. He sat down stiffly on the couch. "Hello."

Carl waved a bony hand. "If you want something to drink, I'm afraid you'll have to get it yourself. I can make it back and forth to the bathroom, but that's about it."

"I'm fine."

"You look tired. Your mom came by, said you would come by when you're done with your pre-Christmas rush thing. Makes sense that people would try to get their stuff in before Christmas."

Lucas nodded. "I'm about at the end of what I can do at one time. I can probably take one more client or two, but anything else will kill me." Lucas cringed internally at the word, but he figured his father was pretty sure that he was dying.

"I probably should get to the point. I'm on some pretty heavy-duty meds." Carl paused to suck in the breath at the end of every sentence, breathe out, and pull some more air in. "Been talking with the nurses, then your mom. Finally I started listening to that woman." He choked, took some time breathing back in again. "She listed exactly what I had done wrong with you. She went over everything, everything she had seen. We both know…"

Carl had a coughing fit, so the nurse came in and injected something into the IV port. When he was able to breathe, Carl started again. "We both know there is a lot your mother didn't see. That priest came by, asked me to repeat every single thing I said to you, trying to remember my exact words. Tried to remember exactly what you said back. A lot of conversations I just didn't remember. I know that you and your mom got real angry with me about it, but I couldn't remember exactly what I said. Ana's been filling me in on a lot of stuff. The priest made me pull out pictures of you as a kid, and then have the conversations again like they were happening. He asked me if that's how you should speak to a child."

Carl's eyes grew wet. "For my dad, John Wayne was his damn hero. That priest, Father Diaz, asked me, 'The real man, or the man in the movies?' I realized that my dad had never met John Wayne, so it had to be the man of the movies. Father Diaz talked about how different times call for different people. He asked how John Wayne would do right now, getting a job, getting a wife with how he treated women. In the movies, not the real man. How a lot of the things in those movies aren't funny today. They're real racist and sexist."

Lucas struggled to keep listening to his dad. The man should have figured out this stuff years ago. He deliberately relaxed his hands, tried to listen.

Carl gasped like a fish, caught his breath, continued. "Then he asked me why I got my panties in a twist thinking you might be gay. Why that would even matter. He asked if you would be less of a son if you were gay. I've never had a priest talk to me like that, but he made me realize that a son is a son. He then asked me if I would have treated my best friend the way I treated you or my wife. Or if I would be arrested if I did any of those things in public. I have to say, I would probably get arrested at least twice over. Ana says, at her count it's probably six times. That doesn't include the shit I never told her, that you probably never told her."

Carl spoke slowly, deliberately, pausing to wipe his eyes. Lucas was stunned that his father was actually crying. Lucas remained silent as his father had another coughing fit, then continued speaking.

"I'm real sorry, Lucas. I can't begin to tell you how ashamed of my actions I am. I know I can't make it right, not with what I say, nothing I can do. Father Diaz explained to me that I was doing what my father wanted, all those years ago. He explained that my stubbornness and my refusal to listen made it impossible for me to admit that I was wrong, which is the first step to change."

Carl gasped, found his voice again. "The thing is, even though Father Diaz is probably going to give me last rites, I know I'm probably going to hell for what I did. I looked at those pictures, I thought about what I said, what I did, and I thought about how scared you must have been. How my actions made you get bullied at school, doing stuff that you had to do. That I made you do." Carl put his head in his hands. "I know that I can't ask for forgiveness, that it's much too damn late for that."

Lucas sighed. He'd been hoping all along that his father would say something like that to him and thought he'd feel elated. Vindicated. But in reality he felt tired and sad and some sort of dark rage.

"I can't forgive you, Carl, not so fast. You said you took on what your father wanted for you, and you projected it toward me. You didn't have any idea who I was, what my talents were, and you didn't bother finding out. I am really, really good at what I do. Literally very few people in the world can do it. I'm the set designer for virtual reality worlds. I create, out of my head, worlds that have never existed and make them real."

Lucas choked, felt his throat dry up. He got up, found a lone Coke in the refrigerator, popped the top, came back, and sat down. "You know how I learned how to do that? It was because I spent so much damn time in my room, staying as far away from you as I could get. I guess because when I was able to get away from you I took my sketchbook and went out in the fields somewhere and made a world where nobody was hurting me."

Carl stared at his son. "Father Diaz said there are many times when I used my words like I was hitting you. That the words were worse because they hurt you in places that nobody can see."

They both sat there while Carl wheezed and Lucas fought to unclench his hands. "I know you can't forgive me all at once, not just on my say-so. I wouldn't expect that. Can you do it piecemeal? Can you forgive me for one horrible thing I did, and accept my apology? Then, maybe tomorrow you can forgive me for some other thing I did. I know it's asking a lot. I know you're still going to be wrestling with this when I'm dead and buried. But I want an opportunity to have a son who doesn't hate me before I die. And that won't be long. I'm not saying that to guilt you into it. I'm saying that because it's true. It looks like I won't see Christmas."

Lucas stared at a wall for a while and thought about something. "You know the time you hit me across the face when I had braces on? I can't forgive you for that one. Let's talk about the time when I was eight, my friend Ronnie got a Star Wars set, and you gave me a BB gun and ammo. The last thing in the world I wanted was a damn gun. So I forgive you for not listening to an eight-year-old who loved Ninja Turtles and Batman and Star Wars. Mama got me what I really wanted, let me dress up like Leonardo for Halloween. She also told me who the real Leonardo was and showed me some of his paintings and drawings. She also gave me a sketch pad and colored pencils. I went from crayons to colored pencils in one day, then she got me an art book about drawing for kids."

Carl stared off into space, then looked back at Lucas. "That eight-year-old boy was an awesome boy. I couldn't understand why you didn't want to run around shooting your gun. Why you put it away, why I never really saw it again. That's what I wanted when I was a kid. But I wonder if that's what I wanted to do because my father made me into that person."

"That's a very large part of the problem. There was nothing wrong with that eight-year-old boy I was. There was nothing wrong with me at all. I was just different from you. And you can't make someone be who you want them to be. If that were true, I would have had the dad that I wanted. One that listened to a little boy talk about superheroes, wanted to just walk around the lake and talk about nothing. You couldn't be bothered. I know you were busy, but you couldn't just take an afternoon and walk around the lake with me?"

"No, I couldn't." Carl clenched and unclenched his gnarled hands. "I couldn't, because I was the ass who didn't listen to your mother and figure out that all of those things that I was working nearly every day to do were losing us money. They were not providing for a family but sinking it. I would have had to admit that a Mexican woman knew more than me about farming, about the land, about what needed to actually be done. I would have had to give up my prejudices on my old ways of thinking, and be a real man."

Carl tried to guffaw, but it sounded more like a hiss. "I'm a complete and total idiot. When I finally admitted to Father Diaz that I was wrong, it was kind of like admitting that I was an alcoholic, or maybe a drug addict, but I'm not any of those. It took forever to get the words out. Then, I admitted to your mother that I was wrong about not listening to her. She cried, she beat the shit out of that pillow over there on the couch, and she told me what a complete asshole I was for an entire marriage. Then she said everything all over again in Spanish."

Lucas gave a gentle smile. "That sounds like her. She gets really angry, but she gets over it relatively quickly."

"I remember how absolutely pretty she was, how much I wanted her. It never occurred to me that you're supposed to treat your wife like your best friend. Father Diaz listed the ways that a person is supposed to be a best friend, then asked me if I believed in those things. I said yeah, sure, then he asked why I didn't treat my wife that way. Then he asked me to list all the things a good father should be and listening to my own kid was not on the list."

Lucas sighed. "All of this happened because you couldn't listen. You also tried to beat me until I respected you. That just proved to me that you were a bully. I don't know anyone who thinks bullies should be respected. Took me a long damn time talking to Father Diaz to get to the point where I didn't want to hate you. He made me realize you had all these damn snakes in your head."

"Snakes? Oh, yeah, that's one way of looking at it." Carl sat there and tried to breathe.

"Were you happy, Carl?" Lucas asked, after a long silence.

"I thought I was, when I was bragging to my friends about the good life I had. Or complained a lot about the crops and the weather. And a wife who didn't understand me. You made it pretty clear that you were terrified of me, and eventually that you hated me. And your mother, she never made any bones about how stupidly she thought I was behaving. Then when she got her act together, and she was doing so much better than me, and you moved out, and she moved out, it finally got through my skull that I was damn lonely. But rather than getting my shit together like your mother did, I decided to double down of being stupid. I decided that if you guys weren't here, I could smoke and drink as much as I wanted to."

Carl laughed, then got through another coughing fit. "Once again, being stupid. Now I get to feel like an elephant is sitting on my chest." He stopped to gasp. "Still smoke, still drink, eat whatever the hell I want. Some teenager delivers it, already cooked. Steak, potatoes, hamburgers, hot dogs, mashed potatoes, biscuits and honey. Anything I ever wanted to eat, and it tastes like ashes in my mouth."

Lucas stared at his father for a long minute. "Because of the medications?"

"No, because I'm dying all by myself with nothing but a TV to keep me company." He held up a gnarled, wrinkled hand. "And yes, I understand it's my own damn fault. Your mother is more right than she knows. Not a single one of my so-called friends has been by to visit. Not one. They haven't come down to play cards with me, to sit and eat my steak and watch TV with me. Not to sit here and hash out old times. Not to drink my whiskey, smoke my cigars, talk about what kings we are. You know why, son?"

Lucas said, "Mama has been saying for years that those aren't actually your friends. That the minute things get tough, they'll be gone."

"She was right. I've even called them up, asked them to come down and see *Bonanza* with me, drink my whiskey, eat my steak. They say something about next week, in two weeks. Haven't heard a damn thing from any of them since I brought home the buck."

Lucas sighed. "I would say that I feel sorry for you, but I really don't. You decided to live this way a long time ago, and no one could get through to you it was a bad way. It would have been fine if you had chosen to live your life and not try to make me live yours. I don't have anything to say about the people who were your friends, because they weren't mine. I do know my friends would show up for me. It wouldn't really matter much what I was asking for, either. If I needed a toothbrush in the middle of the night, money, whatever, they would show up. They may tease me about it, but they would show up."

Carl smiled. "Sounds like good friends. Your mama says you were up with Mitch and James during the last blizzard. I knew Mitch was wild, so angry. Never approved of your making friends with them. But it looks like that is something else I was wrong about."

"The Westons are amazing. Things are going really well. They treat me like I'm family." Mitch laughed. "That means I have to do the cooking, too, when I'm there. One of the women living in one of our cabins, Lydia, made her special dishes for Thanksgiving."

"The one with the dog? Please apologize to her about what I said about the dog. I was just mad because I can't have a dog now, since I'm dying. No one in their right mind would give me one. Your mama was right not to take on any more of them. I was getting to be a drinking, smoking son of a gun around that time. Wouldn't have treated a dog right. I miss those dogs that passed on every day."

"So do I." Lucas stood. "And on that note, I'm going to take my leave. I have to see a woman, pet her dog on the head, and apparently apologize for you. Just so you know, she helped Mama butcher that deer you brought home. The one none of us wanted. My guess is that you were too tired and sick to help. You just wanted to crow about shooting one last deer before you died."

"No, I really did want to fill up the freezer so that your mother would have food for the winter," said Carl with a grimace.

"Carl, we have stores. Mama did not need the huge job of butchering a deer. This is one of her busiest seasons, too. Did you know that she grows poinsettias for everybody so they don't have to haul down the road fifty miles to get them? Did you know that her grains are selling like crazy, that she could barely keep up with the orders? There's so many people wanting and ordering gluten-free everything. She sells a lot of grains, works with Kylee down at the mill, has gone in with her to package and sell the flour. She grows food year-round. This is not a fallow season for her."

Carl nodded, choked, nodded again. "The one last good thing I tried to do, it was a mistake. I didn't listen again, did I?"

"Not one word anyone tried to say to you." Lucas stood up. "I'll work on that piecemeal forgiveness stuff. It kind of sounds like the right way for me to go about it. I'll also talk to Father Diaz, see if he can explain more things to me." He snorted. "I'm going to have to donate a lot when they pass the plate at Mass for all the work he's doing over here, make sure he sees me after he sees you so he doesn't have to make extra trips."

"Son." Carl's eyes misted. "Can you call me Dad?"

Lucas sighed. "No. A dad listens to his kids, wants what's best for them. This is the first day you have ever done anything like really listening to me. In fact, the last time I saw you, you were throwing a roundhouse at my head. This whole time you've been sitting here, you haven't apologized for that, either." Carl stared at his son with rheumy eyes as Lucas turned and walked away.

Lucas put his can in the recycling ,put his coat and snowshoes back on and went over to the greenhouse. He took off the snowshoes and helped Julio fill up the back of the farm truck with poinsettias, with a fat red and green ribbon wrapped around their bottoms with a beautiful red and silver bow. "Church?" Lucas asked.

"Yes," said Julio. "How did the talk with your father go?"

"He said that he was sorry, but I can only forgive him for the smaller things. The things that are farther away from now."

"That makes sense, but it will take forever if you forgive him for every single thing. He had about twenty years to damage you. Would you say a serial killer is damaged in the head? Wait, I said that wrong. What if a rock fell on my head, and after that I became a serial killer?"

"Actually, severe blows to the head can make someone change their personality." Lucas raised his eyebrows. "I get where you're going with this. I'd have to forgive you because you had been hurt and had not been that way previously. It obviously wasn't your fault, it was the fault of the brain damage."

Julio put in the last two poinsettias and carefully scooted them forward. Julio closed the back of the truck and turned to Lucas. "Did it occur to you that your grandfather was probably worse than your father? How many times do you think his father hit him in the head?" Julio turned, walked over to the front of the truck, opened it up, and filled up the back seat of the king cab with more poinsettias. Lucas rushed to help.

"So, I have to forgive my father because he has some sort of brain disease?" Lucas grunted as he pushed another poinsettia into place.

"A thinking disease. Realize that your father did not believe that he had a choice over his actions. Know that your mother did everything she could to stop him, and that she feels terrible guilt over not divorcing him when you were much younger. Even being Catholic, we both agree that she should have done so, but now it is too late. It was like being married to a bull, not a human who can reason for himself."

Lucas sighed. "You're right, I have never really forgiven Mama for not divorcing him."

"She had some wrong thinking." Julio carried a poinsettia in the crook of each arm and one in each hand as if they weighed nothing. Julio put them down on the back seat, slid them over, put up netting that plugged into the seat belts so the poinsettias wouldn't move around. "In that situation, her thinking had been damaged for being in the situation too long. Now she is thinking clearly, and you need to forgive her so that she can forgive herself. She is not *estupido*. She knows you have not forgiven her fully in your heart."

Lucas nodded, handed over the last poinsettia. Julio put it in, then slammed the door shut. "I will go inside and forgive her right away."

"Good." Julio nodded hard once, twice. "I will deliver these to the church, and see if Father Diaz can speak with your father, you, or your mother."

"Please tell him to come and see me when he is already up here talking to Carl or Mama. Please tell him he doesn't have to make a special trip because of me. I may or may not end up forgiving Carl after he dies, but I will try."

"You will forgive him to his face before he dies, because you do not want to be him." Julio got in the cab and drove away. Lucas stared after him, stunned.

Lucas went inside the greenhouse, hugged his mama, and said, "I realize that your thinking was messed up because of everything that happened, and I forgive you for not leaving Carl when you should have."

Ana nodded, and hugged her son. "Thank you," she said and wiped away her tears. "I knew that you would forgive me someday." She turned back to the rows of poinsettias still in the greenhouse. Lucas helped her carry them to the door. Apparently, Julio had to make another trip with the poinsettias somewhere, probably to another church, maybe the Presbyterian one. "Did you have a good talk with your father?"

"He apologized. Not for hitting me in the face when I had braces on, and not for trying to punch me a couple weeks back. He never listened to anything really, just talked about not listening. So I went all the way back to when I was eight, that Christmas."

Ana nodded. "The BB gun."

"It's like he saw *A Christmas Story* and believed all that shit was still happening in the modern world."

Ana laughed, but it was a sad one. "Actually, I think he kind of did. I think he kind of got parenting from very old movies and did not pay attention to the modern world at all."

"You were a great mom." Lucas hefted another poinsettia and moved it to the door. "You listened to me, and even though we didn't have much money most of the time, that never really occurred to me. There was always food on the table, even though I know now there were times that you didn't eat. Plenty of times that we got food from your parents."

"Borrowed money from them, too," Ana confessed. "I paid it all back. Not your father, me." She put her poinsettias down, hugged her son, and then moved more poinsettias to the door. "Yes, I was a good mother, and it is time that I stop beating myself up about it. Am I a good mother now?"

"Other than trying to get me to date people, yes." Ana laughed that full belly laugh of hers. "Now that we've moved every poinsettia here, I am going to go over to Lydia's place because I have to see a woman about a dog."

"I would have suggested that you get a dog years ago. But between September and now, you would forget to walk the dog. The dog will have to live with me for six months and with you for six months. And that would be very weird."

It was Lucas's turn to laugh. "Yes, Mama, it would be very weird." He kissed her cheek, and she drew him into a tight hug. Then Lucas went out to see a woman about a dog.

Lucas hiked out to Lydia's tiny house and was surprised when Luna came running toward him. He played in the snow with Luna for a while then followed the dog back to the little cabin. Lydia opened the door, and said, "Look who came out of his cave!"

Lucas said, "My father apologizes for threatening you about the dog."

Lydia blinked. "That's surprising. He doesn't seem like the kind of person who would apologize for anything."

"This is going to sound really stupid, but can you put on a coat and come with me and do something that doesn't involve talking? Like, seeing whatever the hell is at the cinema. We only have a few screens, so it will probably be boring as hell, but I really can't talk anymore right now."

"I would rather you take me to a bar, feed me bar food, and shoot some pool with me," said Lydia, shivering in the doorway as she toweled off the dog.

"Done," said Lucas. Lydia slammed the door in his face, and came out four minutes later fully dressed, that beautiful hair of hers under a woolen hat, black to match her blue-black hair, and a dark blue coat. She put on her snowshoes, and they trudged toward Lucas's truck. They got in and sang to every country music song about a jilted lover, a pointless job, getting drunk, and something about the weekend. Once they were in the bar and their coats off, Corinne immediately pulled them into country line dancing. Corinne was in some maroon boots with sparkles on the toes, making Lydia laugh.

They danced, sang, then sat down at a table and ate like pigs. They ordered nearly every appetizer on the menu, from jalapeno poppers to breadsticks. Then they all went dancing again and grabbed the pool table when one became available. "This is our last night before we go on vacation! Got my last website up and running!" Corinne was shouting to be heard over a table of cowboys drunkenly singing Christmas carols off-key. A server hustled over to shush the singers.

"One more day and I can say the same thing!" Lydia shouted. Lucas wondered if that meant he was supposed to take her somewhere on vacation. But where the hell would they go? They could go someplace warm, but that would use up most of the money that he had earned from all of this heavy work, and he'd promised his mother rent money in advance. He planned on drawing as many things that came out of his head as he could over the break and find a way to pay his mother a full year in advance as well as saving up money. Then he'd have a cushion and could go wherever the hell he wanted to. Besides, Lydia tended to change into a mountain lion. Where the hell would they go where she could do that?

He pulled Mitch aside and asked him where he was going with his brother and Lydia. "Where we're going, it's a bed and breakfast that caters to people who are...different." He glared at Lucas. "We're going there for two weeks, and I better not see you during that time. Take your girl up to see my mom and dad, spend time hanging out with them. Have a very relaxing family time. Or be at your cabin with her. I don't care. Just don't bother me, my brother, or our girl."

Lucas nodded rapidly as if he were a bobblehead. "Not planning on leaving town."

"Help her decorate something," Mitch suggested. "Women love that. Buy her chocolate, but never buy her any dead flowers. From what I've heard, it's not a good idea to give a Native woman a dead thing. No, give her a living plant. And give something to the dog. That makes women all gooey."

"Okay." Lucas nodded, and Mitch punched his arm. Then it was his time to shoot some pool, and Lucas let the bizarre conversation simmer in the back of his mind.

They drank tequila shots, they danced, and Lucas, James, and Mitch spoke to a lot of their friends while everyone else continued to dance, drink, and shoot pool. They ordered another round of food, this time chicken wings, pork sliders, and cheesy bacon fries, and James and Lucas switched to sodas. Finally, breathless and laughing, Lucas drove Lydia home.

On the way back, Lucas said, "I know you've got stuff to finish up tomorrow. When you're finished, do you want to call me up? I can help you haul the dog stuff over, your stuff too, and maybe you might want to stay at my place for a couple days, a week or two, doing nothing. Would that be good for you?"

"That sounds nice." Lydia's voice was only a little slurred from tequila and exhaustion.

"Maybe we can go into town tomorrow night, buy some Christmas decorations. My house looks like shit without anything in there making it look pretty. We can eat any kind of food you like."

"As long as I don't have to watch a zombie movie. Zombie movies and Christmas do not mix."

"You don't have to watch a zombie movie." Lucas shuddered at the thought, parked the truck, helped her hike over to her place, then went back over to his. He fell into bed and slept like the dead.

HARDWARE

$\mathcal{L}$ucas went to Omar's Hardware. Omar stood behind the desk, a beefy man with a staccato laugh which made him sound kind of like a loon. His daughter, Fatima, could find anything in the store in her sleep. So, if you wanted to know what you needed, where it was, or how to use it, you ask Fatima. Lucas secretly believed that Fatima could build a full-sized house with only the things in her father's store.

Lucas found Fatima restocking the nails. Lucas had no idea what people would be nailing in the middle of winter, but then he remembered all the Christmas decorations. Fatima wore a crimson *hajib* over a loose green top, dark blue jeans underneath, and black high-tops.

Lucas approached Fatima. "I need a tree that a woman would love for my cabin."

Fatima tilted her head. "Lydia is very strange. Smart, funny, deep, willing to do just about anything herself, extremely strong, but she has a look in her eye that tells me that something is really wrong. Anyway, I think the point would be to make her laugh and have a good time. We have a tree from last year. Some guy ordered it and never picked it up. I will not tell who it was because that would be just cruel. It's basically a white tree with blue branches. It's shimmery and silly and would be a lot of fun."

"Okay, I need that then." If Fatima said you needed something, you needed it.

Fatima went to the Christmas tree aisle, grabbed the box, and shoved it into his cart as if she had been lifting a box of foam. "Homemade decorations." Fatima pointed to some boxes. "They are cute, funny, silly. Plus, I would get both the regular silver and the blue tinsel. I would go for a star on top instead of the traditional angel. That's more the style of the tree."

"Okay." Fatima pointed out various ornaments, a Rudolph with a nose that lit up, Santa on his sleigh, numerous gossamer angels, silver and blue glistening balls studded with glitter and plastic gems. There were also various cartoon characters, which made Lucas laugh, so he put those in his cart.

Omar checked everything out, and said, "Do not think that I do not know that my daughter is a treasure," he said, filling Lucas's huge reusable canvas bag up as quickly as he could scan the items.

Lucas parsed that sentence, and lamely said, "She's awesome."

"It is good that you have designs on Lydia and not my daughter," said Omar.

"Omar, I don't mean to be rude, but eww. Your daughter is at least six years younger than I am."

"That is why it is so good," said Omar.

Confused, Lucas paid the bill, got everything into his truck, and then decided that Lydia needed a really good dinner after turning in her last website. He remembered her turkey hatred and her love of bar food, which he shared. He stopped by the bar, loaded up on potato skins, wings, and chicken nachos, minus the beans, because that would completely ruin the mood, plus all of the sauces. He swung by the grocery store and grabbed peppermint ice cream, chocolate syrup, and some cola for some floats. He took his time getting back to the cabin because the snow was starting to fall again. Ice was everywhere because the temperature had gotten a little too high, melted the surface of the snow, then dropped again.

Lucas wasn't stupid. He knew he absolutely should save the trimming of the tree for later. But he did get the tree set up and in its stand. It looked completely silly, but Fatima was right. For some reason it looked correct in that particular cabin. He surrounded the base of the tree with the boxes of ornaments and tinsel, then was horrified to realize that he hadn't gotten any presents yet. Not because he didn't have that many shopping days left before Christmas, but because it would look good under the tree. He put all the food away, made an enormous effort of will to try to eat something else, then realized he could just go back out, go shopping, and get whatever the heck he wanted for the people in his life.

Ana loved handcrafted things, so he knew where to start. Lucas went back to the bar and ate some potato skins and drank a lot of cola because shopping was exhausting. Then he went to see Billie. Billie created beautiful works of stained glass art, and Leelee, her girlfriend, made driftwood sculptures from what washed up on the banks of the lake and the streams that fed it. Leelee included pebbles and created beautiful little environments that often included tiny glass animals that Billie made.

Lucas measured the greenhouse door in his mind, and bought six beautiful panels of flowers, vines, a lake, a river, and the sun and moon. He bought a driftwood sculpture for his mother and Julio, two people of indeterminate genders walking by a glass lake with various glass animals all around. Lucas wanted to show his approval for Julio marrying his mother, which Lucas knew would happen after Carl died.

Lucas found a simple wooden horse carved out of driftwood with a beautiful satiny feel under his fingers. The horse was running, its mane flowing behind it, a wild look of glee on its face, in its wooden eyes. Somehow it felt like caving in, but Lucas bought the horse anyway. Carl might not last until Christmas, and not giving a gift to his father for Christmas just seemed insulting and rude, especially since the man was dying.

Billie was in the back, blowing glass, brown eyes narrowed in concentration, her strong arms holding the metal rod as she spun the glass in the kiln. Lucas could stand and watch her all day, and some townspeople did come to watch the show. Leelee kept her brown hair in beautiful braids, and had a narrow, thin face, dark eyes, and a ready smile. She liked to dress in bolero jackets over her sweaters, and long, heavy skirts over boots in the winter. Her long, elegant fingers made quick work of carefully wrapping all of the presents. Lucas paid for his purchases and let her wrap them, staring in rapt attention at Billie's work.

Lucas walked back to the truck. Lydia's present completely confused him. It seemed like she wanted to live a nomadic lifestyle from the past, but he knew from his work on gaming that people could change at any moment. Lucas decided that anything large would be a bad idea. The woman only carried what she could stuff under her motorcycle saddlebags. The thought of her leaving made him sad, so he pushed the thought away.

Lucas carefully put his purchases in the truck, then got into the cab and turned on the heat. He sat there for a while, thinking. What he needed was a carving, and Leelee was the best. Lucas pulled his sketchbook out of his bag and did several sketches in pencil. Getting the shading right was difficult, because he'd only seen them in their other forms once.

He turned off the truck, went back in, and asked for four carvings of wolves, and two of mountain lions. Then he had to think hard about Corinne's big heart. He decided on a hawk for her, its wings spread in flight. Leelee said she had plenty of wood to work with, and they agreed all of the carvings should fit in the palm of a hand. They haggled a bit on price, then Leelee did a little dance that made Lucas laugh at having her first commissioned work.

Lucas decided he'd given Lydia enough time. He had to be even more careful driving home because the snow was coming down harder. Lydia had to come over pretty soon, or she may have more trouble getting back and forth. He put the presents under the tree, made some hot chocolate and put some cinnamon sticks in the mugs, and texted Lydia. *I have hot chocolate. Are you at a stopping point?*

Give me twenty. Lucas did a happy dance, then he realized he needed some good music. He put on some rock versions of Christmas carols, started reheating the food, then opened the door when he heard Luna outside. He let her in, toweled Luna off, and shut the door when Lydia just stood there, staring at his tree, snow falling out of her hair onto the floor. Lucas helped Lydia get her outerwear off, gave her a towel, poured her hot chocolate, and handed it to her. She sipped it with one hand while brushing off her hair. She stood staring at the tree, then at the boxes on the floor, then back at the tree. She grinned, threw her head back, and laughed.

They were hungry and fell on the food as if they were wolves. Then Lucas put on some country-western Christmas songs, and they did a very odd combination of country line dancing along with trimming the tree. Lydia surprised him by finding the star and putting that on first, then working her way down. They got the lights untangled and plugged in. Lucas was delighted to realize Fatima had put two mesh strings of lights in his cart, designed to be put in windows. He wondered how Fatima had figured out how big his windows were, because, as far as he knew, she had never been to the property. Then he realized the pictures of the cabins were online on his mother's cabin rental website. He used masking tape to hang the mesh, and was delighted to find that he had a five-outlet power strip hiding in his closet. The blue and red lights looked beautiful together, and the mesh ones fit the windows perfectly.

He made his girl peppermint ice cream cola floats, and Lucas, Lydia, and Luna all settled in to watch holiday movies on his bed. "You were busy today."

Lucas laughed and told her about Fatima's gift at figuring out exactly what people needed. "How was your day?"

"Unbelievably exhausting. The last website client wanted so many changes that I was ready to throw the laptop out the window. Which would have been bad because it really wasn't the laptop's fault."

Lucas laughed. "Been there, done that. I remember I once created twenty-seven different levels, with three hidden ones. They were all in different parts of this huge haunted house. It was this Halloween thing." Lydia stared at him out of the corners of her eyes. "If it's a color thing, it really isn't that difficult to change. But, the whole mood of the thing was supposed to be spooky, creepy, with a little bit of humor. They went in and edited out all of the humor."

Lydia dropped her jaw, affronted. "That's remarkably stupid."

"I know. They hired some testers, realized they had a flop on their hands, and asked me to put it all back. I charged them a thirty percent bonus to do it, and got everything done on time. Never worked with those creeps again. Every single thing that they've made since then has bombed, and I think they've gone under."

"Didn't they learn anything from the *Scream* movie franchise?"

"Apparently not. You see, that's the trick with the languages. The parts where I use language have all sorts of in-jokes, satire, even poking fun at the developers. I've been able to pay the guy who makes the languages, Mr. Harris, some more money, giving him the profits for the books that he makes about the languages. They're either hidden within the game, or sometimes sold separately. Anyway, I passed the extra bonus for that stuff on to Mr. Harris."

"How did you meet this guy? He sounds like a genius."

"He is. I took his Global History and Cultures class in high school, which he actually made interesting and fun. I also got my medieval arts certificate from him that informed a lot of my work. I know at least some of how things are supposed to work, and I'm able to put together a good scenario. I'm pretty much at that point where people just give me a very basic concept and say go do whatever the hell you want. Very few people give me something very detailed or exact about what they want. They just point me in a direction, I go, they give me lots of bonus money."

"That's really awesome. You're incredibly artistic. What I do is a lot more mundane. More practical. But these people need to either sell something or to give out information in a way that needs to be clear and precise. I have to be careful because it's really easy to come up with too many pages for a website. I keep it short, simple, and extremely clear. I studied copywriting, and I'm really glad that I did because without it I wouldn't be as good at what I do as I am."

"How long until you think you're going to get more contracts?"

"Not until mid-January at the absolute earliest. I'm thinking mid-February." Lydia sighed. "You didn't happen to buy cookies, did you?"

"No, but I know how to make candy cane popcorn with M&Ms."

"Then, do that. Can I help?"

They made the popcorn recipe and climbed into Lucas' bed to watch a holiday movie, a comedy about a boy, a girl, a snowstorm, and a lot of distance to cover. They switched to another holiday movie, this one about two women who switched houses and fell in love in other countries. The dog curled up on the bed with them under the covers, and they held each other in a nest of pillows and heavy blankets.

Lucas stunned himself by gently kissing her lips. She tasted like peppermint and hot chocolate. He smiled at her, and said, "I won't do anything you don't want. You make the rules here. Whatever you want, we'll do it. Whatever you don't want, tell me to stop, tell me to get the hell away from you if you want to."

Lydia looked at him, eyes glittering. "You do realize that someone is stalking me, and that I could leave at any moment?"

"Seize the day."

"How many condoms do you have?"

Lucas pointed at the nightstand. "Three boxes, in the drawer."

Lydia laughed. "Confidence. I like it." She kissed him, and the movie, the music blaring from the speakers, the cold outside, it all melted away. Lucas felt like they were in some sort of tunnel, some sort of place where only he and Lydia existed. He fell, and fell, and hoped he wouldn't wake up anytime soon.

He stroked her hair, that gorgeous fall of straight blue-black. He managed to get the silver clip out; there was a trick to it he found with his fumbling fingers. He reverently placed the clip on his nightstand. Lost himself in those dark eyes, like the night with shining stars inside. She grinned at him. "I won't break."

"Tell me to stop, and I will," he said. She reached down, grabbed his hardness. He gasped. "I'll take that as a yes." She tightened her fingers on the shaft, reached down with lithe fingers towards his balls. He stilled as the pain started to register; she stilled as well. "I take it, that's a no." His voice was high, squeaky. She smiled a slow smile. She removed her hand, stroked. He gasped. "Good to know my limits." She kissed him, shutting him up.

He expected her to take the lead, but she just kissed him. He stroked her, pulled off her soft fuzzy sweater. To his surprise, she wore nothing underneath. He took his time there, licking and kissing. He wanted her to gasp, moan, and kept at it with the tip of his tongue until her eyes rolled up in her head. *Keep her eyes rolling,* he told himself. He kissed his way down her flat stomach, stroked those hips. She pulled off his shirt and grinned down at him.

He slid off her long underwear and panties, kicked off his own, then dove deep, kissed the inside of her thighs. She grabbed his hand, showed him where and how to place his fingers, how to stroke her inside and out simultaneously. Her breath caught, held, then her eyes rolled back as she arched again and again. Lucas grinned. He was doing better at this than he suspected he could.

He lowered his mouth, used his tongue as he had used his fingers. She screamed, and he stopped, stunned. She tilted her chin down, looked at him under heavy lids. She reached down and drew him up to her, flipped him over. "My body is yours to play with."

"My toy." Lydia reached over, grabbed him. He gasped and lunged toward the box of condoms, nearly dropping the entire drawer in his haste to get it open. He fumbled one box out, then fished out a condom. She took it from him, tore open the wrapper, rolled it on for him. He thought of times tables, then, further under control, held his breath as she mounted him. She took her time. She came, hard, and he rode the wave, releasing himself.

She got up, stumbled to the bathroom, came back with a pack of wet wipes. She got him cleaned up, threw away the garbage, then slid back in bed. "My man."

He pulled her to him, and she lay with her head on his shoulder. "My woman." He stroked that beautiful hair, and they both slid into sleep.

~

*A*na was tired, tipping toward exhaustion. The poinsettias had been delivered, the veggies and herbs had been picked, and grain had been taken out to the mill to be ground into a variety of flours in preparation for a whole bunch of people to decide to get off gluten and eat healthier foods in the new year. Ana had been taking care of the horses for a couple of days, because apparently Lydia and her son were shacked up. That made Ana smile. Lydia wouldn't take any crap from Lucas, and Lucas had to come out of his fantasy worlds and interact with her.

The only cloud on the horizon was Carl. She got his guns back herself. But he didn't seem inclined to use them, which surprised her. She would have thought he would have taken the easy way out. That's how she knew that all those apologies were real, that he had really changed. He didn't apologize for the right things, and the right order, or even really understand all of the damage he had done. But he was making an attempt to clean up what he had done in the extremely short time before he died.

So, she did what she didn't want to do. She went over to the beautiful farmhouse she had abandoned because she couldn't live with the man that lived within it. Father Diaz had instructed her to forgive herself for being the parent that stayed with the man who treated her so badly, who didn't listen to her or to his son. She regretted now buying so much of the farm from him, but she hadn't wanted to lose the farm she had put so much work into. She also wanted him to see very clearly the consequences of his mistakes. He seemed to live his life lurching from crisis to crisis, having no idea how many of them he created himself, or that his actions had consequences at all. She thought it pitiful that he only realized this on his deathbed.

Ana prayed to show compassion toward him instead of pity, but he knew her expressions, at any rate. She tried to smooth her brow, to enter with a gentle smile, but there were still times that she wanted to take that body of his that could barely breathe and throw it out the window.

She didn't want to have any more regrets. She didn't want to look back thinking that she had done the wrong thing. So, she walked in that door that used to be hers, closed it behind her, took off her coat and boots, made some tea for herself in the kitchen, and found Carl propped up on his easy chair. He turned off the television, and she moved the other recliner so that she could face him. "Hello."

"Let me guess. You've been in the barn," said Carl. "Manure and fresh hay with a whiff of grain."

Ana forced a smile. "I've got horse duty today."

Carl sighed. "I realize I was the equivalent of the crazy cat lady, bringing in horses like that." He nodded to himself. "Didn't talk to you about it, just did it." He pointed a finger at her. "And don't think I didn't want to be an asshole and make extra work for you, missy." He sighed. "I used living creatures like pawns in a game with you."

"Done beating yourself up? I know it might get kind of exhausting you having such a long list to go through at all. But that's not why I came." Ana sipped her tea.

Carl wheezed out a laugh, such as it was with his being barely able to breathe. "And why, woman, are you here?"

"Lydia, the one who takes excellent care of the horses when she's not spending a lot of time with our son, is extraordinary. Her dog is amazing too. Luna is a really sweet dog, and doesn't seem to mind how huge the horses are."

"I know I really don't deserve the time of day from you, but could you ask that extraordinary woman to come over here, just for a little while? I'd like to meet her."

"I would suggest dinner, but that will probably wear you out. Maybe just sodas and snacks."

"I'm curious. Why do women feed people when they come over?"

Ana smiled, a genuine one this time. "Hospitality 101." She laughed. "If you offer someone food and drink, that means you want them to stay. If you don't, that's a very clear indication that you only want them to hang around for a little while."

"Social cues," said Wyland, coming into the room. "Something you,

Carl, apparently know nothing about." The burly nurse quickly took Carl's vital signs with practiced ease.

"Exactly. You've got to treat people with a certain amount of respect if you want to get returned to you." Ana sighed, then deliberately relaxed her jaw. "It's not something you demand or require from other people. It's something you earn."

"That's what made my son hate me. That, and not bothering to find anything out about him. Ana, please do me an enormous favor. Please tell me about our son."

Ana stared off into the distance, holding the mug in her hand suspended in mid-air. Finally, she turned back to Carl. "He is sweet, soft, gentle, but strong in ways that you were never able to see. He's on a break now, completely exhausted after doing a tremendous amount of work. He transforms bits and bytes into whole worlds."

She perked up. "You know, I think you need to go traveling today. I've got a virtual reality rig because I wanted to be able to understand what our son was talking about. He talked about this language, or that tapestry, or a space station, or an elf battle. I didn't understand anything at all until I went into the games myself. Then I was stunned and overwhelmed and...awed." She gently put down her cup and stood. "I'll be right back."

Carl was, surprisingly, awake when she came back. The system was a black box with two wireless VR headsets. She set it up, plugged in the power cord, then put the VR set on Carl. She also put rings on his index fingers which would enable him to move about in the game. There were special shoes and even treadmills used for the games, but she made it simple so that Carl could participate. "This is one of the worlds our son did a few years ago. There's nowhere near as much detail. It's a standard story about some elves and a quest and things like that. Just pick a character and walk around in the world a little bit. Don't try to do anything other than that. Just look around. What you see is what our son made." Carl picked out a random character and popped into the game. There was a hallway lit with torches, tapestries hanging on the walls, inlay on the floor.

Ana changed games. "This is the third version of that game, which

our son worked on last year." Again, Carl picked out a random character. This time they were in a feasting hall. Creatures of all shapes,
sizes, and species were getting together, eating from soup tureens,
passing around platters of meats, cheeses, breads. They took little
knives from their belts and cut the bread, meat, and cheese. Flagons of
beer and glasses of wine so delicate they look like they would break if
they were touched were in front of every plate. The tapestries hanging
on the wall were magnificent, scenes from hunting, battles, and
magery. They were extremely vivid and rendered in great detail. Carl
wandered around just looking at things, letting the wash of noise, the
bit of song as a minstrel played in the corner, and the sheer detail
overwhelm edhim.

Ana changed games again. "This is a space station over Earth, a
game our son did about six months ago." Carl randomly picked a
scientist for his avatar, then just stared at the Earth out of the obser-
vation platform. The various screens fascinated him. He went up to a
screen, found that there were advertisements for various jobs, such as
for shuttle pilots, chefs, and horticulturalists. The ads were rendered
in amazing detail. He went to another screen and saw the schedule for
the space elevator. People of all shapes, sizes, and ethnic backgrounds
went by, all in variations of ship suits, wearing boots with soft soles.
He looked around, absolutely stunned at the detail. He walked over to
yet another screen, this one for all the entertainment that was being
offered on the various decks. He touched one, and then saw a level
diagram. He stepped back, stunned.

Anna turned off that game and went over and removed Carl's VR
set and ring. "Can you leave this here?" asked Carl. "This is absolutely
astonishing. Our son did all of that?"

"From what Lucas told me, he does all of the backdrops, the
setting, all the levels. And in that space station game, you can go up
and down an elevator, see the station, or even take the space elevator
back to Earth. He designed all of that. The people walking around,
that's for the game people to do. Some of them are backdrops, but
there are specialists in people in elves and all that sort of thing. Lucas
said he had to specialize in something, and he likes doing the back-

grounds. He says most of the backgrounds of games are lame. Most of them are continuations, the same thing from a slightly different angle or perspective. That drives him crazy. He said that's lazy. He draws a lot, then someone orders a game, and he figures out what will work or not within that world, then he draws it. Then he scans it in, and then makes the rest of the world work."

"I have been a complete ass. Here I was thinking he was wasting his life, and what he's doing is absolutely incredible. And he makes enough money to live on?"

Ana grinned. "That boy just paid me for three month's rent and utilities in advance. He says with the bonuses he's getting, he's paying for an entire year of his health insurance, putting that money aside and savings, then he's probably going to give me a couple more months' worth of rent in advance. He says he wants to end up being able to pay a year in advance because he works incredibly hard between September and now, in mid-December, getting everything in and all the changes made so that the games will come out by Christmas. Then the coders make the people move around against the sets, and everything works."

"I take back every fool thing I said. Invite him over, too, because I need to apologize to him for that."

"Carl." Ana leaned forward. "You could have asked me or anyone else for help. You had enough money coming in for the last couple of years from me that you could have bought a VR set, taken a look at what your son has done. Hell, you didn't even have to do that. All you had to do was go online and look up the games, see what the levels look like there. You could have done that on any computer, even your cell phone. You could have known years ago just how incredible our son actually is."

Carl stared off into space, then shook himself. "It was not admitting to being wrong. First, I opposed everything our son said, all the words coming out of his mouth, because to realize he was right, I would have to admit that I was wrong. And you're right. All I had to do was a little bit of investigation, and I would have found out I was wrong all over the place."

"Do yourself a favor and tell him that when you see him." Ana put the controller rings in a special box, put the small box into the larger one, put in the headsets, closed the lid, and put the box on a nearby shelf. She sat back down on the couch. "I can't guarantee that either he or Lydia will come over, but they probably will. Just do what you've never done before, and ask him what he's been doing, what's been going on. And actually listen. Look him in the eye when he's talking. He keeps looking at the ground when he sees you because he's afraid. Don't let him be afraid anymore."

Lydia finished her tea, stood up, and said, "If you hurt him in any way, I'll take away your pain medication. And I am deadly serious about that. Do you understand?"

"Yes," said Carl, solemnly. "I used to put you down, say nasty things about you for taking our son's side against me. But I was the one taking sides against both of you. I'm sorry."

"Every time I hear that, it just tries to slide right past my ears. All those nights when I cried, wishing I could hear those words out of your mouth. Now, it's just so sad to me because you're saying them so late. Almost too late. I will pray very hard about forcing myself to accept your apologies. It's just that, after all these years, it's very hard to hear. If you had said them five, ten years ago, our marriage would not be destroyed now. It just makes me so very sad that you wasted nearly all of your time."

"It makes me sad, too." Carl sighed gustily. "When I die, do me a favor. Don't bury me in the cold, hard ground. Cremate me, then bury the ashes next to my horse. I know we bought plots years ago, but you should be buried next to the man you really love. The second favor is, please go ahead and marry Julio when you're ready. He looks at you like the sun in the sky or like the harvest moon. I looked at you like that for about a year, and then I forgot what I had."

"Okay, Carl." Ana turned, walked to the kitchen, rinsed her teacup, then put it in the dishwasher. Some sort of pump parts were in there, plastic tubing waiting to be washed. She stared at the tubing, then gently closed the dishwasher, put on her boots and coat, and then went out into the frigid winter day. Then with her tears freezing on her cheeks, she cried. She cried for the man that he should have been, the husband that she had wanted and had never had. She cried for the futility of a man weeks or days before his death suddenly realizing all he has done wrong. She cried because this man, this new man she was speaking to, would have had a chance with her. But it wasn't going to happen. She realized compassion was blooming in her heart.

STRONGER

*L*ydia was saddened to have to climb out of her haze. She had moved into Lucas' cabin. She brought over her computer, the clothes she needed, the food out of her refrigerator, and the dog bed, food, and toys. Lucas threw the dog toys all over the cabin. That surprised her. She didn't think she would want to move in with someone, even on what she was considering to be a vacation.

Second, she realized she was getting stronger when she found she could lift the dog without even thinking about it. When she was finally able to leave the dream world of the bed, snacks, movies, and binge watching television shows, she took Luna out to the lake, and Lucas often came with her. They snowshoed all over the place, had a tremendous amount of fun, and Lydia realized she wasn't getting winded. That completely stunned her.

Lucas took her to the Weston's farm twice a week for something-- a game night, barbecue, holiday party, or movie night. Lucas would stay behind with Corinne, playing board or video games, while the rest of the pack changed and ran through the snow on four feet. Cats sometimes got into small groups of two or three or maybe four. But they didn't tend to run in packs. Mountain lions were extremely solitary beings.

Lydia felt so stunned. She was around Lucas nearly all the time. She spent a lot of time with the large family, the Westons. She met with Ana and Julio, had dinner with them a few times.

She had even been over to see Carl. The cancer had done a number on him, causing nearly a complete change of mind and heart. Lydia used everything she had learned as a Hatathli woman. She said to Lucas, "Look into his eyes. Listen to his words. You do not have to change your heart. His time for words is passing."

"I will. For you, not for that asshole."

Bit by bit, Lucas relaxed more and more, unclenched his fists, even slouched into the couch from time to time. It was Luna that actually changed Lucas' mind. Luna's compassion from the old man shamed Lucas into behaving better. She would go over, place her head under the old man's hand, and he would stroke her silky ears. *I still want to throw the old man out the window* was the thought he kept in the taut lines of his shoulders. Lydia touched his knee and Lucas tuned in again.

"That game, that one with the space station." Carl gestured. "I don't know how you did it, son."

"One panel at a time." Lydia kept her hand on Lucas' knee. He still hated the word "son," as he didn't feel Carl had earned the title of "father."

"He draws in between jobs, has ideas ready to go." Lydia smiled.

Carl sighed. "I sucked as a dad, son." He sighed. "I hate that you flinch whenever I use that term." Carl stroked Luna's head some more.

"Forgiveness is a mountain, and we don't have much time." Lucas' voice was more tired than sad.

"Okay. Okay." And then they would talk about the horses.

The sense-of-family thing was very strange. Lydia had her mother, and her father wasn't there very often. When he was, he had all Lydia's attention. Then, after her father died, the medicine man had come by, but he had never lived in the house. Renault had his own place where he could do work with the people of the village. He was almost never there, having so much work for him to do covering such a wide area of the reservation. Lydia had never begrudged Renault his work. She knew how desperately important it was. But Renault was rarely at her home. He took her with him when he could.

There were times when Lucas was somewhere else mentally, then his sketchbook would come out, and beautiful worlds would come out from under the hand that held the colored pencils. Then Lydia would leave him in his world and go on a walk and take the dog out on an adventure. Then she would come back, eat something, play around on her computer. It was a very calm, happy life.

This togetherness stuff was odd for her. Ana treated her with absolute respect, as did Julio. Carl was struggling to make some sort of connection with his son before he died, and Lydia was there to support Lucas navigating this new world that he didn't think was going to happen.

Then, of course, there were the Westons. They were always doing something; cooking, eating, drinking, talking, playing a board game, putting together a puzzle, watching something, playing a video game, or changing and running off into the woods in the dark. Lydia got used to spending nights out, Stretcher on one side of the trail and Lydia on the other, making sure that the wolfpack stayed safe. Lydia had never been around wolf shifters before. What she found was some sort of wild abandon. They took such joy in being outside. And Lydia didn't have to be constrained in any way. She could openly talk about being a shifter.

Apparently, there was a shifter Council, its goal to protect the shifters, making sure they weren't discovered. If you wanted to come out and say you were a shifter, you could do that as an individual. But you had no right to involve the rest of the pack. That automatically made you a loner, which was kind of a dangerous situation for shifters whose animals ran in packs. The main laws were, don't get found out, and don't expose anyone else. Lydia had no intention of breaking either law. The third law, more an underwritten one, was never, ever try to harm another shifter. Shifters were rare, and therefore must be protected. The exception was a shifter that was willing to break their own laws. Then, their own pack or a small group of shifter enforcers would find and deal with such a threat.

Adoption was also a problem, with situations like Lydia's mother's where the parents had no idea that the child would change arising from time to time. Every group of shifters had people ready to adopt a child at a moment's notice. Shifter children were rare and extremely well protected. Lydia had more than one conversation with Gunny, Rachael, James, and Stretcher, finding out about her people, shifter people. With this family, she knew she could call and they would help her with any need.

Mitch, James, and Corinne were off at the shifter retreat place. She learned from Rachael that Mitch was volatile and needed to keep himself very relaxed. Lydia found out the address and website information about the shifter B&B from Rachael. The place looked beautiful, and Lydia decided to go there at some point.

Lydia's discussions with the Westons about shifter secrecy and security brought up an interesting theory. What if Lydia's stalker was someone who didn't like shifters, and the only shifter she knew of was Lydia? Lydia looked at every picture that Hella Girl sent her. Her friend's aging forward-reverse software was truly incredible. But Lydia couldn't find anyone that looked like the shooter. Not classmates, or teachers, not the bus drivers or somebody that worked out in the university gym. Not her hiking instructors, either. Getting pictures of all the rez people was much harder, but Hella Girl kept at it. Lydia couldn't understand why she didn't recognize this woman at all while the woman had an obvious hate on for Lydia.

There were people who wanted to turn furry, but since it wasn't a virus, that wasn't possible. There were also people who believed any of the things that happened in movies would occur, and therefore hated shifters out of their own ignorance. Hella Girl put names and faces to as many of the crazies she could, and turned over that information to the FBI as well. But none of them happened to be the person that shot Lydia.

Lydia no longer believed that her stalker thought she was dead.

The stalker probably didn't know where she was. Years of living a low profile came in very useful.

~

*L*ydia's speculations came to an abrupt halt when Carl's slow downward spiral accelerated. Lucas and Ana took turns being with Carl, Lydia looked after the horses, and Julio looked after the hydroponics farm.

They had Christmas early for Carl, on the sacred day of the winter solstice. Lucas put a small present in the old man's hand and helped him tear off the paper. Carl looked at the wooden horse running into the wind, and tears streamed down his face. "Thank you, son," whispered Carl. For once, Lucas didn't flinch at being called "son."

Ana handed Lucas his present from Carl. Lucas opened it up and found top of the line portfolio paper, a wooden box with a hundred shades of colored pencils, and several erasers. Lucas was stunned, tears streaming down his cheeks. "I didn't recognize your dreams, son, or your skill. You're a very hard-working artist, and you do tremendous work. I played your games. I keep dying," he said, and attempted to laugh. "Like I keep doing in your video games, but I'm doing it here, too. Anyway, I had a lot of fun, far more fun than I ever did watching old *Bonanza* reruns. You do things that make people live in other worlds, and I didn't understand it before, but I think I do now. I'm really sorry that I drove you away so hard that you wanted to live in other worlds instead of this one. If there's any advice that a foolish old man can give you, remember that you live in this world, too. That you need to do things in this world to make it better."

Ana smiled through her tears at the breakthrough between father and son. Luna sat at Carl's feet, ready to lick his face, accept a scratch behind the ear. Luna's great compassion towards Carl had melted the ice around Lucas's heart. Lydia was delighted that Luna was such good medicine for both father and son.

Lydia went to check on the horses, leaving the dog with Carl, who needed the dog more. She fed them their evening feed, and then she came back into the house, ready to prepare something for dinner. But it was not to be. Julio was at the front door, and he said quietly, "Carl has passed. It was good, this Christmas for him. The coroner is coming. Ana and Lucas must be together now, and you shall be on the outside for a few days. Please do not take this amiss. They need to heal because of the mess Carl left for them."

Lydia looked up at Julio, and said, "You are like my second father. He is a medicine man for my people. I think, with the proper training, you could be very similar to him."

Julio shook his head. "My place is here with my woman. We shall cremate this man who caused so much destruction. Then, when Ana's tears have dried, she will turn to me, and I will turn to her. This coming year, which may have begun in sorrow, will end in great joy. Whether or not you and my new son stay together, you will come back and dance at my wedding."

"If I'm still alive, I will be here."

Julio snorted. "Whoever did this to you is a coward, shooting you from afar with a poisoned bullet." Lydia raised her eyebrows. Julio smiled. "I talk to the Westons, as does Ana. Find this person and take this problem away." Lydia nodded and went in to hold Lucas in her arms. He let her go, then held on to his mother. Lydia called Luna, and they hiked back to her cabin, leaving the family to grieve.

~

The service was two days later; there was no point in delay. There were only a few people at the graveside, actually urnside, service. Father Diaz was quick and brief, and Ana shared the memory of the beginning of her marriage to Carl. Lucas described the one time that his father complimented him on his art, on his deathbed. Clarence and Skeeter were there, but they kept their so-called funny stories about Carl to a minimum, partly because it was below freezing outdoors, and partly because Father Diaz kept gimlet eyes on them. The little horse Lucas had given to his father was embedded in the marble plaque, right next to the plaque for Trigger, his beloved horse. Sadness smothered them like a blanket, but nobody cried.

Then, everyone scattered, but not before Ana very loudly and clearly asked Carl's two so-called friends where they had been while he was dying. When they brought cards over and played with him, watched a television show, had a smoke or drank some whiskey with him. After initially trying to argue back, the two men slunk away. Ana decided not to have a wake because Carl really didn't have friends.

Christmas was two days after the service. Lydia decided to spend a private Christmas Eve with Lucas, and to go over and give the presents to Julio and Ana before leaving to be with the Westons. Lydia knew that Lucas needed his mother, and that she needed him.

They had a quiet late lunch; Luna got a bone that she nibbled in front of that ridiculous, happy tree. Lydia gave Lucas little glass paperweights to hold down his sketches on his drafting board in the shapes of various characters from the games Lucas had helped design. She had worked with the glassblower Billie on them. There was a human, a dragon, an alien, and an elf. "Loriana! Skyright! Yaequal! And Quird! Awesome!" He stared at her, goggle-eyed. "You went to Billie!"

"She's an amazing glasswright." Lydia smiled. "She did them pretty fast too." Lucas' eyes filled with tears. "There's no crying on Christmas Eve!" Lydia barked. Lucas bellowed laughter.

Lydia opened her present, a carving of a mountain lion on a rock, eyes closed in slumber. She absolutely loved it and held it close. "This is the woodcarver's work. Leelee, Billie's significant other. It's...it's special." She tried not to choke up too much, but her voice still came out raspy. "My other side. My puma. She's so lovely. I was so busy hiding her. Me. Myself. Both parts. Dating was kind of hard, because, hey, let's have some fun, did you know that I turn into a mountain lion?" Lucas choked out a laugh. "But this...it's special. Easy. Fun. Relaxing." Luna stood up, walked over, and flopped into Lydia's lap, chew bone and all. "Oof. And I have a dog."

Lucas grinned, then leaned over and kissed her. The kiss got deeper, and Lydia leaned in. Then there was a knock on the door. "Are you expecting anyone?" Lucas shook his head, and *oofed* as he stood up from where they had been sitting on cushions by the tree.

Lucas opened the door, and Ana was all smiles. Lydia saw the corners of her eyes crinkle, the sadness deep within those brown eyes, but smiled back. Luna carefully put her bone down, then went over to kiss Ana's hand. Julio came in behind Ana and shut the door. "*Mijo! Feliz Navidad!*"

"*Feliz Navidad*, Mama." Lucas hugged his mother close.

Lydia stood and took the two presents out of Julio's hands. "Welcome!" She stood on her toes and kissed his cheek. "Can I get you some hot chocolate?" She knelt and put the presents down under the tree. "I have the spicy kind."

Ana grabbed Lydia in a hug as Lydia stood up. Lydia righted herself, careful of the dog at her feet. "No, we open the presents now. Oh, my! What did you give my boy?" She carefully fingered each paperweight. "From your games. I recognize them." Ana turned to Lydia. "I knew you were good for my boy."

Lucas snorted. "I'm not a boy anymore. Let me pour you some chocolate. Come, sit." They sat down at the tiny table while Lucas poured the Mexican hot chocolate spiked with cayenne pepper and cinnamon, Lydia brought out the two folding chairs, and they sat and drank.

Lucas handed his mother the unwieldy gift from under the tree before he sat down. Ana opened it and stared at the figures walking along the glass lake on the driftwood sculpture. Julio leaned over and fingered the tiny glass animals. Tears began to stream down Ana's face. Lucas handed her a tissue box. "Mama, don't cry," he said helplessly.

"No, *mijo*. These are good tears."

Julio kissed Ana's head. "I thank you. You have made your mother and I very happy."

Lydia waited until the tears stopped to open her present. It was a necklace of lavender blown glass with matching earrings. She grinned. "Leelee has been busy. It's really lovely." Then Julio and Ana exclaimed over the stained glass panels that would go in the door to the greenhouse, a bowl of strawberries, fields, a mountain, a black-berry bush.

Lucas wiped his eyes and opened his present. It was an easel with multiple clips that could be raised and lowered, even hung on a wall. "Wow, thanks Mama!" He hugged his mother, then Julio gave him a side-hug.

They chatted about nothing for a while. Finally, Ana said, "Will you be at midnight mass, mijo?"

"I will," said Lucas. "Lydia can't go. She will be…"

Ana reached out, brought the little carving of the puma to the table. "I know where she will be. This is you?" Lydia nodded. "So beautiful." She kissed Lydia on both cheeks. "So good for my boy!"

Lydia grinned. "I try."

Lydia and Lucas got in the truck, along with the dog, to have Christmas Eve dinner with the Westons. There was more loot at the Weston's farm. Lucas got a special, thin case for his portfolio that would fit in his backpack, along with loops for fifteen of his brand-new colored pencils. He loved it. Lydia got a soft robe in a dove gray, and she promptly put it on, making everyone laugh. The Westons loved the miniature figures of the wolves and Stretcher's mountain lion. They plied Lucas and Lydia with ham, biscuits, roasted apples with cinnamon and walnuts, and peanut butter pie. Lucas kissed Lydia goodbye, then went home to take his mama to midnight mass with Julio.

After several Christmas movies, with toffee pecan popcorn balls and sodas to go with it, the midnight hour came and went. Everyone wished each other Merry Christmas and went to bed.

On Christmas morning everyone slept in very late, then had a mushroom cheese quiche with bacon crumbled on top and a cinnamon swirl coffee cake, along with hot chocolate. They lay around in their sweats and robes, played around with puzzles, and watched television.

~

Those two days of normalcy Lydia kept deep within her mind, and she felt enormous gratitude to have those days there. Because, at around seven the following night, her whole life changed. Lucas had come back, and he was in the kitchen getting more chocolate pecan popcorn balls when the text came in.

The text from Hella Girl was short and sweet. *Found the bitch.* Lydia pulled up and expanded the picture. The hair was lighter, the nose blunter, the jaw stronger than their initial blurry picture showed. But Lydia would bet that girl was half Crow, half Hispanic. The girl had dyed her hair several shades lighter, making her hair honey brown instead of Lydia's black. Lydia could see why Hella Girl's software hadn't been able to find...Celia Munoz. Her driver's license picture was for a much younger Celia. Lydia racked her brain and just couldn't find the woman in her head.

Gunny knew the look in Lydia's eyes and stopped putting together his puzzle to come over and look over her shoulder. "She looks Crow and probably Hispanic."

Stretcher stood up in one liquid movement. "Found the shooter? When do we leave?"

"Get packed," said Gunny over his shoulder. Stretcher moved to her room in the back of the house.

He turned back, and Lydia scrolled down to get the rest of Hella girl's texts. *Girl was raised on the Crow reservation, at the edge. Her mama claims that your dad was her dad on the birth certificate, and tried to get money from him. He demanded a genetic test; she refused. Said that her word should be enough. He refused to pay a dime until she got the test.*

Lydia read the information to Gunny. "She's not a shifter," said Gunny. "Your dad stood by you; he would have stood by his other daughter if he really had one. My guess is this girl never turned furry, and he had his answer."

"What?" asked Lucas, trying to make sense of the information that was coming in.

"Shifting is a dominant trait, which is why shifters use about thirty forms of birth control when they're not ready to settle down," Gunny explained.

"Bad pizza," said Lydia, making Rachael laugh. "It's the reason for my existence. My mom was on birth control pills, but ate bad pizza two days before she met my dad. He used condoms, but apparently something went wrong."

"How old is this girl?" asked Rachael. Lydia told them.

Gunny nodded. "Four, nearly five years younger than our Lydia, according to her driver's license. I get what you're saying. At that point, he knew about Lydia's existence because he met her when she was three. So, he would have been doubly careful with anyone that he met."

"So, that's why you have the…" said Corinne, making a hand gesture that mimicked an injection.

"Birth control you only need four times a year," said Stretcher, coming out of her bedroom with her go bag on her back. "Hella useful for shifters. We need to know where she is. This background is interesting, but not so relevant at the moment."

"That's the other thing that took so long to put together," said Lydia, still scrolling down her screen. "This woman, who thinks she's my sister, knew she had been seen, did things with her hair and makeup, and has been using fake IDs to get jobs. Her arm works, but not so well. Looks like healing took time for her too. Right now, she's working at a bar in a small town in Arizona under the name Sadie Mills. She takes money out of the only ATM in town, so we got her on facial recognition, plus her bank account is in her real name. They must be paying her under the table."

Gunny pulled up a map on his own phone. "She may be in the middle of nowhere, but she is near the White Mountain Apache." He grinned ferally. "I have been to Council meetings where I have met two of their shifters." He started typing rapidly with his thumbs.

"Hold on a minute. I'm the one she shot. I need to be there." Lydia stood and headed to the bedroom for her travel bag. "Rachael, I hope you're good with Luna staying here," she called over her shoulder.

"Anytime you need to hunt feral pretend younger sisters, we're here to help." Rachael rose and went to the kitchen to make sandwiches and to put sodas and cold packs into small travel carriers. Gunny rose and walked to his bedroom, speaking rapidly in Apache.

Lucas followed his girlfriend and her dog into the bedroom in a daze. "Well, we can just let the Apaches take care of it. You can stay here, forget the whole thing happened."

Lydia stared at Lucas as if he had grown two heads. "One, this person shot me, not anyone else. Two, she shot a shifter with silver bullets. Shifters must be the ones to take her down. Three, she's deluded herself into attacking a woman that she apparently believes is her sister. That's majorly twisted, and my dad is dead, so what is the point here? We can't compete for affection for a dead man. Also, according to the map link, she's not currently on the reservation. She's about thirty miles out. That means she needs to be herded onto the reservation before we do anything. We can't let our secret out." Lydia made sure she had everything and zipped her duffel closed.

"So, you're just going to kill the woman who thinks she's your sister? Isn't that just a little bit twisted on the other end?"

"One, she shot me and nearly killed me. I don't know what is going to happen when I confront her, but I'm not going to only use harsh language. Two, we have very specific laws about this."

"Laws you didn't know about until you got here." Lucas narrowed his eyes, planted his feet.

"Laws I obeyed when I didn't know them because they're obvious. This woman, no matter who she is or thinks she is, hunted a shifter with a silver bullet. That cannot be allowed to stand. It's a shifter thing. I'm sorry you don't understand it, but I don't have time to talk with you about it anymore." She walked around Lucas as he stood there, his jaw hanging open. She turned. "Go home, be with your mother, Lucas. I've got this." She turned and stalked over to the door.

They got everything together and put it by the door, duffels and food and drink for the road. They put on boots and coats and headed out. Gunny and Lydia took Gunny's monster king cab, and Stretcher took Rachael's smaller truck and followed. They took it slow navigating themselves out of town, but they made good time on back roads. They got on the interstate. Hella Girl kept them updated on information she had received, mainly that the woman had bought several weapons, and had probably made her own silver bullets using a mold. The shooter had both a handgun and a rifle, each registered under fake names.

Gunny and Lydia both thought it unlikely that Celia carried a rifle around with her where she was. So the key was to confront her at work, herd her onto the highway, and get her onto the reservation without giving her the ability to go home and get the rifle. She probably had a handgun with silver bullets on her, and that would be dangerous enough. They stitched together a plan, stopped at a rest stop and filled Stretcher in. Gunny discussed it with the Apache people, who would meet them there.

They got a hotel room with double beds and slept for a few hours, then checked out and went after Celia late in the afternoon. They drove up to the little roadhouse by the side of the road, snow falling into a ravine in the back. There were only three trucks and an SUV in the parking lot. Gunny pointed at the building with his chin. "Not exactly a jamming place."

Thom, an old Apache with a lined hatchet face, got out of his truck. He wore a long black duster, battered jeans, and ancient hiking boots. He shook Gunny's hand. "Gunny," he said.

"Thom," Gunny said.

"They are mountain lions?" John asked, pointing with an elbow at the two women. Stretcher and Lydia both coughed. The old man grinned. "We will take the back door. One of you confronts the shooter, and she will either run out the front or the back. Then, we get her where she needs to be."

"Sounds good," said Gunny.

The Apache took the back door, Lydia walked in the front, and Gunny and Stretcher were ready with the trucks.

Lydia walked into the roadhouse dive. It was dark, a low wooden structure with a bar, barstools, a wooden floor, and heavy beams in the ceiling. An ancient country tune from the Man in Black played on the jukebox. Lydia looked straight at Celia and said, "Hello, Celia. You shot me, but didn't kill me. Bad mistake on your part."

Celia dropped the mug on the ground that she had been holding. It bounced, spewing beer everywhere. The bartender, a tall, gangly woman in a cowboy hat, stopped cleaning a glass. There were a few patrons, most with their heads down over their beer, who all turned to watch the show. Celia, wearing jeans, cowboy boots, and a sweat-shirt with the name of the bar on it, bolted out the back door. The Apaches herded Celia to her car. Lydia turned around, ran out the front door, and hopped in the truck with Gunny. The girl drove an ancient Pinto with both snow tires and chains, so it was very easy to hem her in, a truck in the front, two trucks in the back, forcing her to head toward the reservation.

"Off road," said Gunny to Stretcher on his cell phone, and Stretcher slowed while Gunny moved up beside Celia with the truck and forced her off the road. Celia stopped in a spray of gravel, then got out and ran, pulling on a sheepskin-lined leather stadium jacket, but found it hard to run in her boots in the thigh-high snow. No rifle, so she apparently hadn't put it in the car. Lydia really didn't care if she was cold or not as adrenaline thrummed through her veins. She took her time, stalking her prey, as Stretcher cut Celia off. Gunny got out, a gun in each hand. He knew better than to get between a cat and its prey.

Lydia bellowed. "Stop! Celia Gomez, you stand accused of shooting me, a shape-shifter, in the shoulder with a silver bullet. Do you deny the charges?"

"You're a fucking skinwalker!" Celia turned and shouted, her face contorted with rage.

"That's why you went all murderous bitch on me?" asked Lydia, confused. "I am a shifter. So was my dad."

"That's a lie, like all the other lies! Our father was no skinwalker!"

"He was a shapeshifter, not a skinwalker. People can't take on the skin of animals and walk around in them. That's just crazy." Lydia stalked closer to Celia, not bothering to hide her intent. "That's how he knew that you weren't his, why your mother refused to take a genetic test proving that he was the father. You didn't turn all furry, did you?"

"Liar!" screamed Celia, patting around for the gun in her pocket. "Your mother was a skinwalker! She forced our father to renounce me!"

Gunny stepped forward with a gun in each of his huge hands and pointed one at her head, one at her heart. "Stop patting your pockets looking for your gun loaded with silver. You shot a shifter with silver bullets which carries the consequences of death. The fact that you shot someone you believed to be your sister makes you a crazy, pseudo-fratricidal bitch."

Lydia stood firm against the wind. "I'll prove I'm not related to you. I'll take a test. There will be no familial match, and this tower of lies you piled up will crumple. Then, when you know the truth, I will hunt you down, and consider whether or not to claw your eyes out of your head. In the meantime, you'll be held in a tiny jail cell and permitted to exercise for about an hour a day. And you won't have any access to silver weapons."

"Liar!" Celia screamed again, and she turned and bolted for an empty spot in the woods. She turned and shot with that little pea shooter of hers, but they easily ducked her wild shots. They were about a thousand feet above sea level, and they had picked their spot well. Lydia knew what that break in the trees actually meant. Lydia slowly went after Celia. Celia kept looking back, terrified, but couldn't hit anyone because she was running on snow. Stretcher came up at her from the side, still at an unhurried pace. Then, Celia, not looking where she was going, fell with a scream that pierced the night.

Luckily for Celia, it wasn't a cliff face, but a steep drop-off. Celia landed hard against a rock jutting out of the earth with an audible crunch of bone. Her gun went flying. Stretcher and Lydia looked down and saw Celia laying on her side.

There was only one way to handle the situation with such a steep embankment. Stretcher stuffed her clothes into her backpack and changed. Two Apache coyotes and wolves came from either side and slid down the embankment with her. They each caught some clothing in their teeth, and hauled a screaming Celia back up the embankment. Gunny went back to the truck for the first aid kit, which included a roll of duct tape. Plus, he had enough gauze to wrap a mummy. They immobilized the arm and shoulder with sticks, gauze, and duct tape, tied the still-screaming woman to the backseat of Gunny's king cab truck, and Lydia climbed in to help Gunny get her to the hospital. They left Stretcher behind with the Apache wolves and coyotes to change back and drive to the hospital.

The doctor took one look at the duct tape and raised her right eyebrow. Gunny shrugged. "What? It's on her clothes, not her skin, and you'll have to cut that shirt off anyway."

Celia had to have surgery to repair the entire upper arm and shoulder. When she woke up, she kept ranting about her sister and skinwalkers and some wolves that tried to kill her. The tribal police came, and Gunny and Lydia said that the woman had shot a mountain lion, believing it to be Lydia. Lydia said she was not, and had never been, related to the woman. The tribal doctor, not the Western one, took a saliva sample from each woman.

By the time a DNA test had proven that the women were not sisters, Celia was in a psychiatric hospital, getting her shoulder tended to as well as having therapy to determine why she felt the need to shoot a woman who wasn't her sister. They didn't know what to charge her with because the mountain lion had survived and had supposedly been sent to some sort of rescue facility. The government officially didn't know that there were other shifters than wolves.

Since the mountain lion had not been threatening anyone, the tribal police charged Celia with shooting an endangered species. They confiscated all her weapons and forced her to pay a large fine to go to wild animal rescue and rehabilitation. Celia had also been guilty of stalking, and Hella Girl had abundant proof of that once Celia's accounts had been hacked.

Celia chose the psychiatric hospital over prison, and the tribal police impressed upon her what would happen to her if she ever tried to harm another shifter, either by stalking or more overt means. Gunny, Stretcher, and Lydia trusted the tribal police to make everything right, and made it home before the new year began.

MISUNDERSTANDING

*L*ucas couldn't understand everyone's blasé reaction to the woman Lydia, Gunny, and Stretcher had gone after landing in a hospital with a smashed shoulder and arm. Or about her ending up in the mental hospital. "She's still alive," said Stretcher.

"You should have seen those two cats stalking her." Gunny stood proudly. "She had nowhere to go. I will say this for her, she could have given up, and instead she ran off a damn drop-off."

Lucas cringed. "If she had given up, would you have killed her?" Gunny shrugged, which drove Lucas crazy. Rachael tried to talk to him about following the law, and that Celia seemed to be completely insane. Rachael was actually concerned about leaving her alive because there was no guarantee that the mess in her skull would become anything less than homicidal.

Lucas couldn't talk to his mother about the whole thing because she didn't really know much about the shifters. Certainly not that they dispensed their own justice. So, when Mitch, James, and Corinne finally came back, he went to Mitch's garage and laid out the whole thing.

Mitch listened while cutting front fender pieces off of a mangled Harley, its entire front end smashed. He heard Lucas out, then said,

"Well, it seems to me that Celia was kind of like this dude, the one that survived this crash. He asked me to rebuild his Harley for him. He got a broken leg. By the time he gets home, I'll have it working for him. He had his lights on, and he and the truck in front of him were both parked at a stoplight in broad daylight. The kid that drove up behind the bike had been smoking pot, and he just didn't notice that both vehicles were stopped although their lights were all on. And, once again, the whole broad daylight thing. The kid's gone to jail for substance abuse, is getting his license taken away, and will probably have to attend some sort of program for that."

Mitch went over to the little refrigerator, popped the top on a Coke, and offered one to Lucas, who accepted. "There are consequences for your actions. Celia, though, didn't think there were any consequences. Now, let me ask you a question. What would you do if you found out you had some sort of secret brother? That your father got drunk and had another child by another woman?"

Lucas popped the top on his Coke, then thought for a minute. "That's actually not outside the realm of possibility. He did drink and smoke a lot and wasn't home a lot, went to the bar with his friends as soon as he ran out of chores at least a couple times a week. I guess I would be shocked for about a minute and a half, then I would see if there was something I could do for the guy. I doubt Carl would have spent a dime on him."

"Would you hunt him down, stalk him, try to destroy his credit, take away his livelihood? Would you sneak around in the dark and shoot him in the shoulder?"

Lucas shook his head. "Of course not, but that woman was crazy."

Mitch put his Coke down, got the front fender off, and put it in the recycling bin. Mitch picked up his metal shears and went after another piece of twisted metal. "So, mental hospitals. They get some drugs in you, get you stabilized. Now, I know that the vast number of mentally ill people are not violent. This woman is. She shot your girlfriend. Do mentally ill people go off their meds?"

"All the time."

"So, because your girl was kind enough to do it your way, now for the rest of her life she's going to have to look over her shoulder, make sure no one is trying to destroy her credit, destroy her relationships with her clients, and isn't going to step out of some dark alley and shoot her in the damn head. And you're standing here blaming Lydia for not being broken up that this woman is in the hospital?"

"There is a restraining order against her."

"And how many women have been killed even though there was a restraining order out against their stalker?" Mitch moved his shears, trying to pull out a tenacious piece of bent and broken metal.

Lucas sighed. "You make me sound like a complete idiot." He looked at Mitch's biceps. "And that I'm going to have to get a gun, bulk up, learn how to fight, and learn how to protect my girlfriend."

"Yes to all of those. Gotcha." Mitch pulled the metal piece out with gloved hands and dropped it into the recycling bin. "We in the animal kingdom know that a truly crazed animal needs to be put down. Medications, the law, finding out that Lydia really wasn't her sister, warnings from shifters and the Apache Nation, absolutely nothing will ensure that that crazy bitch will not hunt Lydia down again. So, yes, your naive outlook has put both of you in the crosshairs. I really hope that Lydia decides to stay here, despite your stupidity. That way, she'll have enough Pack around to protect her."

Lucas sighed. "You make me sound as bad as Carl."

Mitch stood and looked directly into Lucas' eyes. "Your father didn't see or accept who you really were until his damn deathbed. You need to accept the fact that Lydia is a shifter. Someone or something may die because of that. She's extremely powerful, but the first time you saw her, she had been shot by a silver bullet. When will it enter your thick skull that she is different from you? You cannot question her or her judgment ever again. She followed the law, both human and nonhuman. She treated a woman who is batshit crazy with kindness. I think she did it because of you."

Mitch put down the cutter on his bench. "I strongly disagree with this, because I think Lydia set us up to have to deal with this woman again. But, unlike you, I will not question her because I'm not stupid enough to question the judgment of a woman. Especially one who could go up against me and either her human or shifter form and win easily. If you love her, and I think you do, you're going to have to get a lot stronger, a lot tougher, and a lot less naive. And you can never, ever make my mistake, and leave your woman alone."

Lucas looked out the window at the boxing setup on the breezeway between the garage and the house, the heavy leather bag, the speed bag. Lucas knew the kickboxing stand had been taken inside, and that all three of them beat the shit out of the thing on a regular basis. "You have a problem with teaching me how to fight?"

"No. Just know that I'm going to whip your ass." They set up some times to spar. Mitch refused to take any money, saying it was part of his shifter duties.

Lucas drove back to Lydia's cabin, hoping she was still there. He needed to make an apology, and fast. He found her stretching on the banquette she shoved together for her bed, and the dog was on the floor stretching too. He laughed as he took off his boots. "Are you teaching that dog yoga?"

"She already knows Downward Dog."

Lucas groaned at the joke, shed all of his outerwear, including the snow boots, and sat down on the floor. The dog crawled in his lap. "I am really sorry I've been an idiot about that woman. We have no guarantees that she won't attack you again."

Lydia sat up. "About that. I got two texts, one from Hella Girl, one from the tribal police. Last night, Celia used a bed sheet and her sling and killed herself in the middle of the night." Lydia shook her head. "Word got back to her people. My people. Believe it or not, I got a personal apology from the Crow medicine man. He's asked me to come and visit, to learn the ways of my father. He said that he tried to teach my father, but understood my dad's need to play music."

"I'm really sorry she's dead. I'm also relieved that she won't get out and do dangerous things to other people anymore." He stared as Lydia stretched, loving the movements of her upper arms, her shoulders, the concentration on her face. "Are you going up there?"

"Going to Montana in the middle of winter?" She snorted. "I told him I would give him two weeks in the summer. I usually have this huge dip in new work in late May and early June."

"I do, too. What's up with that?"

"I think it has to do with budgets and mid-year goals. Would you like to come with me?"

"If you'll have me." Lucas hung his head. "I apologize for not trusting your judgment. That was stupid."

Lydia smiled at him. "Yes, it was. To be blunt, that woman would have gone through much less pain and suffering if she had died immediately. But cats don't look backwards. We look forward." She stretched again, touched her toes, rolled her spine back up. "I guess what I'm asking is for you to come and meet whatever family I've got left. The medicine man says I have a distant female cousin somewhere, and that I'm distantly related to him, too."

"Wow, meet the family, big step," said Lucas. Lydia coughed. "I'd be honored."

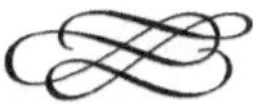

*A*na and Julio got married in the backyard behind the farmhouse, not in the church as everyone had expected. It had been six months since Carl had died, and Father Diaz gave his approval over the strenuous objections of the now-retired Father Monaghan. Lucas gave away his mother, her sister Connie was her maid of honor, and Luna was the ringbearer, carefully holding the little pillow with the rings sewn on in her teeth. People from the church, the little town, and of course all the Westons were there. The music was beautiful, the chocolate cake frosted with caramel was delicious, and the tacos were incredible. Then the line dancing began, and everyone hit the wooden dance floor set up on the lawn.

Lydia sighed during a break in the dancing, a cup of spiked punch in her hand, and talked to Lucas. She had on a gorgeous simple lavender silk dress that brought out the sparkle in her eyes, the blue-black in her hair. She was wearing her Christmas gift from Ana at her neck. "I'm sure they'll have a lovely honeymoon in Florida. I really didn't want to delay going to the Crow Nation, but I guess I'll just have to not take on any new clients for a little while."

Lucas shook his head. "We don't have to take care of the horses. Julio's niece Lupita will board them at her place. She thinks they would be fantastic for trail rides, but they would spend most of their days just relaxing and eating grass in the paddock. If they get along with the other horses and they're happy there, Mama may sell them to Lupita."

"Wow. Wait. Does that mean, after we get this place cleaned up after the party, we can drive to Montana?"

"Well, the caterers and the people we rented the chairs and the little arbor thing from will actually be cleaning up. They were very careful with the food, and I don't think there's going to be anything left over."

Lucas laughed as Lydia spilled punch on the ground while dancing. "Hey, don't get any punch on that dress! We need it for our wedding!" At that, all the Westons turned and looked directly at them. Lucas sighed, pulled the ring out of his pocket and got down on one knee. "Lydia, you're beautiful, incredibly strong, highly intelligent, and you don't let me get away with anything."

There was a scattering of laughter, and the newly wedded couple stopped dancing and started walking slowly towards them. Ana was crying, and Julio was smiling like the sun. Someone silenced the band. "I know I'm still young, that you're older than me emotionally and mentally. But I promise to try to grow up fast. I would love to marry you, to spend the rest of my life with you. I know this will probably mean a long engagement, because you're working on a lot of things, but I would love for you to be my wife."

Lydia looked down at him, with that half smile on her face that meant she was about to do something he probably wouldn't like. "Did you know that I found that ring about two weeks ago? Did you know that I already applied for a wedding license?"

"I pretended to be you," said Mitch. He took Lydia's glass of punch, handed it off to his brother James. "So, it's kind of a surprise for you, but when Lydia says jump, you jump. Besides, you're already dressed up."

Lucas stared at Lydia's face. He slid the engagement ring on her finger, stood up, and said, "I suppose that since the priest is here…"

Mitch smiled at Lucas and patted his jacket pocket. "I have the rings right here." He reached out and led a stunned Lucas to the arbor. Gunny offered his arm and walked Lydia to the other end of the aisle, Luna at her side. Everyone put down their plates and drinks, and rushed to sit down again. Father Diaz stood up next to Lucas, and the band played the wedding march again. Lucas looked at his woman and wondered if his heart could withstand all of the shocks she tended to give him. It didn't matter; he was getting married to the most beautiful woman in the world. Cat. Whatever. Whatever she was, he would love her forever.

<<<THE END>>>

Thank you!

Thank you for being one of my beautiful, amazing readers! I can't do what I do without you! If you liked the book, please leave a review! I read them all, looking to improve my craft so I can write more fun stories for you.

Thank you to my beta reader, Lynda. My editor, iWordyNerdy, is amazing, and so is my critique partner, Alyssa. Crooked Sixpence created my incredible covers. Any errors left in the manuscript are entirely my own. Please let me know what they are so I can fix them in your online review! Or, you can contact me on social media at Facebook: Facebook.com/lj.hawke, Instagram: Instagram.-com/ljhawke, and Twitter: Twitter.com/Hawkelj, and my website: ljhawkeauthor.com.

Books in the Forever Loved series:
Forever Charmed
Forever Claimed
Forever Wild
Forever Challenged

ABOUT THE AUTHOR

L. J. Hawke is an author, university professor, and an avid reader. She writes what she loves to read—paranormal romance, urban fantasy, and science fiction, as well as some nonfiction titles in her fields of expertise. She can be found petting her cats while writing, or with a backpack on her back, traveling the world—after calling the cat sitter.

One last thing...

If you enjoyed this book or found it useful, I'd be very grateful if you'd post a short review on Amazon. Your support really does make a difference, and I read all the reviews personally so I can get your feedback and make this book even better.

Thanks again for your support!

www.ingramcontent.com/pod-product-compliance
Lightning Source LLC
Chambersburg PA
CBHW022202050726
47590CB00002B/614